W9-AUT-322

FLIP
THE
BIRD

FLIP THE BIRD

KYM BRUNNER

HOUGHTON MIFFLIN HARCOURT | BOSTON NEW YORK

WWW.HMHCO.COM

Text set in Apollo MT Std

Library of Congress Cataloging-in-Publication Data
Names: Brunner, Kym, author.
Title: Flip the bird / Kym Brunner.
Description: Boston : Houghton Mifflin Harcourt, 2016.
Summary: "A teenage falconer in training runs up against trouble
when he finds himself falling for a girl who is part of a radical
animal rights group"—Provided by publisher.
Identifiers: LCCN 2015044086 | ISBN 9780544800854 (hardback)
Subjects: | CYAC: Falconry—Fiction. | Dating (Social customs)—Fiction. |
BISAC: JUVENILE FICTION / Animals / Birds. | JUVENILE FICTION / Boys
& Men. | JUVENILE FICTION / Family / General (see also headings under
Social Issues). | JUVENILE FICTION / Lifestyles / Country Life. | JUVENILE
FICTION / Social Issues / Peer Pressure. | JUVENILE FICTION / Social
Issues / Self-Esteem & Self-Reliance. | JUVENILE FICTION / Nature
& the Natural World / General (see also headings under Animals).
JUVENILE FICTION / Sports & Recreation / General.
Classification: LCC PZ7.B828453 Fl 2016 | DDC [Fic]—dc23
LC record available at https://lccn.loc.gov/2015044086

Manufactured in the United States of America
DOC 10 9 8 7 6 5 4 3 2 1
4500617164

This book is dedicated to all of my feathered friends and the One who created them.

FLIP
THE
BIRD

ONE ····🦅

TODAY WAS THE DAY I'D BEEN DREAMING ABOUT practically my whole life.

Too bad it was sucking big time.

I'd been given one job: to grab the plastic critter cage from my room with the mouse inside and bring it with me. Simple. Go to my room, pick up the container, and walk to the truck.

Somehow I'd managed to screw that up. I still couldn't believe I had left the mouse behind. I'd even fed him a cheese curd last night and everything. We were practically bonded, the two of us. I looked down at my dark brown I'M NOT LAZY — I ACTUALLY ENJOY DOING NOTHING T-shirt, wishing I had done something productive for once.

"You're such a moron!" my brother, Lincoln, roared from the back seat of Dad's tricked-out pickup truck when my mistake was discovered. Lincoln was only eighteen, but he thought he knew everything. "What'd you do with it?"

Whoever called it "brotherly love" wasn't talking Lincoln and me. "I . . . I must have set it down somewhere in the house," I stammered. "I don't know."

I did know but wasn't about to admit it out loud. After I'd grabbed the cage, I'd walked through the kitchen, and there, right in front of me, was an unopened bag of chocolate mini doughnuts. And since doughnuts are more like memories than actual food at my house because they're never around for long, I had set the cage on the counter so I could scarf down a couple. Or maybe eight, I'd lost count. Was it my fault I'd grown six inches in the past year and was now six foot two and ravenously hungry all the time?

The sound of Dad's tires screeching to a halt directly in front of Pete's Pet Emporium snapped me out of my doughnut dream.

"You've got two minutes to buy a new mouse and get back out here, or that hawk we saw will be long gone," Dad warned, his bushy gray eyebrows pinched together.

"Yeah, I got lots of stuff I need to do before I meet up with Lauren," Lincoln chimed in, flexing his softball-size muscles as he stretched. "So make it snappy, butthead."

After seeing Dad's eyebrows of anger, I held myself back from rebutting Lincoln's butthead comment. Especially since I owed him one for convincing Dad to let me buy a new mouse instead of abandoning our trapping expedition altogether. I tore out of the truck and dashed into the pet shop, thankful they were open this early.

The bell jangled noisily as I whipped open the door, but it was barely audible over the squawking, barking, and bubbling of the overstuffed shop. Pete, the short, balding dude who owned the place, wasn't at the register, so I rushed toward the back of the shop, where the mice were kept. I whizzed past a family crowded together in the puppy circle, playing with a yipping ball of brown fur and made my way down the narrow fish food aisle. Where the heck was he?

"Yo, Pete? I need help real quick," I called out, hating to sound like a pushy customer, but my apprenticeship hinged on me trapping this hawk today.

"He went into the back room," a female voice said from behind me.

"Thanks." I turned around to see who had spoken. My jaw dropped when I saw her, forcing me to use every ounce of energy I possessed to shut it again. Standing in front of me was the prettiest girl I'd ever seen in my almost fifteen years on earth. She looked about my age, with elbow-length hair the white-blond color of candlelight. She wore a blue T-shirt with white wording and some graphics, which I was dying to read, but I didn't want to be a jerk and stare at her chest. Well, not while she was looking at me, anyway. I did manage to notice, despite the limited ogling opportunities, that she had more curves than a French horn.

Instead of walking away, she said, "What are you buying?"

Her question startled me. I hadn't expected someone who looked as if she could be in a Victoria's Secret ad to actually speak to me, but then again, why not? I wasn't the handsomest guy around, but my little sister, Maddie, and her friend Hannah always giggle and call me Hottie Pants, so I figure I'm not too bad —even if the girls are only ten.

"Oh, just a mouse," I told her, sounding way too cheerful.

Then I cringed at how lame it sounded to be buying a dinky little mouse. Why hadn't I said I was there to buy rat poison or bear feed—something more manly? If I could somehow slip it into the conversation that I'd be using the mouse to trap a dangerous, flesh-eating hawk, it might make her hang around for a few seconds longer.

"A mouse? That's so sweet!" Her face lit up as if I had just given her the diamond stud that blinged from the side of her nose. After seeing how excited she was by my buying a mouse, I was glad I hadn't specified I'd be using it as bait for a hawk's breakfast. "Do you mind if I watch while you pick it out?"

Was she serious? I wouldn't have minded if she tied me down and poured red ants on my face, as long as she continued to talk to me. "No, that'd be awesome!" I gushed, sounding more like my little sister than the rugged guy I'd been faking I was.

I needed to calm down or she'd think I was a loser. I've talked to plenty of hot girls before, although to be honest, they've usually just given me my change and I've said thank you.

She blessed me with a blue ribbon smile—the kind you get for Best in Show at the county fair. "Cool! I've been in here wandering around, waiting for my parents to finish shopping at the hardware store down the street. Sad how all these animals are locked up though, isn't it? I wish I could set them all free."

"Yeah, real sad," I agreed quickly, even though I thought it a bit extreme to want to free animals in a pet shop, but that was girls for you. Always feeling sorry for the weak and the meek.

Come to think of it, perhaps this could work in my favor. "So where you from?" I hoped that she would say she had just arrived in town and was moving in next door to my house.

"Up north. Not too far away." She shrugged. "Want me to show you where the mice are?"

"Sure, that'd be great." I acted as if I didn't already know it was the third tank to the left of the storage room door. As I walked behind her, admiring the view, I ran my hand through my hair, wishing I'd brushed it this morning. While I had heard that girls liked guys with thick wavy hair, I wasn't exactly positive they liked tumbleweed heads.

We stopped in front of the twenty-gallon tank filled with a swirling mass of mice, but I was still watching more of her than the mice. I wondered if there was something slightly off about her judgment. I mean, the only time I'd seriously attracted the attention of a really hot chick was when I stood next to the chicken incubator at the Museum of Science and Industry tapping on the glass. I rubbed my jaw, thinking the heavy stubble that accompanied my recent growth spurt must be responsible for this new-found female attention.

She clapped. "They're all so adorable! What color are you getting?"

I wondered what color mice juvenile red-tailed hawks preferred, but figured as long as it was furry and breathing, the color was inconsequential. "I haven't decided." I remembered to lower my voice to sound more manly. "Pick the one you like."

"Really?" She looked up at me, her eyes wide with excitement. That's when I saw that her eyes were sage green with light flecks of yellow in them. How cool was that? I'd never met anyone with eyes that color before and was pretty sure I never would again.

The door to the storage room burst open, jerking me out of my drool fest. What was I doing standing here chatting when my hawk was waiting for me? Pete came out carrying bags of cedar shavings. "Pete!" I called out, waving a hand in the air. "If you have a quick second, I need a mouse right away." I hoped he would pick up on my need for speed.

He stopped and looked at me. "Another one? Your dad was in last night."

"Yeah, I know," I responded, purposely being vague. "Emergency replacement."

He nodded. "Okay, okay. Just let me set this stuff down."

"What do you mean, 'emergency replacement'?" she asked, gracing me with another dazzling smile. "Do you have a whole slew of guard mice at home and one quit?"

She's sweet, obviously has good taste in guys, and has a great sense of humor? I couldn't believe that I'd finally met the girl of my dreams, right there at the pet shop. "Worse than that," I replied. "The commander lost his battle with German Cheezles today. Nastiest case I've ever seen."

She laughed heartily, not one of those stupid giggles I'd heard on the lips of all the dumb girls Lincoln used to date before he met Lauren. She leaned closer to the tank, her green eyes darting from side to side as she watched the mice. "They're all so cute."

"Yep, hard to pick one, isn't it?" I knew I needed to blow out of there soon, before my dad stuck his head in the store and bellowed for me to hurry up. Talk about embarrassing.

"Oh my gosh! Look at that one!" She pointed to a mouse licking its paws. "It's tan and has a white spot around her nose. You like her?"

"That's the same one I was looking at!" I exclaimed, feigning amazement.

She playfully smacked my arm with the back of her hand. "Liar!"

I laughed, thrilled that she had made skin-to-skin contact, even if it was only to hit me. I suddenly feared that I might have chocolate doughnut bits stuck between my teeth. When she wasn't looking, I did a quick tongue sweep to clear any debris.

"All right. Here I am, Mercer." Pete bustled toward us holding a white Chinese takeout container poked with air holes, identical to the one I'd left in the kitchen.

Dream Girl's head spun toward me so fast, the tips of her hair grazed my forearm, giving me the cheapest of cheap thrills. "Your name's Mercer?" She seemed intrigued, like many people do when they hear my name for the first time. I contemplated telling her that she'd misunderstood and that my name was actually Bill Gates Jr. But since my financial status pretty much hovered around zero on any given Sunday, I decided humor was the better route for me. "Yep, it's Mercer — a favorite name of hit men and male models alike."

She bit her lip coyly. "Which one are you?"

"Both." I aimed my finger gun into the air, shot it, and blew on the end before stuffing it back in its holster. Then I struck what I hoped was a modeling pose, hands balled in fists on my hips. "Armed and ungodly handsome. That's me, ma'am."

She laughed. "Did you know that Mercer is the name of a city in Wisconsin?"

My eyes widened in surprise. Not many people had ever heard about that little town way up north by Lake Superior. "Know it? My parents named me after it. It's the loon capital of the world, you know." I held my hand over my heart as if proud of that fact, but decided not to share that it was also where I'd been conceived. That sick little factoid would remain my secret.

She laughed again, making my spirits soar. I was just getting up the nerve to ask her what her name was when Pete lifted the cover of the tank and handed it to me. "Hold this." We'd bought so many mice from Pete over the years that he knew exactly what I wanted it for, so he reached in and grabbed the first tail he could.

"No, not that one!" Dream Girl cried in dismay. "The tan one with the white nose!" She tapped on the glass, pointing out the intended victim.

Pete shot me an exasperated look over the rim of his wire glasses.

I nodded sheepishly. "Yes, the tan one, please."

Pete shook his head and sighed, setting the white one back in the tank. It took him a few tries, but he finally managed to grasp the tail of the tan mouse.

"Yes, that's the one!" She grinned at me proudly, as if she had birthed the rodent instead of simply picking it out. I decided right then that I wanted this girl to be the mother of my children, even if they ended up tan and furry with little white noses. But first, I'd have to ask for her number.

Pete put the mouse in the box and we followed him to the register. As he rang me up, my future wife turned to me and said, "What are you going to name her?"

I had never named my bait before but figured it couldn't hurt. "Not sure. Got any ideas?"

"That'll be a dollar and twenty-two cents." Pete handed me the carton.

"What do you think of Cinnamon?" She bit her nail, like she was worried I'd say no.

I pretended to consider it a moment while I dug my wallet out from my back pocket. "Cinnamon, huh?" I said. "Yeah. I like that name."

Pete rolled his eyes and held out his hand for the cash. Dad's truck horn blared as I opened up my wallet. It was as empty as my trap. I patted my pants pockets, feeling for change. Panic raced up my gut and lodged in my throat. "Oh no! I spent my last dollar at lunch yesterday. Let me run out to the truck."

Pete threw his hands up. "Mercer! I've got a ton of customers here."

"Sorry." Not only sorry, but mega-humiliated. What kind of girl would want to marry a guy who couldn't come up with two bucks to pay for a lousy mouse?

Dream Girl smiled at me and plopped her yarn purse onto the counter. "I got it."

I would rather have gouged out my eye with the fish tank thermometer than let her pay. "No, that's okay. My dad's right outside." Four steps later, the cash register drawer slammed shut. I glanced back and saw Pete handing her change before he rushed off toward the puppy circle.

The horn blared again, this time longer. "Hold on!" I yelled over my shoulder.

She handed me the white carton. "Well, here you go. Have fun with Cinnamon!"

I started walking backwards, an indelible grin on my face. "I will! And thanks!"

She nodded, waving. "No problem. Just take good care of your new commander."

"You bet," I assured her, thinking it depended on how she defined "care."

I gave her one last look and dashed outside. Three steps onto the sidewalk, I realized I had forgotten to ask for her phone number, her name—anything! How stupid was I?

As I flung open the truck door with my container in hand, I had to wonder exactly which one of us was the man and which one was the mouse.

TWO ·····🦅

THE MOMENT MY BUTT CHEEKS HIT THE SEAT, DAD floored the truck and pulled a U-turn.

"What took you so long?" he snarled. "That hawk is probably long gone by now."

"There were a lot of customers," I explained, buckling my seat belt. I tossed a look over my shoulder at Lincoln. "Including one insanely gorgeous customer in particular who picked out my new pet mouse." I grinned broadly as I held up the box, gently petting the outside of it. "We named her Cinnamon."

"You were flirting with a girl while we were out here waiting?" Dad turned left on County Road Q so fast that my head grazed the window. "Where are your priorities, Mercer?"

Where were *his*, I wondered. "It wasn't just any girl, Dad. She was the prettiest, sweetest, coolest girl I've ever met in my life. And she followed me around the store and actually laughed at my jokes."

Lincoln's eyes widened. "You told her you were buying the mouse as a pet? What a great ploy, little bro-mite." He laughed, showing off that perfect smile of his that made all the girls go crazy. "Picking up chicks at the pet store? Brilliant!"

"Don't encourage him to lie, Lincoln." Dad shook his head.

"Build a relationship based on honesty, Mercer. That's more important than going out with as many girls as you can."

Lincoln laughed again. "Going out with as many girls as you can might not be as important as honesty, but it's way more fun. Right, Mercer?"

"You know it." I didn't actually know it, but I bumped knuckles with my brother anyway. Though he picked on me, I couldn't deny this: Lincoln was the master at snagging girl-friends. As soon as he'd break up with one girl, he'd have a new one on his arm the following weekend. Well, until he met Lauren, that is. He'd been with her four or five months now. At least he knew a good one when he saw one. Lauren was gorgeous, smart, and super sweet. Why she was with my brother was the mysterious part.

"Being a man is doing what you want, when you want," Lincoln assured me.

"Not true," Dad said, using his Joe Falconer voice. "Being a man is doing what is right even when you don't want to."

I coughed out "Buzzkill," earning me an exasperated look from Dad but another round of knucks from Lincoln. Dad suddenly grinned. "Will you look at that?" He pointed out the front windshield. "Today's your lucky day, Mercer."

If it had been my lucky day, I would've had the courage to ask Dream Girl for her phone number. Still, I knew what he was really referring to, making my excitement ratchet up to high. I scanned the telephone poles, hoping this hawk was a lot like me —content to lounge in one place for hours. Holding my breath, I gasped when I spotted my future hunting partner still perched there, grooming himself, as if he'd been waiting for me the whole time. "Yes! Thank God!"

If everything went correctly, that juvenile red-tailed hawk would become my hunting partner for the season, and then I'd release him back into the wild in four months. Human and hawk working together in perfect harmony. At least that's what Dad always says.

"Get the trap ready," Lincoln urged, referring to the bal-chatri on the floor by my feet, the humane contraption where neither hawk nor bait is injured in the process. I slid the tightly meshed wire trap with the zillions of monofilament loops onto my lap as Dad spun the truck around.

I pried open the holding pen in the center of the trap and shook the mouse inside. "Go get 'em, Cinnamon." I checked to make sure the hatch was securely locked and that the brick used to weigh the trap down was firmly in place. Since both things passed my inspection, I got on my knees and leaned my body halfway out the window, turning my head so my hair wouldn't obscure my vision.

If Mom had been in the truck right then, which was a pretty hilarious idea, since she's never anywhere but at work, she would have used this opportunity to tell me I needed a haircut. But after today's pet shop incident, I had even more proof that girls liked how I looked, so it was staying just the way it was — on the longish side and kind of messy.

Dad cruised along the shoulder, waiting for my signal. I spied a narrow patch of low grass ahead and timed my throw accordingly, hurling my shoebox-size contraption off to the side of the road. I watched the trap, along with the mouse, somersault a few times before coming to rest ten feet to the left of my intended spot — in a huge mass of overgrown weeds.

Lincoln chuckled. "Nice shot, dingwad."

I kept my cool and patted my headrest twice, unlike my first attempt two days ago when I'd stupidly shouted, "Pull over!" at the top of my lungs, making the red-shouldered hawk I was after bolt all the way to the next county. Dad got ticked off, but, hey, he should have told me about that headrest-tapping thing ahead of time. It was yet another case of Mercer's Law: if anything in the universe went wrong, blame me.

Dad stopped the truck thirty yards farther ahead. I kept my eyes on the hawk, willing him to swoop down and attempt to munch my mouse. "C'mon, big guy, free food," I urged quietly.

The hawk fluffed his feathers and repositioned his feet.

It wasn't the killer response I'd hoped for, but at least he hadn't flown away. And thank God I didn't have a cold. Lincoln still hadn't let up on me for sneezing and scaring his red-tail away while he was attempting to trap his apprentice hawk a few years ago.

Dad leaned over and checked my trap's position. "Not sure

this will work. Only a foolish hawk would expend energy trying to land prey among that much cover." He grabbed his metallic green thermos and unscrewed the lid.

I felt the need to defend myself. "What do you mean, 'that much cover'? Bella caught a rabbit in thigh-high alfalfa last year!" I said, reminding him of Lincoln's northern goshawk.

Lincoln tapped his chest over his tight-fitting Gold's Gym T-shirt. "That's because Bella learned from a master."

"Master-bator maybe," I quipped.

"Hey, watch your mouth," Dad chided me as he poured coffee into the thermos's lid. "And you're not a master falconer yet, Lincoln." Dad glanced at him over his shoulder. "But you're close, I'll give you that. One day you might even turn out to be as good as your old man."

"Maybe even better," Lincoln teased, but I doubted he was joking.

Part of me wished I could do a Dorothy and splash coffee on Lincoln's conceited face and watch him melt.

Dad smiled as he raised his cup. "You just might if you keep at it." Swirls of steam rose into the air, filling my nostrils with an awesome aroma. Weird how something that smelled so good tasted like sewer runoff.

"Come on, hawk. Be hungry." I stared at the bird up on the telephone pole, begging the falconer gods to toss some luck my way for once. That's when I noticed that the mouse was motionless in the bottom of the trap. Had I killed Cinnamon on the throw? Would a hawk even go for a dead mouse? There was no way I was asking, or I'd get Falconry Lecture 234. I assumed mouse tasted the same, dead or alive, but couldn't be sure. The thought of doing a taste test both disgusted and intrigued me, but with eight waxy doughnuts sitting in my gut, I abandoned the mind movie before I upchucked.

To my relief, Cinnamon began running around, frantically trying to find a way out of her prison. "Whew! I thought I killed my bait for a second there."

Lincoln cleared his throat. "If you toss the trap sidearm, it'll spin rather than flip. Unless maybe you're not strong enough to do that." He reached out and squeezed my bicep—hard. "Geez, Mercer. Your arms are like spaghetti noodles. You'd better start lifting weights. A bird gets heavy after a couple of hours on the fist."

"I do lift weights!" I protested. It was true. Every time one of those weightlifter commercials came on, I did ten biceps curls with each arm.

"The TV remote doesn't count," Lincoln said, laughing. "You've got a long way to go to get these guns." He showed off his bulging muscles.

"Big deal," I scoffed, but I secretly flexed my arm muscle by my side, making a mental note to do more weightlifting starting tomorrow. My biceps couldn't handle another one of Lincoln's death grips.

I wanted to tell my brother to cram it, that having strong

muscles wasn't important to be a good falconer, but I didn't want to listen to Dad go on about how Lincoln had a point, blah, blah, blah, so I shut my trap and sat there silently. Ha! Shut my trap. Wasn't that a metaphor or something? And then, out of nowhere . . . *whoosh!* That red-tail swooped toward the tan and white fur ball with the same energy I devour all my meals. Sidearm, my butt!

The hawk pounced on my trap, attempting to extract the mouse with his talons, but Cinnamon remained safely inside her holding cell. Seconds later, the hawk became hopelessly snagged in the slipknots we'd rigged all around the outside of the bal-chatri. The red-tail flapped his wings, trying to untangle his feet, but lucky for me, the harder he pulled, the tighter the slipknots gripped his industrial-strength yellow legs.

"It worked!" I screamed, my voice two octaves higher than normal.

"Way to go, Apprentice Boy." Lincoln patted my shoulder hard, but I didn't care.

Dad set his coffee into the holder. "Let's go take a look and see what you got."

I prayed that what I got was one badass hawk who'd help me win the Best Apprentice award at the falconry meet next month, proving to Dad and Lincoln once and for all that I wasn't as incompetent as they seemed to think I was. And I'd finally gain their respect.

To be honest, I wasn't sure which prize I wanted more.

THREE

I NEARLY KILLED MYSELF WHEN I DASHED OUT OF THE truck, missing the step. I landed like a felled redwood, but leaped back up to check out my new hunting buddy. I prayed he had a striped tail, the sign that he was a juvenile rather than the rusty red of an adult, or I wouldn't be able to keep him. Young, inexperienced hawks for young, inexperienced falconers —a perfect match.

Not to mention that it's also the law. And there was no way I was going to lose my hunting license after it had taken me so long to earn it. I'd finally checked off all the boxes the Department of Natural Resources required to legally trap a hawk: minimum age (I'd turned fourteen last March), passage of the falconry exam (I'd gotten a sterling 98 percent), inspection of my future hawk's living quarters (you could lick ice cream off the floor), possession of a hunting license (paid the fee myself), and sponsorship by an experienced falconer (Dad). Check, check, checkity-friggin'-check.

Lincoln stood alongside me, watching as the bird tried to free himself from the fishing line nooses that entangled his legs, his wings flapping wildly. "It's kind of small. Must be a male."

"Who cares?" I knew females were bigger and stronger hunters, but with my track record with human females, maybe a male was a better choice for me. We'd be two guys hunting in the wild —on the prowl and doing whatever we wanted. Perfect partners, if you asked me.

"He's small but healthy." Dad rubbed his chin. "He'll grow."

"Yeah, he'll grow." I shot Lincoln a smug look. "He's just a baby."

Slowly, so as not to freak the bird out more than he already was, I crouched down to get a better peek at the red-tail, *my* red-tail, and was awestruck by how cool he was. His toes were the shade of yellow kindergarten paint, and the feathers across his back had at least seventeen shades of brown. His fluffy leg feathers fluttered in the breeze, and his curved gray beak looked ideal for nabbing enormous amounts of prey. When I checked out his eyes, my jaw dropped for the second time that day.

This hawk had sage green eyes with yellow flecks—same as Dream Girl.

I wasn't the type of guy who read his horoscope or tossed salt over his shoulder when he dropped a fork, but I knew this was more than a silly coincidence. No way. This was one huge premonition: Dream Girl, dream hawk, same day. I couldn't believe my good fortune. My mind drifted for a second, wondering if this was a sign that I'd eventually catch up with Dream Girl again.

Gazing back at my new hunting buddy, I observed the chubby face and the downy chest feathers of a juvenile. Didn't fool me. I knew deep down he was one fierce hawk with a thirst for blood. With this guy by my side when hunting season opened, I'd finally get my turn to be large and in charge instead of merely a bush beater for all the other falconers.

I knew it was probably a little childish to want the Best Apprentice pin so badly. I should have been content with manning my own hawk — getting him to trust me so we could be teammates — but I couldn't help myself. I'd been dreaming about becoming a falconer for as long as I could remember. And I'd been to more falconry meets and hunting trips in my fourteen and a half years than most people had been to church in their entire lives. That should count for something, right?

Dad squeezed my shoulder. "All right then. Work on getting him hooded while I get the other supplies."

I glanced at Dad to make sure he wasn't kidding. Though it was common to place a leather hood over our raptors' eyes to keep them calm, I figured a wild hawk wasn't about to accept one without some training first. "Who, me? By myself?"

Lincoln laughed. "No, he's talking to the red-tail. Of course, you."

For ten minutes, the two of them stood there ordering me around without lifting a finger to help. After I got the hawk hooded, I suffered only one mishap when attempting to disentangle his feet from the fishing line nooses, earning me a nasty talon gouge on the back of my hand. It hurt like hell, but I was so happy to have trapped this bird, he could have bitten off my pinky and I'd still think he was cool. In fact, the more I thought about it, the more I realized that sporting a missing digit would help prove we're a couple of tough dudes and people should back off.

No one could say I didn't have goals.

Dad said, "Good job. Now carefully place him in the carrier and let's get him home." He unlatched the inside chamber of the trap and shook Cinnamon to the ground. She took off, disappearing under a shriveled cornstalk. So much for saving a memento of my true love.

As Dad set the trap into the back of the truck, Lincoln helped me get the red-tail's wings folded so he wouldn't break any of his beautiful feathers on the ride home before I placed him in the darkened carrier. "Don't worry," I reassured my new hunting partner as I closed and locked the door. "I'll see you in a few minutes."

As I reached for the truck's front door handle, Lincoln elbowed me in the chest. "Get in the back, Apprentice Boy."

"Whatever you say, General Falconer." I saluted him with my middle finger and a wide grin, scuttling into the back seat before he could punch me.

"Did you just flip the bird at your brother?" Dad asked the second I got in the truck.

"Did I what?" I looked at Lincoln, who shrugged, and then at Dad.

"You know, flip the bird. With your middle finger?" Dad started the truck.

Lincoln and I immediately cracked up. *Flipping the bird* was the dumbest expression I'd ever heard. Why would anyone call it that? I looked at my finger and smiled. An idea began to form in my mind, but I kept quiet.

"Everyone says 'flick him off' these days, Dad." Lincoln slid his seat belt across his chest, clicking it into place.

"Fine. Mercer shouldn't be flicking his fingers at people," Dad said, maneuvering back onto the road. "It's what people do when they don't have a large vocabulary."

Dad obviously still thought of me as a ten-year-old. When I'm married with kids, he'll probably still be bugging me to use my napkin. "Me dumb. Don't know words," I joked from the back seat. "Bird hurt me." I showed Dad and Lincoln the back of my hand, fresh blood oozing out of a red smeary mess.

"Whoa. That's nasty." Lincoln popped open the glove box and handed me some napkins.

Dad shook his head. "You shouldn't have moved so fast around him, Mercer."

Was it my imagination, or did it seem that Dad cared more about the hawk than the buckets of blood pouring from my wound? It'd be nice if he didn't treat every conversation as another opportunity to school me. "Yeah, I guess not."

As Dad drove through town on our way home, he and Lincoln gave me tips on all that I'd need to do before putting my bird into the mews. A mews is a falconer's always-plural word for "cage," but also the term for the entire barn. One mews, two mews, everywhere a mews, mews. All this secret language was unnecessary, in my opinion; I would've been fine keeping my hawk in a cage in the barn, but whatever.

Dad hung a right at Nelson's Gas, so I joked, "Hey, look. We're passing gas. Boy, does that stink."

"Shut up, you dork." Lincoln grinned. "Did you think of a name for your bird yet?"

"As a matter of fact, I did." My idea from a few minutes earlier rushed back to mind. "I decided to call him Flip. As in, Flip the Bird. Get it?" I eyed Lincoln, gratified when I heard him laugh. That made the name even better.

"Don't be stupid," Dad barked. He opened his window a bit more, making me wonder if he took my gas joke seriously. "Name him something dignified—a name he can be proud of."

"A name he can be proud of?" I repeated. "He's a bird, Dad. And because you're requiring me to release him at the end of the hunting season so I can start fresh with a new hawk next year, I'll only have him a few months. Then off he'll go, back into the wild. He'd be as happy being called Flip as he would Butt Nugget."

"Butt Nugget. Love it." Lincoln chuckled under his breath, making that name a serious contender too. The whole reason I wanted a funny name was to show Dad and all his falconer buddies that they didn't have to take falconry so seriously all the time. They all acted as if the falconry codes had been handed down to Moses along with the Ten Commandments. Every falconer except Dad's best friend, Weasel, of course. That guy didn't take anything seriously, which was probably why I liked him so much.

Dad smoothed his mustache. "How about Arthur? As in King Arthur? Falconry's been around since 2000 BC, you know."

I grimaced. "Probably why Arthur sounds like an old man's name."

"If you think this is so humorous, maybe I should pull over and let the hawk go." Dad braked then—I guess to show me he was actually thinking about it.

Lincoln turned toward me and discreetly rolled his eyes. We both knew Dad was exaggerating only to teach me a lesson. Still, I needed to calm him down. "C'mon, Dad. Just because Flip's a cool name doesn't mean I'm not serious about becoming a falconer."

"Doesn't seem like you're serious." Dad frowned, apparently still not convinced.

Time to reason with him man-to-man. "You named your kids Mercer, Lincoln, and Madison after the towns you conceived us in, but that didn't mean you weren't serious about becoming a father, did it?" Truthfully, though, after I'd found out about the disgusting way in which I was named, I was thankful I wasn't called Room 241 at the Holiday Inn.

"Don't disappoint me, Mercer. That's all I ask." He stepped on the gas, and that was that.

Now if I could just find the guts to remove Flip from the carrier when we got back home, I'd be taking the first step toward that seemingly insurmountable request.

FOUR ······🦅

WE TURNED OFF THE MAIN HIGHWAY AND ONTO THE dirt road leading to our neighborhood. The truck's wheels kicked up stones and sent dust clouds flying out behind us as we drove the half mile to our house. As we pulled into our driveway, Dad whistled. "That sign sure looks great, doesn't it?"

He was referring to the recent addition of an illuminated sign on our front lawn that boasted BUDDIE BIRD REHAB CENTER, and below that FALCONRY DEMONSTRATIONS AVAILABLE. At the bottom it read RICHARD BUDDIE, WILDLIFE REHABILITATION SPECIALIST, along with his phone number. While it's a nice sign, and Dad totally knows his stuff when it comes to rehabilitating injured raptors, I wasn't sure exactly whom he expected to see it, as we get only about two cars per day driving past our house.

When I told Dad he needed to do more in the way of online advertising, he made a face and shrugged. Guess he didn't think I knew much about social media either. Now if Lincoln suggested a bigger online presence, Dad would be hosting Twitter parties every Tuesday night.

Dad stopped in front of the house to let Lincoln out. Before Lincoln hopped out of the truck, he turned to me. "Congratulations, bro. Have fun with Flip today." He held out his fist, bumping mine straight on before he slammed the door.

As I watched him walk away, I wished for the tenth time that I'd thought to ask Dream Girl her name. She was so into animals, I bet she'd think Flip was cool. She'd even forgive me for Cinnamon once she knew the mouse was out running free in the field somewhere. For exactly how long that freedom would last would safely remain unknown.

Dad and I drove around to the back, where the white barn stood perpendicular to our house. There it was, Dad's pride and joy, the fantasy raptor facility he had built to his specifications. He drove in through the side garage door, staying only long enough for me to unload Flip's carrier — it nearly detached my arms, but I managed to do it — before he backed out. It was as if he was afraid the birds would twist the doorknobs with their beaks and come flying out at the exact moment the garage door was opened. Talk about overly cautious — he was worse than my grandma on an icy pavement without her cane.

Before I took Flip out of his carrier, I searched the rehab center for the equipment I needed. Dad's shelves were stuffed with every type of bell, gauntlet, hood, telemetry device, and disinfectant that Northland Falconry Distributors sold. Finally, I grabbed a bolt of tan kangaroo leather, a jar of lanolin oil, pliers, and a handful of tannery tools, dumping them all on the table. After flicking on the light, I got to work fashioning Flip's new leather gear. I'd made and replaced enough ankle cuffs, jesses, and leashes that I could do this blindfolded.

A short time later, Dad walked up behind me. "How's it going?"

"Great so far," I replied, not looking up.

He watched as I methodically traced and carved anklets and jesses from the supple leather before rubbing heavily scented lanolin oil on them. "Nice workmanship," he proclaimed, nodding his approval.

At last, it was time to outfit Flip with his new attire. With his hood still on inside the carrier, Flip's sensory system was set to calm, making it easier to attach the equipment to his scrawny legs. First came the anklets, followed by the sturdy eight-inch leather jesses—which allowed me to hang on to Flip so he couldn't fly away until I wanted him to. I added a swivel and a leash, and he was good to go. Actually, good to *stay*—at least until the end of the hunting season. After turning off the lights in the rehab center for a more subdued setting, I slid my thick gauntlet onto my arm before getting my bird up on my fist, quickly looping the leash between my pinky and ring finger.

When Flip was out of the carrier, I slowly removed his hood, sending him leaping off of my fist as if my glove were made of lava instead of leather. A bird hanging upside down was not good. I'd seen enough birds bate like this, so I knew what to do: place my hand on his back and gently lift him onto my fist.

Dad said, "Don't make eye contact. Just keep calm and he'll eventually give in."

Flip bated seven more times before he finally stayed put for a minute. I stood stone still, noting with each exhale that Flip's breath had an earthy odor, kind of like the way the air smelled after a summer rain.

"There you go," Dad said quietly. "That's the first step. Take good care of him, Mercer, and he'll be yours soon enough."

"Cool. I plan to," I replied, not turning toward Dad for fear my head movement would send Flip dive-bombing off my fist again. "And in exchange, this guy is going to help me win the Best Apprentice award." I grinned. "Amazing that I caught a bird that's as unbelievably handsome as its owner, huh Dad?"

Dad rolled his eyes, smiling. He pointed toward the mews. "Enough flattery—for both of you. Go show him his new home."

"Already?" My excitement plummeted. "Can't I hold him awhile?"

"Not today. He's stressed enough. We'll try feeding him to-morrow, although I doubt he'll eat for a few days. Put him in his mews while I clean up here."

I didn't want to put Flip away just yet, but it wasn't as if I could go out into the yard and play a game of fetch with him.

I couldn't wait to show him off to Reed and Charlie, my two best friends. They'd been hearing me talk about getting my own hawk for a long time now. Reed had told me that trapping and then hunting with my own hawk would make me the coolest guy at Woodley High. I'm sure he meant after himself because Reed never had trouble in the popularity department. Just one more reason I liked hanging out with him so much. I'd text both him and Charlie later this afternoon and tell them the good news.

Dad picked up the bolt of leather and the bottle of lanolin oil. "Oh, and by the way, Maddie let the original mouse go free. Said she found it on the kitchen counter next to an empty bag of doughnuts." He raised his eyebrows.

"Oh, yeah! Now I remember," I said, as if this was news to me. Dad shook his head and started toward the house.

With Flip on my wrist, I sauntered to the door connecting the rehab portion of the building to the sacred area known as —cue the church music—the Mews. After passing through, I shut the door firmly behind me, not gagging the way I used to do when I was younger. On the scale of disgusting odors, wild bird smell lies somewhere between compost pile and garbage dump— not horrid, but not an olfactory picnic either. I strolled down the long hallway lined with wooden doors, each with a large barred opening for us to peek through. Our birdie hotel currently had twelve residents—eight permanent ones, two healing ones, and two hunting birds.

"Make that three hunting birds now," I told Flip while heading toward the last mews, which would become his. On the way, I passed Monocle, our one-eyed great horned owl. She immediately started "herking" away at me, making me grin. Monocle is, and always will be, my favorite bird here. I laughed at her impatience. "Give me a minute, Mon."

It's like this: whenever Monocle sees me, she makes a noise with her throat that sounds like *herk*, which she repeats louder and louder until I spend time with her. We got her as a cute little owlet after a farmer's cat dragged her to his door—apparently by the eye, stupid cat—and I've taken care of her ever since. Lincoln jokes that Monocle's the only girl who has ever had the hots for me. I don't mind his teasing because I love that crazy owl right back.

The only part that sucks is that Lincoln is right.

"Sorry to tell you this, Flip, but Monocle will always come first in my book." Flip's talons grasped my gloved wrist harder, which was maybe his way of saying he wasn't too thrilled with that pronouncement. Opening the door to Flip's bathroom-size mews, I checked to make sure everything was exactly the way I had set it up earlier this week: three perches at different heights, one swivel perch bolted to the center of the floor near ground level, and a small warming hutch for winter—although raptors rarely, if ever, needed protection from the elements. There was even a night-light so my overprotective father could check on them one last time before he went to bed. He'd walk along the length of the barn, peering through the series of thinly spaced vertical bars that were covered with delicate screening to keep out disease-carrying mosquitoes, which lined the entire front wall of the mews.

I attached a leash to the ring on Flip's jess, tethering him to the floor post. "Here you are. Mews sweet mews." He bated again, but hopped back onto the perch seconds later, giving me an adrenaline rush as I savored my falconry milestone. I had done it—I officially had my own hawk.

Flip stood motionless, his mouth frozen in a slightly open position—kind of like how my dad looks when he falls asleep on the couch. His pupils widened and narrowed in photographic precision as he gazed at me, his soft, puffy chest feathers beckoning to be touched. I wanted to somehow let him know that I would indeed be taking good care of him.

"Hey there, fella. It's your old pal, Mercer." I knelt down and gently stroked his chest. Flip reached out to touch me too, this time goring my right forearm.

"Ah, man!" I yelped, moving out of his reach. Bright red blood filled the narrow gouge on my arm.

"What did you expect?" I whipped around and saw Dad standing there. "You can't pet him, Mercer. He's a hawk, not a puppy."

I pressed hard against the gash. "Thanks for the news flash."

"Now, now. I didn't mean anything by that. He'll begin to trust you soon enough, but you can't rush it." He held the door open for me and jerked his head toward the house. "Come on.

Let's leave him be for now. Go sanitize that wound, bandage it, and get cleaned up. Maybe let a razor take a trip around your face too?" He smirked at me, but I knew he wasn't joking.

Now he's giving me lessons on how often I should shave? "Why? I'm not going anywhere."

"Actually, I was hoping we could surprise Mom for her birthday by taking her out for lunch."

Whenever free food's on the agenda, I'm usually a willing participant. But lately, suffering through the diatribes of my sister, Maddie, about the trials of fifth grade severely lessened my mealtime enjoyment. Not to mention that Dad would probably make a big deal of my ineptitude in getting footed twice by Flip. "Not really in the mood. Can you bring me something back?"

"C'mon, Mercer." Dad sighed, almost pleading. "Let's do this as a family for Mom's sake. What do you think about taking her to Elliot's Pine Log?"

What I thought was that Dad should be elected president of good ideas. Elliot's Pine Log served the juiciest steaks, coupled with enormous baked potatoes. "Now that's a different story. I guess I am pretty hungry."

"What else is new?" he joked. As I walked away, Dad added, "Oh, and one more thing."

His tone made me think he had something positive to add. Had he forgotten to compliment me on my accomplishment of trapping my first hawk? Was he going to tell me how well I had crafted Flip's new leather jesses and anklets, fitting him perfectly on my first try?

I faced him, eager to hear what he had to say. "Yeah?"

He slid his hands in his pockets. "It's my duty as your sponsor to remind you that falconry is extremely difficult for first years to grasp, so don't get your hopes up for earning that Best Apprentice pin at the meet next month. Falconry is all about camaraderie and becoming one with nature—not competition. Worry about doing the best you can and be satisfied with that, okay?"

I tried not to let the disappointment show in my face. "Sure. I get it. Thanks, Dad." But as I trudged toward the house, I knew deep down that he had never given that speech to Lincoln. Guess Dad's lack of confidence in me didn't bother me as much anymore. It was one of those facts of life that I had to accept, or it'd eat me up inside.

Besides, there was always the chance that I could prove him wrong.

FIVE ···🦅

O N THE RIDE OVER TO MOM'S WORK, I WAS TRYING
to locate the exact spot of the itch on my back when Maddie
launched into a saga about some loudmouth classmate none of us
knew or cared about. "Anastasia told us that her mom is going
to buy her whatever car she wants when she turns sixteen, but
I think she's lying. I mean, her mom wouldn't even let her join
Creativity Club, so you wouldn't believe it either, would you,
Mercer?"

"What?" I stopped scratching for a second when I heard my
name. "You must have mistaken me for someone who listens
when you speak."

"Very funny." She scrunched her nose and stuck out her
tongue.

Dad pulled into the Illinois University of Rockford parking
lot, saving me from death by boredom. I noticed a group of about
fifteen people near the entrance to the lab, walking back and
forth and holding signs. Lab workers on strike? Students against
science? Two people held a large white banner that read HALT
THE SLAUGHTER — LET HUMANS AND ANIMALS LIVE TO-
GETHER.

HALT. I'd heard that name before but couldn't quite remember what it was. Based on their signage, they seemed to be

insinuating that the lab was preventing humans and animals from living together . . . and then slaughtering them? That didn't make sense. Mom told me that she cured diseases at work, never anything about animal torture. What was going on?

I hopped out of the truck and craned my neck to get a closer look.

"What's happening, Mercer?" Maddie sailed past me.

"Someone's yanking your chain." I tugged on her ponytail, evoking a loud "Stop it!" from her, which made me laugh.

"Hold up, you two," Dad called from inside the truck. "My wallet fell under my seat."

"I'll meet you there," I said, curious to see what all the commotion was about.

"Don't start anything with those people!" Dad warned. "Maddie, stay here."

Don't start anything? Me? Dad had the wrong brother. Lincoln was willing to risk life and limb to be at the center of a controversy, but he had the muscles to back it up. All I wanted was a backstage pass. I hurried my scrawny butt over there, eager to find out the scoop.

From a safe distance, of course.

As I neared Mom's building, two fine-looking girls tromped toward me in skimpy homemade dog costumes. Gotta love Indian summer weather in mid-September. The girls held a banner between them that read DON'T KILL LABS IN YOUR LAB. Yellow Labrador puppies pranced along the bottom of the sign, the last one with a gun against its head. The image was totally creepy, but I forgot all about it when the girls turned and walked the other way. Nice tails, girls. Walk slower.

At times like these, I wished I had the face of Reed and the confidence of Charlie, because that combination would have girls flocking to me like Canada geese heading south for the winter. I relished the image of a squadron of girls in a big V rushing toward me with their arms outstretched. They could goose me all they wanted.

A middle-aged guy with a ponytail muddied up my view by holding a cardboard sign in front of my face. Stepping back, I read KILLING CANINES IS DOGGONE CRUEL, in squiggly red letters that I guessed were supposed to look like dripping blood but appeared more like smeared ketchup. Ugly Ponytail Guy got right in my face and huffed, "Don't use pugs to test your drugs!"

"Don't look at me, dude." I held my arms up in surrender mode. "I don't do drugs. Or pugs, for that matter."

Five steps later, another hot girl, this one in a skinny white top and Dalmatian pajama pants, stepped off the lawn and blocked my path. Her nose was painted black and she had little whiskers drawn across her cheeks. Not only that, but her blond hair had been pulled up into ponytails on the sides like a floppy dog's ears. The hypodermic needle poking out of her chest with fake blood smeared around it was over the top, but hey, whatever made this chick happy was fine by me as long as she kept prancing like that.

"Oh my God!" The girl waved her hands in the air excitedly, making her pamphlets flutter. "Mercer, right? From the pet shop this morning? What are you doing here?"

My mind became as jumbled as the mouse tank. Dream Girl? At my mom's work? I peered closer, and sure enough, a small diamond stud twinkled on the side of her smudgy black nose. My heart started pounding as I nodded, grinning uncontrollably. I lifted my chin toward the commotion behind her. "I was kind of wondering the same thing about you."

She laughed heartily as a heavyset woman in a one-piece purple jump suit tapped her on the shoulder. "Off the sidewalk, Lucy. It's against the rules."

So her name was Lucy. I thought it fit her perfectly — fun and cute. But what was with the no-sidewalk rule?

"Sorry, I forgot," Lucy said to the frizzy-haired lady before turning to me. "Want to walk with me a second?"

"Sure." I'd walk with her for a few billion seconds if she'd let me. We stepped onto the grass, sliding in line behind two little girls wearing Scooby-Doo costumes. "I thought you said you were from up north."

"I am." She nodded, her floppy ears nodding with her. "Or maybe I should say *was*. We moved to Woodley two weeks ago." She shrugged. "Guess it doesn't feel like home yet."

She lived in Woodley too? How incredible was that? Elation flooded through my body, making my heart rate leap. That meant that unless she lived way out past McKinley Road, there was a really good chance that she went to my high school. "Funny you should say that. I've been here two years and it doesn't feel like home yet to me either."

Dad and Maddie scurried past the assembly line of protesters. Ugly Ponytail Guy yelled at them too. "People who kill innocent animals will burn in hell, and their carcasses will be thrown to the dogs."

I turned to Lucy. "What's with all the death and destruction?"

She tilted her head slightly, squinting in confusion. "Haven't you heard what they do here? We're here to protest the university's testing procedures—ones that include injecting dogs with drugs to kill them."

"Are you sure?" With one quick toss of my head to get the hair out of my eyes, I glanced down at the literature she had given me and saw a woman in a lab coat smiling as she held a knife to a dog's throat. What kind of weird prank was this? "You know this is a college, right? Not an animal shelter."

"They 'claim,'" she said with air quotes, "that they're doing scientific research, but in reality, they're injecting Botox into boxers and performing cosmetic surgery on baby pigs to test new plastic surgery procedures. Totally disrespecting the right of all creatures to live naturally."

Killing dogs and giving pigs plastic surgery? There was no way my mother was performing those sorts of atrocities. Although, now that I thought about it, I'd be lying if I didn't say

I'd be at least a little curious about what a pig with a face-lift would look like. The thing is, I had always imagined Mom was, I don't know, examining things under a microscope. I was definitely going to ask her about this at lunch. "Wow. Well, it's nice of you to help out."

"Thanks!" Lucy beamed. "Protecting animals makes me happy."

"Me too," I agreed, hoping she'd realize that we were both nature lovers. How perfect was that? Of course, she showed it in a different way than I did, but what did that matter?

Before I could ask Lucy more questions, behind me Dad snapped, "Back off, lady."

I whipped around to see the crazy woman in purple yelling, "Dogs are humans with fur and they don't deserve to suffer anguish and humiliation at the hands of murderers!" Her eyeballs bulged so wide open, they looked like they'd fall out if she sneezed. I almost laughed, thinking she was being theatrical on purpose, but no one else seemed amused, so I fought the urge.

Dad pulled Maddie closer to him, scanning the area. The second he spotted me, his eyes narrowed and he angrily beckoned me over. I gulped. "Uh, can you hold on a second?"

"I'm not going anywhere. We're walking in circles anyway." Lucy smiled and slipped back into line.

Before I could even get within five feet of my dad, he sputtered, "What do you think you're doing?" His face reddened the way it does when he trips over my shoes.

I shrugged, not sure why he was so uptight. "Nothing. Just talking to a girl from school."

Between clenched teeth, he spat, "No, you're not. Let's *go!*"

I could tell by his expression that this was an order, not a request. But I wasn't about to walk away a second time without at least asking for my dream girl's number. "Gimme one second, okay? I just need to ask her something." When his nostrils started to flare, I brilliantly added, "It's about homework."

Dad stared at me and then at the protesters. "Make it fast. And don't mention anything about your mother." *Duh,* I wanted to say, wondering exactly how stupid he thought I was.

As I walked back toward the protesters, the woman in purple began swaying back and forth with her eyes closed, chanting some gibberish about salvation. I spied Lucy heading back toward me, but how was I going to ask her for her number with all these people yelling out slogans and my father waiting impatiently twenty feet away? Talk about awkward.

As Lucy approached, she had a curious look on her face. Her gorgeous green eyes searched out mine. "Hey, I just thought of something. You're not here to visit someone who works in the lab, are you?"

I could tell from her tone that the correct answer to her question wasn't "as a matter of fact, my mom's the director here." So instead I winced, pretending I'd rather cut my leg off with a butter knife than associate with someone who worked at this slaughterhouse. "What? No. We're here to pick up some forms about college for my older brother for next year. He's a senior."

If Lincoln had been there with me then, he'd have used this opportunity to say, "But as long as I'm here, can I pick you up too?" But that wasn't my style. Not that I had a style, because I was such a newbie at this. I cleared my throat, deciding I'd just need to come out with it. I swallowed, feeling an unnatural smile spread across my lips. "So I was wondering if—"

"Stop the slaughter of innocent dogs!" the crazy woman shrieked, collapsing to the ground in a heap at my feet.

My anxiety was already pumping at full speed, but this shot it through the roof. Had she actually passed out, or was this part of the act? I knelt down by her side. "Are you okay?"

"She's fine," Lucy intoned, sounding embarrassed. "She has low blood pressure and when she gets excited, she sort of faints. Happens all the time. C'mon, Mom. Stand up."

Holy crap! Purple jump-suit lady was her mother? Lucy and I each grabbed a flabby arm and got her back on her feet. "There you go," I said, trying to sound positive. "Feeling better?" How did Lucy have such a nutjob for a mom and still turn out so nice?

"Thank you, young man!" Lucy's mother chirped. The color started returning to her chubby cheeks. "It's rare to see such a gentleman in a fella who's only . . ." She paused, waiting for my response.

"Fourteen," I replied, immediately regretting it. I should have said I was fifteen or sixteen because according to my brother, Dr. Lincoln of Loveology, girls wouldn't date younger guys.

"I am too!" Lucy said cheerfully, making me a bit more confident about my chances of getting her number.

Her mother bustled off to rejoin the group of protesters when I heard Dad's undeniable you're-grinding-down-my-last-nerve voice. "Mercer, *now!*"

Lucy bit her lip, glancing at the entrance to the lab. "You'd better go. Your father seems really anxious to get those forms."

After giving Dad the one-minute sign with my finger, I started to panic. How awkward would it be to just straight out ask for her phone number amid all this chaos? But then, somehow, the world's greatest idea came to me. If I pretended to be interested in this dog protector club or whatever of hers, she'd totally think I was the right guy for her. Then voilá! I could have the prettiest, coolest girl around. "How can I get more information about your club?"

"You want to join HALT?" Lucy's green eyes opened wide with delight as if I had just rescued her puppy from a burning building. "That's so cool! If you want, I could call you tonight and tell you all about it. I totally wouldn't mind."

And as it turned out, neither would I.

"That'd be great." Freakin' amazing, in fact. I whipped out my wallet, handing her one of the fake business cards I'd made in graphic arts class that read JACKASS OF ALL TRADES, MASTER OF NUNS, with my name and phone number on it. Maybe it wasn't the best impression of me, but it was probably the most accurate. Except the nun part. I didn't know any nuns, but if I did, I bet I could be their master. If they'd let me, that is.

"Talk to you later then, Lucy." I gave her a head nod, trying to remain calm, but inside, my heart was leaping like eleven lords. After I turned toward the entrance, one glance at my dad's face made me pick up the pace. While I'd expected him to shower me with remarks, I hadn't expected a deluge. Literally. Droplets of liquid fury pelted my cheek as he spoke.

"What's wrong with you?" Dad looked at me, his eyebrows pinched together. "Don't you know who those people are? Why were you talking so long and what did you give her?"

Maddie stared at me, her arms crossed. "Yeah!"

I ignored her, realizing Dad was in no mood to appreciate my smooth move with Lucy. So I said, "We're working on a project together, so I gave her my phone number, that's all." Then I pushed past them, hoping to cut off any further discussion. After navigating the revolving doors, the echoey quiet of the university building made the protesters' voices resemble the buzz of a fluorescent light in its final hour. Hopefully that would calm my father down as well.

Once inside, Dad strode toward the elevator, waving me on. "As far as that girl is concerned, as soon as your project is done, you stay away from her. She's bad news."

"Yeah!" Maddie repeated, sneering at me. "You made us wait for you because of her!"

"Big deal. I've waited for you plenty of times." Seriously, though. Why was Dad so worked up? I knew if I asked him for specifics, I'd get a ten-minute sermon about some obscure thing someone had done to him twenty years ago. So I kept my smile hidden as I buzzed with anticipation, wondering if Lucy would actually call.

SIX

WHEN WE WERE FINALLY HEADING UP TO MOM'S
floor, Maddie fixed her hair, gazing at herself in the shiny
surface of the elevator's front panel. "That whole thing was scary.
Why did those people say Mom's work kills dogs?"

It's got to be some stupid mix-up. Forget it and move on. We
had better and juicier things to think about, like Elliot's prime
rib with creamy horseradish sauce on the side. My mouth watered picturing it.

As Dad put his hand on my sister's shoulder, I noticed that
the lines around his eyes resembled finely chopped coleslaw in
the subdued light of the elevator. Or maybe I was just project-
ing my hunger onto his face. Either way, he looked worried. "It
probably has something to do with the heart attack study they're
conducting right now. It uses dogs as test subjects, and, yes, some
dogs do lose their lives during the testing period, which is un-
fortunate. But Mom and the other scientists here make humans'
lives better by discovering drugs that help premature babies'
lungs to develop, or stop the spread of skin cancer, or prevent
people from having seizures."

So it seemed that at least some of Lucy's statements were true.
No mention of face-lifts or Botox, though. Knowing how quickly
a rumor could spread at school and—let's face it—how juiced

up it became each time a new person told the story, I wished I knew exactly what was true and what was juice.

"But that's so sad for the dogs." Maddie puffed out her lips in full pout mode.

It was kind of depressing. I mean, a dog *could* be a nice pet — for a family who didn't have thirteen birds of prey to take care of. But, sad as it was, if a few dogs' lives saved millions of humans' lives, maybe it was worth it. I wondered how many dogs they used before the study was over. And where'd they get the dogs anyway — pet shops, dog shelters, back alleys? I doubted Mom would divulge that information to me. After all, I was merely a boy who lived in her house. Okay, so that was mean. But ever since she'd gotten this facility director's job two years ago, she spent way more time there than at home, as evidenced by her being here on a Saturday. I missed the old mom, I guess, the one who got home at five every day and didn't work on weekends.

After exiting the elevator on Mom's floor, we signed in and received our visitor's badges. Two clean-cut guys in lab coats passed us, engaged in a heated discussion about bacterial infections. A sick feeling jumbled up my stomach. I was wondering if those guys were on their way to slaughter a shepherd or inject drugs into a pug. We walked to the reception area outside Mom's office, admiring the large gold plaque on her door: DR. SHALENE BUDDIE, DIRECTOR OF RESEARCH. Dad whispered to Marla, Mom's secretary, that we came to surprise her, so she shouldn't announce we were there.

We tiptoed past Marla, who smiled and waved to me. We huddled outside Mom's office door, and on the count of three, Dad whipped it open. Maddie and I leaped into the room and yelled, "Surprise!"

Mom glanced up from her computer. "Hey . . . what are you guys doing here?"

Whoopee. Uncork the champagne.

Dad closed the door. "We're here to take the birthday girl out to lunch."

"Aw . . . how sweet. Give me one sec." Mom typed a sentence or two and closed her laptop. I knew deep down she was happy to see us, but her commitment to this place seemed to take over her personality. Here at the university she was Dr. Shalene Buddie, a brilliant medical researcher, but at home she turned back into regular old Shay, a mom who liked red wine, medical mystery TV shows, and dark chocolate Milky Way bars. She looked at her watch, pursing her lips. "Hmm. I've got a mountain of work that's due today, but I suppose I can take a short break for lunch, right?"

"Hello? It's your birthday!" Maddie exclaimed, as if that trumped everything else. I remember when I was little the shock of being told I had to go to school on my big day.

"Thanks, baby." Mom smiled at her, but I could see the tension in her eyes, her forehead, her neck. She looked at the rest of us. "I have one project I need to check on before we go, but it's on our way out. Give me a minute to freshen up."

After pulling out a small makeup bag from her bottom desk drawer, Mom twisted the top off a lipstick tube. As I watched her paint her lips, it occurred to me that Maddie had Mom's dark blond hair but Dad's brown eyes, and I had Dad's brown hair but her gray-blue eyes rimmed with navy. Guess that proved we were all genetically linked. Our craving for Milky Way bars might have been a clue too.

Dad cleared his throat. "Just so you know, Shalene, some of those HALT protesters hassled us out there on the way in."

Hassled us? More like completely enthralled us with their beauty and charm. But I wasn't about to contradict him. No one wanted to see Uptight Sputtering Man reappear.

"What? Why didn't anyone inform me?" Mom punched two numbers on the speakerphone, her mouth tight with anger. Why had Dad brought that up now? My stomach growled as we watched Mom tap her foot, waiting for Security to answer. We all stood frozen, listening, while the phone buzzed.

"Security. Max here."

"Max, it's Dr. Buddie. HALT's out front again, and they're breaching the security line. I want you to go warn them that if they step one foot onto the sidewalk or touch the visitors in any way, we'll have them arrested for trespassing and assault; you got that?"

"Yes, ma'am. Right away," Max answered. "I'm heading there now."

"And if they ever show up again, I expect to be notified

immediately." She ended the call and picked up a manila folder off her desk.

Part of me wanted to lighten the mood with "Hey! Lucy can touch this visitor any time she wants!" but I kept quiet. Though I wasn't exactly sure where I stood on the whole dog issue, I knew everyone was blowing things out of proportion around here. Arresting them? On what charges? Touching the university's sidewalk? How petty could my mother be?

Mom smoothed her gray flannel skirt and heaved a huge sigh. "I probably shouldn't be going to lunch while those protesters are here——" Maddie cut in with some loud whining, but Mom silenced her with an upheld hand. "But if we keep it under an hour, I'll do it. Okay with everyone?"

Maddie cheered, but I shifted my eyes to Dad, wondering if he'd declare that we needed to change plans. Elliot's Pine Log was only a few blocks away, but it was kind of fancy. It seemed to me that the fancier the place, the slower the waiters. Dad hurried ahead to open the door for my mom. "No problem," he declared emphatically. Maybe I'd get that steak, after all.

We were hurrying down the hall when Mom suddenly said, "Stay here, guys. I'll be right back." Her black heels clicked against the shiny tile floor as she made a beeline to the door marked AUTHORIZED PERSONNEL ONLY. She slid her ID through the slot and disappeared inside.

A moment later, we heard the faint sound of a dog barking somewhere deep in the lab. I swallowed the bit of hot bile that rose up my throat. So there were definitely dogs here, but unless I was hallucinating, that one sounded alive to me.

"Dogs are the best," Maddie said to a man in a lab coat striding by. "Why do you have to kill them?"

"Shut up, Maddie!" I elbowed her hard.

"Sorry about that." Dad held one hand up in apology. The young scientist smiled uncomfortably and continued his jaunt down the hall.

Dad gave Maddie a look of reproach. "That's private business, Madison. Mom can tell you more about it later. Just stand here quietly."

After what felt like ages, Mom burst through the door like a busy waitress bringing out an order. Or maybe that was my hunger insinuating itself into my perceptions again.

"Okay, I'm all set now. Follow me," she said brightly. "My car's parked in back."

We hurried to match Mom's brisk pace. Dad said, "Do you want to ask security to come out with us, Shay? Just in case?"

Mom shook her head. "Nah, I think we're okay. HALT goes for drama and media attention. Nothing exciting about the employee parking lot."

We took a different elevator down, which led us to the back entranceway. We stepped outside, temporarily blinded by the sun. Mom scanned the lot, shielding her eyes. Before we could go anywhere, a rusty green station wagon pulled in front of us and stopped.

The driver had his window down, his arm hanging out. "Well, lookee who we have here. We hit the jackpot, boys. It's the director of this hellhole."

The back and passenger doors opened and two guys around Lincoln's age slipped out. One guy had on a Cubs hat and the other had arms the size of ham shanks. What was going on?

"Security's on their way!" Mom called out to them, fumbling around her waistline for her walkie-talkie.

When they started walking toward us, their jaws set tight and eyes trained on Mom, a blast of intense panic hit my chest. They didn't look like the protesters out front.

Dad strode toward them, his hands held high, as if trying to placate them. "Look, fellas, we're with our children. We don't want any trouble. Get back in your car."

"Security needed in the employee parking lot!" Mom barked into her walkie-talkie, her voice shaky. "Now!"

I grabbed my sister and pulled her close.

"What are they doing, Mercer?" she asked, glomming onto my waist.

I ignored her, watching as Mom thumbed through a set of keys on a large ring.

The jerks kept coming, not saying a word.

Dad's tone changed in a hurry. "I *said,* get back in your car, boys." He blocked the space between us and them and then turned to yell, "Shalene, kids! Get back inside!"

My ears were ringing. Should I run for help, bring Mom and

Maddie inside, attack? "Leave my mom alone, you maggots!"

I admit that wasn't the boldest move I'd ever made, but I didn't think I could take on two buff college guys without a weapon, nor with my sister wrapped around me in a death grip. I looked around for something to threaten them with — a stick, a big rock, anything — but there were only a few pebbles and an old food wrapper.

I spied a chunk of loose curb, but before I could pick it up, the Cubs hat guy yelled, "You like the blood of innocent dogs on your hands? Here you go, Director of Death!" Before I knew what was happening, the two guys ran full speed toward us.

Maddie screamed, "Watch out, Mom!"

The shorter, buff guy pulled the lid off a pitcher and flung the entire contents on my mom, creating a waterfall of thick red liquid, drenching her suit. The scent of tomato soup punched the air. Chunks of what I assume was fake fur pebbled the ground.

"You're all going to jail, you punks!" Dad grabbed the buff guy by the shirt, but one strong push almost knocked Dad down, so the guy got away.

"You got to catch us first!" the Cubs hat guy replied, laughing as he ran.

That did it. They thought this was funny? Freaking my mom out? Scaring my little sister? "You jagoffs!" I screamed, my face flaming hot. I knew what I had to do. I took two steps toward the loose cement chunk, dragging Maddie with me. She let out a loud shriek and let go, burying her face in her hands.

I ran and picked up the loose chunk of curb and chased after them. Mom yelled, "I'm fine! Forget it, Mercer!"

But I wasn't about to forget it.

Blind with rage, I watched the two guys jump into the car and start driving off.

Dad snapped, "Let them go, Mercer!"

I could still hear Maddie screeching in the background as Mom shouted, "Get their license plate number!"

Screw the license plate; they were getting away! I bolted after them, racing through the parking lot, cement chunk in hand.

"Mercer! Don't!" Dad called out. "They could have weapons!"

What were they going to do? Fling empty soup cans at me? Before they could get any farther, I stopped and whipped the curb hunk as hard as I could at the back window of the station wagon. It fell short, the piece skidding across the blacktop and landing under a gray Buick. Me and my stupid, weak arm muscles! Never again, I vowed.

I walked back toward my family, embarrassed. Mom had her arm around Maddie, who was still sobbing her guts out. "It's okay, Maddie. I'm fine, honey."

"Are you sure, babe?" Dad pulled out a handkerchief from his pocket and handed it to my mother.

"Yes, just aggravated; that's all." Mom looked at Dad. "Call the police, okay?"

Dad stepped away, sliding his cell phone out of his back pocket. A moment later, two university security guards came bustling over. They were too late to catch the guys in the Chevy but just in time to get an earful from my mom for failing to man the back entrance — the same back entrance that Mom herself had said the protesters would never hang out at, but I wasn't about to bring that up.

After the cops arrived, I sat on the curb next to Maddie, listening as my parents rattled off a description of the three guys in the Chevy wagon. We all added what little we knew, but there wasn't a whole lot to say. After that, Mom announced she'd work from home for the rest of the day. I totally understood why we had to scrap our plans, but I couldn't help mourning the loss of medium-rare sirloin steak and the huge baked potato with all the toppings. Friggin' protesters had ruined my mother's suit and our awesome lunch. Damn them!

As we waited for the police to finish their investigation, the unsettling thought that these guys were part of Lucy's group crossed my mind. God, I hoped not. There was no way I could even think of going out with Lucy if she did stuff like that to people like my mom. But I wasn't ready to give up on my dream girl. Not yet. Not before I'd had a chance to figure things out.

My parents decided to pick up Mom's Camaro the following day, so we all headed to Dad's truck. He grabbed a blanket out of the back and placed it on the passenger seat for my mom to sit on, while Maddie and I slid into the back seat. The little drama queen kept making gagging sounds every few seconds, so Dad gave her an empty grocery bag "just in case." The smell of the rotting tomato soup concoction was pretty horrendous, so Maddie and I opted for a windstorm over a stink tornado, and Dad kept the windows halfway open the whole way home.

Mom pulled napkins out of the glove box and blotted her sleeve vigorously. "Those HALT people are brainless idiots." She tsked loudly, dabbing and blotting at spots on her blouse. "They think it's noble to fight for animals, but they have no clue that the whole point of our testing is to save their sister, their husband, or their own sorry selves. Ridiculous."

My heart sank. So those guys were part of HALT after all, it seemed. For several minutes, I stared out the window of the car, watching stores whiz by, emotionally spent. Figures that I'd finally meet a cool girl who might even like me back and now it was over before it had started. Why would Lucy be part of a group that did nasty things like throw fake animal fur and spoiled soup on scientists? I ran a hand through my hair, pissed off. This sucked.

"Mom?" Maddie asked, her voice high and whiny. "Why don't you just do your testing on mice? That way people wouldn't be so mad at you."

I tuned in, curious about the answer to this one myself.

Mom turned around partway and faced her. "Because a dog's cardiovascular system is very similar to ours. No other animal species mimics what happens to humans so closely. For this study to yield any sort of useful results, it has to be canines."

"But dogs are so *cute*," Maddie insisted.

Mom's face softened, but I could tell she was trying not to lose it. "Yes, dogs are cute, honey. But they're also really important to our research. The FDA doesn't allow us to test our new drugs on humans until extensive trials on animals have concluded."

"So you're *required* to test on animals first?" Somehow I was relieved to hear that the scientists at Mom's work didn't have a choice.

She nodded, looking a bit surprised that I didn't know this already. "Absolutely. The FDA needs indisputable success in the clinical trials before they approve a new drug." She tossed a piece of soggy gray fur out the open window.

"So they should be protesting the FDA people, not you?" Maddie asked.

Mom smiled. "Well, the FDA probably wouldn't be too happy about that either. But yes, in a way, you're right. I can't change those laws, even if I wanted to, which I don't. While I dislike taking a dog's life, I'd be horrified to test our drug on humans. *That's* inhumane."

Dad piped in with "I guarantee if one of those HALT people had a heart attack, they'd be begging for these drugs. Wish they'd ask questions before acting on things, that's all."

That's when I decided to take my parents' advice. Instead of acting against Lucy, I'd ask questions, perform my own clinical trials, and hope for indisputable success.

SEVEN 🦅

WHEN WE GOT HOME, I INHALED TWO CHEESE sandwiches and half a bag of beef jerky — an unsatisfying replacement for prime rib — but I cheered up on the way to the rehab center to work with Flip. The second I walked in, I caught a hint of the aroma I craved — a blend of leather, dust, and lanolin oil — and sucked that scent into my lungs like a chain smoker. Dad had Sasha, our sharp-shinned hawk, on his fist, bringing her to the examination table for her daily weigh-in.

I watched as he set her on her T perch on the bird scale. "When you're done with Sasha, can we work with Flip?"

"Hold on, Buddie Boy. We have something to discuss first."

My anger simmered as I gripped the edge of the worktable. Why did Dad insist on calling me that lame nickname after I'd told him a thousand times I didn't like it? But getting into an argument over it was off the list for today. I needed his help manning Flip. So I sat on the stool and waited while he worked the soap up into a lather, methodically washing every surface of his hands.

He finally turned off the water with his elbow and grabbed a paper towel. "We haven't discussed your apprenticeship duties yet. Before you work with Flip today and every day, I'll need you to hose down all thirteen mews. I'm releasing Lincoln of that

59

duty and handing it over to you. Let me know when you're done. Then we'll start manning your hawk."

"We have to wait until I clean *all* the mews?" I threw my hands up in exasperation. "That'll take me at least half an hour!"

"More like an hour if you do a good job." He eyed the scale, pausing as he observed the digital readout. "I tell you what — skip Flip's mews for today so you don't frighten him." He woke his laptop with a tap of a few keys and noted Sasha's weight on his daily log. "Why are you acting so shocked? Cleaning the mews is one of the burdens of being an apprentice and you know it."

I did know it. I complained only so he'd think I was overwhelmed and wouldn't add any more responsibilities on top of all the cleaning. Serious about falconry? Definitely. Dedicated to cleanliness? Not so much. I'd helped Lincoln with this particular job many times. The process was the same for each mews: remove the bird, attach it to the holding perch in the hallway, go back with the hose, and obliterate every mushy, gray mute pile lying on the floor that you cared to notice, change out all the used food and water bowls with clean ones, and then return the bird to its home. Do that thirteen times without having a major artery clawed open, and you were hired.

I strolled into Monocle's mews first, wasting a solid ten minutes with her so Dad would think I'd spent an entire hour cleaning. I scratched between her ear tufts and on her chest while she stared back at me with her gorgeous yellow eye. I found an especially good spot on her neck, so she rubbed her face against my hand in pleasure. I chuckled, thinking Monocle was one seriously cool owl. Even though Dad was adamant that rehabbed birds of prey are not pets, I'd always thought of Monocle as my dog substitute. Although, after what I found out today, maybe I'd better keep Monocle as far away from Mom as possible.

Lincoln peered in through the steel bars of the mews I was cleaning. He had a barbell in each hand and was doing biceps curls, a softball-size mound appearing with each flex of his arm. "Make sure you do a good job over by Bella. She ate a whole pigeon last night, and she's been slicing it out like an automatic rifle all day." He let out a blast of laughter, as if cleaning massive amounts of his bird's crap was funny.

"I've been slicing a lot today too." I squirted his chest with a blast of the hose.

Now *that* was funny.

"What the hell?" Lincoln looked down at his bare chest. "You ever do that again, you're dead meat." He pointed a barbell in my direction, which would have worried me if there hadn't been twelve steel bars between us. Even Lincoln wasn't strong enough to pry them apart.

I hoped.

"My hand slipped, sorry!" I needed to soothe the savage beast that was my brother because he was unpredictable when angry. Wish he'd lighten up. As I watched him skulk off to continue his workout, I wondered, were big muscles really the key to getting girls to chase after you like a free coupon to Starbucks?

I was definitely going to hit the weights later on. Maybe it would help me win Lucy over.

Speaking of which, I thought I'd better rehearse what I'd say to Lucy if she called. While I was thinking about possible funny lines, a gruff voice behind me asked, "Where's that butt-ugly apprentice I heard is around here?"

I grinned, recognizing Weasel's voice. Since he was Dad's closest friend and falconer confidant, I knew him almost as well as I knew my father. I poked my head into the hallway. "Sorry, I can't help you, pal. Only extremely good-looking apprentices work here."

Weasel tugged at his crazy beard, which he probably hadn't shaved since he was a toddler. It had intermingled patches of brown, red, and gray hairs throughout, and if you looked long enough, probably a few missing children as well. "Eh, you'll do." The toothpick poking out of the side of his mouth wiggled up and down as he spoke. He looped his thumbs through his suspenders and twanged, "So I hear you done got yourself a hawk, boy."

"Yup. Wanna see it, mister?"

"Why you think I came? I tell you, boy, you is ugly *and* stupid." He looked serious for a second, and then gave me that whacked-out belly laugh of his, the kind that makes you laugh too. "How's it going, Skinny?" He pulled me into a headlock and messed up my hair at the same time.

"Pretty good." I wiggled out of his embrace, flicking my hair out of my eyes.

He poked my ribs. "Don't look like it. When you gonna get some meat on those bones?"

Dad appeared out of nowhere, answering for me. "With as much meat as Mercer eats, you'd think he was prepping for the Caveman Olympics." He smiled, but it quickly faded. "I noticed you cleaned the mews like a caveman too, Mercer. You're going to have to do way better than that in the future."

I hunched over and took a few loping steps toward Dad, doing my best caveman act. "Ooh, ooh. Me clean cave good."

Dad shot me his Joe Falconer look. "I'm serious. No more half-ass jobs from now on."

Weasel chortled. "Yeah, they'd better all be whole-ass jobs or you're out of here, boy."

"Don't encourage him, Weasel," Dad said, but I saw him wink. He looked at me. "Well, what are you waiting for? Go get Flip so we can start his training."

Finally! I practically ran to Flip's mews and peeked in the window. There he was, my new hunting buddy, waiting for me. I turned the doorknob and Flip leaped off his perch faster than a high-rise BASE jumper. Make that a low-rise jumper, since the floor post was only six inches off the ground. But we had to tether our new birds to the post or they'd fly around, crisscrossing the mews like a game of tag gone wrong when you went to retrieve them. After they were "manned," or spent enough time with us so that they came to trust us, which took anywhere from a few days to a week, we could let them fly anywhere they wanted inside their mews, but Flip was far from ready for that.

Spying Dad's flannel shirt hanging on a nearby hook, I decided to put it on for a little extra protection. After sliding my elbow-length glove on to my left hand, I took a deep breath and walked in. Flip hissed and flapped his wings as if his tail was on fire. I inched forward until he relaxed before unhooking his leash and grabbing hold of the jesses that were attached to his legs. Flip began bating again, flapping his wings a hundred miles an hour in my face, but I hung on and righted him back up each time he landed upside down. He eventually tired and grabbed on to my heavily protected forearm with his steel claws, panting like crazy.

All his hostility toward me made me wonder how the heck I was going to transform Flip from "wild hawk who reviled the sight of me" into "ace hunter who killed like a trained assassin" in twenty-three days. Flip needed to snag some major game at the falconry meet, or I wouldn't have a chance of winning the Best Apprentice award.

I joined Dad and Weasel out in the training area, the only swath of grass that we keep trimmed in the entire football-field-size lawn that lies between the house and the pond way out back. We call the pond Buddie Waters, named after some famous old blues guitarist my dad loved. It was my favorite place to hang out. You could swim, fish, take out a paddleboat, or just sit and vegetate.

Heading to the rounded steel bow perch, I knelt down and Flip stepped onto the pipe wound with rope. So far, so good. I hooked his leash onto the metal loop.

Dad spoke quietly. "Now walk backwards toward me slowly."

I backed up about five feet, stopping just in front of him and Weasel. Weasel handed me a small chunk of rabbit meat from one of the pockets of his green falconer's vest. "Now hold it out on your fist where he can see it, Skinny. When he flies toward you, stand perfectly still."

I did exactly what Weasel said, but Flip kept flying off the perch, trying to get away instead of coming toward me. And each time, it took him another fifteen seconds of flapping around before he landed back on the perch. Flip sat there breathing heavily, his wings held away from his body in an angry posture. "What's wrong with him?" I asked Dad, the heat of frustration warming my face. "Why won't he come to me? Isn't he hungry?"

"Settle down, Mercer. It'll happen," Dad responded calmly. "All in good time."

"Try it real nice and slow," Weasel coaxed, patting my back for encouragement. "Once he figures out he can't go anywhere, he'll settle down and see the food."

After five more failed attempts, Dad sighed. "Well, that's enough for today."

I spun toward him. "Enough? I didn't do anything with him

yet." Even though Flip wasn't playing nicely, I wasn't ready to put him back in his mews. If Dad and Weasel were both experts, why didn't they do whatever it was they did to calm a skittish hawk?

Dad stroked his mustache. "Relax, Mercer. You did do something—you've started socializing him. That's it for tonight. Put him away and we'll try again tomorrow."

Right when I was about to storm off, Weasel put his hand on my shoulder and squeezed. "If you stress Flip out too much, he'll develop a fear of you. You don't want that now, do you?"

I shook my head no, but secretly I wanted to ask how Flip could be any more afraid of me than I was of him.

Dad motioned with his head toward the mews. "Only give him a small portion of dinner so that he's hungrier tomorrow. Little baby steps."

Weasel smiled at me. His beard moved in any case, so I think that meant he smiled. "Once ol' Flipper realizes you're in this together, things will get better, I promise."

"Yeah, I know." As I walked back toward the mews with Flip bating like crazy on my arm again, I wondered how'd I get this lunatic bird in shape to hunt in time for the meet if he wouldn't even fly five feet to get some free food from my hand. Maybe Dad and Weasel were just being nice and didn't want to tell me that Flip was a dud. A sick feeling hit me like a punch to the gut as a new idea crossed my mind: maybe they thought *I* was the dud.

I weighed out two ounces of thawed rabbit meat and plopped Flip's dinner into his bowl. He opened his mouth in alarm. Couldn't he understand that I was his guardian, not his enemy? "See you tomorrow, Flip. Hopefully you'll start to trust me." I trudged into the rehab center to wash up. When I was halfway through scrubbing rabbit guts off my fingers, Mom yelled from the house, "Mercer! Your cell phone's ringing!"

Lucy! I shut off the water, and without bothering to dry my hands, I sprinted out of the rehab center screaming, "Don't answer it!"

That's when I fell over the hose that some stupid Apprentice Boy forgot to wind back around the hose reel and nearly broke my neck.

EIGHT ····➤

IT'S A GIRL," MOM MOUTHED AS SHE HANDED ME MY phone, a confused look on her face.

"Yeah, so?" I was a little irritated that she had answered my cell, but even more irked that she seemed so surprised that a girl was calling me. I snatched the phone from her, bits of grass and mud still clinging to my forearms from my fall. I played it cool, leaning against the kitchen counter as if talking to the hottest girl in town was no big deal.

I reached for the deepest tones of my voice range. "Hello." Mom rolled her eyes before turning around to pour herself a glass of juice.

"Mercer? Is that you?" Lucy asked.

I decided to forgo the bass tones, not sure I could keep it up anyway. "Yeah, it's me."

She sounded relieved. "It's Lucy Wendel. To talk to you about HALT, remember?"

I jerked my head, nervously glancing at my mother. She didn't flinch, so she obviously hadn't overheard the dreaded word *HALT*. "Of course I remember." I didn't tell Lucy that her phone call had practically been the only thing on my mind the entire day.

Since I felt pretty self-conscious talking to Lucy with my

mother listening, I headed downstairs. It was comfortable enough in the basement—two navy leather couches, a flat-screen TV, a pool table, and a dartboard—but more important, it was nearly soundproof.

For the next ten minutes, Lucy babbled excitedly about how HALT was so wonderful because society had such a blatant disregard of the rights of animals. She explained that many HALT members were also vegetarians, because the need for animals would decrease over time if people didn't buy meat products, thereby saving thousands of animals' lives. I thought the whole idea of boycotting meat sounded like wishful thinking, but I said, "Uh-huh" and "You're kidding me!" at all the right spots, and that seemed to do the trick. Lucy was convinced that I was convinced, and that was all that mattered.

"So what do you think?" she asked breathlessly. "You want to join?"

Getting a girl to call me and talk about her club was way different from actually being a member. My stomach contents jostled at the thought of being part of the very group that had attacked my mother. Would joining HALT get me the private key to Lucy's heart, or was this how she treated all potential new members? I decided to ask a few more questions. In the name of scientific testing, of course. "How often would I see you? The group, I mean. Like meetings."

I shook my head at my stupidity. Any more slips like that, and she'd hang up.

Lucy cleared her throat. "Well, my friend Haley and I are starting up a teen HALT chapter at our school this year. She was one of the yellow Labs protesting with me." She giggled. "Do you go to Woodley High?"

I confirmed that I did, and she answered with a cheerful "Awesome! Me too," making me give a silent yet exuberant thank-you to the god of good-looking girls. She continued, "I thought maybe you could, you know, be part of the club too. With me."

"That might work," I said, struggling to maintain my cool when all I could think about was that Lucy went to Woodley! First, how incredible would it be to see her every day, but second, how had I missed seeing her in the hallway the first three days of school? I must have been sleepwalking.

"Cool!" she chirped. To my eager ears, it sounded like she meant it too. "Oh, but there is one thing you should know before you join." She sighed into the phone, making me worry that what was coming next was an admission that I'd have to arm-wrestle her boyfriend for the job of treasurer. "You'd be our first guy in the club. I know that would suck, but maybe you could eventually convince your friends or whatever."

Yeah, it'd totally suck being the only guy in a group of overly enthusiastic girls who didn't want to hurt animals. I could already picture myself entertaining Lucy and her friends with stupid jokes or wowing them with the new muscles I'd be building as soon as I started lifting those weights. That's when I heard the door leading to the basement open, followed by Dad's booming voice. "Mercer, get your butt up here and roll up the hose!"

"Be right there!" I shouted back, glad when I heard the door close again.

"Was that your dad?" she asked tentatively. There was no way I was going to explain that, at this very moment, we had thirteen birds housed in the rehab center — large, mean birds who ate fluffy little bunnies — and that I'd carelessly left the hose unwound, the same hose that, incidentally, washed away the bones of the birds' victims. Better for her to think that my dad had some anger management issues instead of me having laziness ones.

"Yeah, he wants me to do some chores. Before I go, I just wanted to say that I think you're doing a real nice thing." I cringed at my choice of words, thinking I sounded like a total wimp. I cupped my hand over my mouth so as to speak directly into the phone in case anyone upstairs could hear me. "And that I'd be happy to join HA — your club."

Though I knew I'd never protest at my mom's workplace, I figured they did other things I could get on board with. Hopefully, Lucy would be so completely smitten with my charm that soon enough it wouldn't matter to her if I went on her protests or not.

Or that I liked to hunt with hawks in my spare time.

Or that I regularly ate cows, pigs, and chickens in addition to freshly killed pheasants or grouse, courtesy of Dad's falcon,

Troy. I grimaced at the thought of how much stealth I'd need to pull this off, but there was no turning back now.

"Great. I can't wait to see you at school on Monday," she cooed. Was that a touch of flirtation I heard?

I almost blew my cover by blurting out an excited "Me too! I think I love you!" but I lowered my voice and gave a manly "Cool. Me too."

After we hung up, I raised both fists into the air while doing a three-second victory dance. If I could pull off playing Mercer, Protector of All Animals for a bit, perhaps there was a chance Lucy would go out with me. I didn't know how long it would take to win her over, but she sounded like she was digging my Father Nature side.

On Sunday morning, after three reminder yells from Dad to get up and clean the mews, I rolled out of bed, worried that the next time, he'd show up with a cattle prod in hand. I wrestled my black CEREAL KILLER T-shirt out of the drawer and threw on the crumpled jeans that were on the floor from yesterday. If I could barely see the rotten tomato soup splatters, I figured no one else could either. There was a bit of an odor when I sniffed my pants up-close, but nothing a shot of Intimidate cologne wouldn't fix. Three squirts later, I was good to go.

When I got downstairs, Maddie was sitting at the kitchen island with a plate of microwaved pancakes, watching some lame teenybopper show. She had her hair pulled back into the same messy hairstyle I'd seen on girls my age at school, along with her usual array of pink glittery attire. In honor of my T-shirt, I inhaled two bowls of Cinnamon Toasters, but was still hungry. When I glanced at Maddie's breakfast, the scent of the warm maple syrup made me drool. I waited for her to get distracted and then snatched the last pancake off her plate.

"Give that back!" Maddie lunged for the pancake. On the way, she bumped her glass, sending a huge *sploosh* of milk across the table. "Now look what you did, Mercer!"

It was hard to drum up any sympathy for her — she should have known better than to leave food unattended when I was around. "You want this back?" I made a show of licking the entire length of pancake before offering it to her. "Here you go, Sister Dearest."

"I'm telling Dad, you big jerk!" She huffed and puffed more than the Big Bad Wolf. "You eat it now."

"For me?" I gave her my biggest movie star smile, touching my chest. "You shouldn't have." I folded the pancake in half and took two huge bites. "Thanks, toots." I winked.

"Pig." She even talked like the wolf.

I was headed toward the family room when I spied a Waupaca Comets window decal stuck on the patio door. A pang of homesickness hit me square in the chest. "Where'd this come from, Maddie?" I pointed at the decoration from the high school I would've attended if we hadn't moved.

Maddie glared at me, her arms crossed. I could tell she was torn between wanting to be the one to broadcast this insignificant bit of news and torturing me by keeping me in the dark. Seconds later, she spilled. "Lincoln found it in the junk drawer this morning, so he stuck it there."

I felt somewhat comforted that Lincoln seemed to miss Wisconsin as much as I did. When Mom got the director job at the university's science lab, we moved from the coolest place on Earth to this quasi-rural town of Woodley, Illinois. Not only did I have to leave behind all my friends, but living in Illinois now made us FIBs—"Effing" Illinois Bastards—a term every Wisconsinite over the age of eight knew. Whoever made up that acronym of shame wasn't "fibbing." Sorry to say, some of them —I guess "we" would be more fitting now—even deserved it.

Every weekend in winter and all summer long, thousands of FIBs packed up their cars and headed to Wisconsin to escape their polluted, congested Chicagoland so they could inhale some clean Wisconsin air. During hunting season, everywhere you turned there was a FIB. They seemed nice enough—unless you talked football with them—but what I hated most was seeing them take down prize Wisconsin quarry, while some locals went home empty-handed. That part sucked. Like when the opposing team wins the homecoming game—it just doesn't seem right.

After my breakfasts, I went outside to clean the mews. Since I knew Dad would be watching me like a hawk, ha-ha, I hosed down all thirteen way better than I had yesterday. I gave a relaxing back rub to Monocle while she brushed her head against my hand. An hour later, I strolled into the rehab area. Dad had a new patient in the Raptor Restrainer, and he stood there clutching his chin, as if deciding what to do.

"Hey, Dad." I plopped on a stool. "I finished cleaning. I'm ready whenever you are."

He glanced up. "You'll have to wait a bit. I'm trying to decide what course of action to take with this female Cooper's hawk."

"What's wrong with her?" I scooched my stool closer, wanting a front-row view of my father in action. Not only did he possess the knowledge to cure a million avian illnesses, mend broken bones, and recognize exactly what type of infection a bird had simply by looking at it, he was also the Superman of the raptor world, zooming in faster than a speeding bullet to rescue injured birds. People called from all over the Midwest, looking for my dad's help. Good thing he was such an expert because one bad move with raptors and the DNR swooped in and removed all of your birds. Kind of like the FDR or whatever the organization Mom said watched over her drug testing. My favorite part of this whole rehabilitation thing was that after the bird healed completely, we released it back to the wild. Just as I'd do to Flip in a few months. Seeing a wild raptor get a second chance at life choked me up every time.

Another well-guarded secret of the rugged-but-majorly-sentimental Mercer Buddie.

"She's got a nasty case of bumblefoot." Dad turned on the hinged light and pulled it toward the hawk, lifting her foot so I could look underneath. "See those lesions?" He pointed to two red, puffy holes oozing fluid on the bottom of the hawk's foot. "This is why a falconer has got to keep his bird's perches wide enough so that when the bird is standing on them, her talons don't come around and pierce the bottom of her own foot."

"Whose hawk is it?" I was curious to know how far this falconer had driven to bring his bird to Dad. So far the record was 785 miles, all the way from Wichita, Kansas.

"Shockingly, she's from a fairly well-known zoo. It might be forgivable if she belonged to an ill-trained apprentice, but a zoo? They shouldn't be allowed to keep raptors if they don't know what they're doing." He frowned, shaking his head. "I'm required to report all zoo injuries to the licensing board, so they'll have to deal with them. Not going to give her back until they assure me things have been corrected." He strode to his medicine cabinet and opened the door. "You want to help me with the meds?"

"Sure." While I waited for Dad to get the supplies he needed, I scanned his personal Wall of Fame mounted over the examination table. There were at least ten plaques citing various accomplishments: MR. RICHARD BUDDIE, MIDWEST FALCONER OF THE YEAR; RICHARD FRANCIS BUDDIE, MASTER FALCONER; RICK BUDDIE, WILDLIFE REHABILITATION SPECIALIST. And there were a ton more in the drawer. I bet he had more certificates than the raptor workers of all the nearby zoos combined.

He set a variety of colored tubes and sterile tools wrapped in plastic on the table before putting on a pair of disposable medical gloves. "This zookeeper is lucky that he brought this hawk in when he did. Bumblefoot can be a killer, but I think this one will be okay."

As I watched my father squeeze a small blob of pinkish ointment onto a cotton swab I considered rehabbing birds for a living when I got older. Helping sick and injured birds seemed like the coolest thing ever. My dad didn't make a lot of money, but if I could find a wife like my mom — pretty, smart, and who brought in the big bucks — it'd be awesome. Although if I could marry a girl like Lucy, I bet I wouldn't care how much money we had.

Dad's voice broke into my daydream. "Hold her foot for me, okay?" I applied steady pressure so the hawk couldn't move as he dabbed antibiotic on the oozing wounds. "When we're through here, I'll check your cleaning job, and then we'll get started with today's training session."

I winced at the suggestion that I needed checking on. "You don't have to check. I did a good job this time."

"*This* time?" Dad raised his thick brown-gray eyebrows. "How about *every* time?" I rolled my eyes after he turned and walked to the medicine cabinet to return the ointment. "Go have Flip fly off the perch to you a few times and then I'll meet you out back in five minutes. Okay, Buddie Boy?"

"Sure thing, Dick." I knew I was pushing it, using the old-fashioned nickname for Richard, but how many times did a guy need to ask his dad to stop using his childhood nickname? "Kidding," I added quickly, giving him a fake smile and a shrug. Maybe this time he'd take the hint.

"Not funny, Mercer."

"I know. Sorry." As I walked away, I felt guilty. If only Dad treated me the way he treated Lincoln, things would be fine between us. When would he see I wasn't a kid anymore?

Passing Liberty's mews, I spied a nasty chunk of something white and lumpy underneath her perch that hadn't come off with the hose earlier. If Dad saw that, he'd probably ask if I wanted Lincoln to go over the disinfecting directions with me again. No, thanks. Part of me wanted to leave it there, telling myself that I might as well act like a little kid, since Dad treated me like one. But I knew if I did that, I'd remain at the bottom of this family totem pole. So I went and obliterated the heck out of it with the heel of my shoe.

After depositing the mute pile into the trash, I washed up and grabbed a bag of rabbit tidbits out of the fridge. I hoped Dad was right about Flip being hungry today. To be honest, I didn't know if my arm could take being held out in the extended position for as long as I'd held it out yesterday. With a heavy sigh of apprehension, I slid into position against the wall inside Flip's mews. Sweat started to build up under my arms as I stood there motionless, waiting for him to notice the food in my hand. Three heart-pounding minutes later, it happened. Flip flew to me, just as Dad said he would. I brought Flip outside on my fist, happy I hadn't needed Dad's help. I knew that wild birds were much harder to work with than imprinted ones. Imprinted birds were raised by humans right out of the egg, so they practically begged to be trained.

Dad was waiting for me when I got out to the training area. He had me practice basic retrieval techniques for the next thirty minutes, but like yesterday, it didn't go well. Flip didn't seem to understand that I wanted him to fly after the swing lure—a long rope with a piece of rabbit skin attached—and catch it in his talons. At first he ignored the swing lure completely, but then Dad showed me how to load it with bait, and things got a little better. Flip eventually caught on, but then, even after he knew what he was supposed to do, he still acted like a rookie, snatching the lure only two out of nine times.

"Is it me or is it him?" I asked, wanting a straight answer.

"I guess he feels compelled to live up to that ridiculous name you gave him."

"Ha-ha." If this were anyone but Dad, I'd probably have shown him the literal version of Flip's name.

"I'm teasing, Buddie—I mean, Mercer. Flip doesn't trust you yet, which is the falconer's greatest obstacle. But the more time you spend with him, the sooner he'll love being with you."

I nodded, the burning tension in my chest easing. As I walked back to the mews with Flip on my fist, I wondered whether the same tactics would work on Lucy. If I spent time with her to get her to trust me, would she love being with me too?

There was only one way to find out.

NINE ····➤

WHEN THE ALARM BUZZED FOR SCHOOL THE next morning, I hopped out of bed on the first ring. I needed extra time to shave the stubble on my jaw and upper lip without cutting myself. I figured toilet paper wads stuck on my face with dried-blood glue might not be hugely attractive.

After a shower and one small nick on my chin, I lingered in my closet. It took me a while to decide which of my T-shirts would make Lucy think I was funny but not morally repulsive. I settled on my blue I'M ONLY SMILING BECAUSE THEY HAVEN'T FOUND THE BODIES T-shirt along with my second-favorite pair of jeans—both clean. I got dressed and flew downstairs a minute before Lincoln and I were slated to leave for school. He had started being prompt after he discovered that Lauren arrived early. Maybe he was worried some early-bird nerd would snatch his chick.

"Ready to go, Merce?" Lincoln grabbed an apple out of the wire fruit basket. He took a huge bite, chewing loudly.

"Yep." I zipped my backpack and hoisted it onto my shoulder. I grabbed three granola bars out of the box on the counter and stuffed them in my pockets. "Bye, Tattleson."

"Don't call me that!" Maddie complained shrilly. "I don't tattle anymore."

Lincoln and I looked at each other, and we both burst out laughing. I told her, "Keep telling yourself that, Maddie, and maybe it'll come true."

We hopped into what Lincoln called his "rusty but trusty" silver Caddy, which was the size of a rowboat. He started the car and paddled down the driveway, cruising toward school with the music blasting.

"So did you and Lauren have a good time last night?" I shouted over the music, hoping to get some insight on what to do if and when Lucy and I started going out.

As things stood now, I'd kissed only two girls in my life. Beth Simmons in seventh grade, who didn't have the decency to close her eyes. I know because I checked, resulting in a very awkward moment, for sure. And then Marcy Feldman at the eighth-grade graduation dance last year. She had eaten a ton of garlic bread before she came out and didn't have any breath mints. Let's just say that getting bitten in the lip by Flip would be more satisfying than either of those kisses were.

"We had an okay time." Lincoln lowered the radio volume to a humane level. As we drove past our neighbor's gray barn, a few sheep turned to stare, so I stared back. "We watched a funny movie, but we could have had a *better* time, if you know what I mean."

Apparently Lauren wasn't throwing herself at Lincoln like all the other girls he'd been with. "She wasn't 'in the mood' last night, huh?"

He shook his head. "Not any night. Not with anyone. That's what she told me, anyway. But she's got a smoking-hot body, so it's worth the wait." He laughed, glancing my way.

I smiled but couldn't resist telling him what was on my mind. "Yeah, but she's really smart and super nice too. I mean, that's what you like about her too, right?"

"Yeah, yeah. Of course." He made a face as if I was an idiot for pointing that out. As he pulled into the school parking lot, he said to me, "Speaking of hot girls, what happened to that chick at the pet shop? The one you told you were a mouse lover?"

I grinned. "Actually, I found out she goes here."

"Lucky for you, little bro-mite!" He grabbed his binder from the back seat.

As we got out of the car, I realized that falconry and girls were pretty much the only two things Lincoln and I talked about. We joined the swarm of kids herding toward the school entrance. "So little Mercer finally has a girlfriend? Good work, my man." He congratulated me by patting my back hard, making me stumble.

I fought the urge to yelp. "She's not my girlfriend yet. I just met her."

"Then get some balls and ask her out. Don't be such a wuss." He hurried off, calling out to some dudes ahead of us.

Still feeling the sting in my back, I stumbled through the glass doors of Woodley High.

Going back to school after a weekend off was usually a drag, but I couldn't wait to get this day started. I walked with the flow, keeping my eye out for Lucy. Sadly, I didn't see her then or following any of my first four classes. It was Mercer's Law at work again. When you wanted to find someone during passing periods, say a cute girl who you still couldn't believe actually called you, she wasn't anywhere to be found. But when you wanted to avoid someone, say an egotistical chiseled brother, it seemed my tender shoulder inevitably found his fist. Three times that morning, to be precise.

I congratulated myself on not falling asleep through any of my morning classes, but when fifth period came, I practically sprinted for my locker. Those three granola bars did not cut it. I dropped off my books and darted to the cafeteria before I died of malnourishment. I bought two foot-long hot dogs, a jumbo bag of cheddar potato chips, and a large Coke before heading to the table that Charlie, Reed, and I had occupied all last week.

Within two minutes of sitting down, my first dog was gone. Man, the food was way better here than in middle school. So were the girls. I couldn't help noticing all the pretty girls of every size, shape, and color who walked by. If things didn't work out with Lucy, at least there would be plenty of options at Woodley. My heart sank a bit at the thought, though.

I almost fell off the bench when I caught a glimpse of Lucy walking across the cafeteria. Sure, I was excited to see her, but that's not why I almost fell—Charlie had flung himself next to me, and at five foot seven and a hundred ninety pounds, or so he claimed, his body was like a wrecking ball.

"Hey, Mercenary. What's up?" Charlie tore open a packet of hot sauce with his teeth.

I resituated myself back on to the bench and mumbled, "Not much," barely able to form words. With her back to me, Lucy stopped at the table kitty-corner from ours and placed one knee on the bench, scanning the cafeteria. She had on a tight white T-shirt with a U.S. flag blazoned across it and a pair of frayed jean shorts. I wondered if I should I call out her name or wait until she saw me.

Two guys with golf shirts tucked into their jeans temporarily blocked my view as they walked by with their trays, doing double takes as they passed her. I heard one of them say, "God bless America," followed by a hysterical fit of laughter. Dorks.

"I must say, I'm feeling rather patriotic today myself." Charlie squeezed the hot sauce onto his taco. "All I can say is Lucy is one lucky gal."

I spun to look at him, my hand frozen inside my chip bag. "Wait. You know her?"

"Not yet. But she's in my fourth-period Lit class, and after she starts going out with me, that's what everyone will say. Lucy is so lucky to date such a hot motocross biker." Charlie curled his hands into motorbike position and revved his engine, but with a farmer's tan and a few extra chins, he looked more like a Harley has-been than a pro racer.

"One with a spare tire." I smiled, poking the extra layer around his middle.

"That's not a spare tire. That's fallen chest muscle." He patted his belly roll affectionately.

"I could use some of that myself," I admitted, laughing. "The amazing thing is, I met that girl on Saturday. Twice, in fact. She even called me."

"No, she didn't, you lying piece of toe skin." Charlie pushed my shoulder, nearly sending me to the floor. Again.

I was beginning to feel like the target in a Whac-a-Mole game. "Seriously! I just didn't get a chance to tell you. She asked me to join her animal rights group, and I said yes. Not sure what it's all about, but if it means I can hang out with her more, I can do that." I grinned.

"I can be an animal if that's what she wants." Charlie raised his eyebrows twice and growled noisily. "Heck, I'd swear on my mother's grave that I was a Baptist preacher if she liked that sort of thing." He placed his hand on my shoulder, gently this time. "Hallelujah, my good friend. Go in peace."

"You can't swear on your mother's grave because she's still alive, you big idiot." I swatted his hand away.

The thing was, Charlie fantasizing over Lucy made me realize that one of the other hundred or so guys in school who weren't shy around girls would be asking her out any minute while I stood by and watched it happen—if it hadn't happened already. I looked over at her unpacking her lunch and sighed. As much as I wanted to ask her to hang out, the fear of putting myself out there and having her relegate me to the friend zone made me reconsider. That was probably why I'd had so few dates. With owls, however, I was a real charmer. If I didn't get over my fear soon, Monocle would have a good shot at becoming Mrs. Mercer Buddie.

Lucy gave an enthusiastic hello as two other girls sat down at her table. One of the girls was tiny, with straight pumpkin-pie-colored hair, and the other one, with a bright green streak in her hair, looked vaguely familiar. After a few seconds, I figured it out.

I elbowed Charlie. "Hey, Chubs. Isn't that the girl who works at Dairy Barn?"

"Hmm . . . let me think." Charlie's hand discreetly made its way into my chip bag as he considered my question. I slammed my hand on top of his, stopping his progress. He managed to snatch a few chips despite my best efforts. "Ah, yes. A girl with my dream job. Maybe I should go over and say hello to those fine ladies."

"No, wait!" I swallowed hard, holding my hand up. "Let me talk to Lucy first and then you can go."

Charlie eyed my chips. "Sure. Go ahead. I'll wait here and guard your lunch."

"Fine." I pushed my bag closer to him as I planned my attack. I'd walk over and say, "Hey, Lucy. How's it going?" And she'd say, "Oh my gosh! It's you, Mercer! I haven't stopped thinking about you since our phone call." I'd take a seat, we'd talk, and by the end of lunch, she'd realize what a studly mouse-lover I was and ask if I was going out with anyone. I could totally do this.

"Well, here goes nothing," I told Charlie, standing. I took a deep breath and walked toward the girls' table—and promptly zipped right past Lucy without saying a word.

It was painfully clear that I was indeed a wuss.

TEN ·····🦅

AS I SNATCHED A HANDFUL OF NAPKINS I DIDN'T intend to use, I convinced myself that I'd already done the hardest part—talking on the phone with Lucy and making plans to get together in the future—even if only to join some dumb club. The rest was simple. Smile and say hi. How hard could that be?

As I approached the girls' table for the second time, my chest tightened. To my horror, Charlie stood there, his arms outstretched, a giant grin on his face. "Hello, my lovely ladies. Allow me to introduce myself. My name's Charlie and I happen to be the finest stain removal expert in all of Woodley High. If any of you ever need me to dab at a ketchup spot on your chest or brush crumbs off your lap, I'm your man. I'll be at the table right over here"—he turned slightly to point at our table—"if you need assistance."

Lucy and Dairy Barn Girl looked at each other and burst out laughing, while the redhead didn't look quite so amused. I tried to make eye contact with Lucy, but she was laughing so hard, she didn't see me. I sat down at our table, disappointed in my lame performance. I spotted Reed standing by the cashier with a tray of food in his hands, looking bewildered. I stood for a second and held up my hand until he saw me. Already knowing what would follow, I watched in depressed amazement as all the girls flanking his path kept their eyes on him as if magnetically attracted to him, unable to look away.

Ever since I'd known him, Reed had been a chick whirlpool, engulfing all females within eyeshot of him. Old or young, pretty or average—it didn't matter—they all got sucked in. Reed was nearly my height, had a curly brown 'fro, broad shoulders, and a deep dimple in his chin—a combination that made girls go crazy. When we studied Greek gods last year, Trina Becker even wrote Reed a letter addressed to Adonis. Reed thought the whole thing was weird, whereas I secretly wished a girl would write a letter like that to me.

Didn't they care that Reed had flunked a grade? Okay, so he had to repeat kindergarten, but still. While he didn't have trouble getting girls to like him, the only girls I'd ever heard Reed get really excited about were the ones on his Garage Girls calendar. He was a total gearhead, just like his dad. Charlie and I joke that Reed would eventually marry a girl only if she had spinners on her shoes, racing stripes, and a plume of black exhaust trailing behind her.

Reed plopped down across from me, his tray loaded with food. "Hey, Merce. Congrats on your hawk, man. That's awesome." He gave me a high-five.

I slapped him back, keeping my voice low and the wording

vague on the tiny chance that Lucy was eavesdropping. "Thanks. You guys will have to come by after school one day so I can show him to you." I'd fill Reed in later on the other Herculean feat I would be attempting soon—asking Lucy out.

"What are we, birdbrains?" Charlie stuck his thumbs under his armpits and squawked. "Of course we'll come. Birds of a feather flock together and all that. That's quite a feather in your cap, young man."

I tilted my chin down and peered at Charlie with mock exasperation. "Enough."

Reed laughed. "Hey, did you guys see these burgers? They're the size of monster truck wheels." He took such a huge bite that his cheeks bulged and he had a hard time chewing.

"You think you took a big enough bite?" I asked, laughing. "Your burger's half gone."

Reed nodded, unable to speak. With a sigh, I snatched my empty bag of chips from Charlie and tilted my head back, letting the crumbs slide into my mouth.

Charlie smiled. "If you think that's impressive, tomorrow I can teach you the fine art of spitting without drippage."

Reed burped. "Sign me up," he said, stuffing the rest of his burger into his mouth.

I was about to say, "Me too," but a rebel crumb scrambled down my throat, making me choke. I reached for my napkin to spit out my food—hopefully without drippage—at the exact moment Lucy and her friends approached our table. I turned my head and spat the whole disaster into my napkin, shoving the balled-up mess into my lunch bag and crunching it closed.

Lucy held a pink clipboard in her arms and had a smile on her face, Dairy Barn Girl toyed with a green strand of hair, and the ginger wore a T-shirt that had a picture of a dead cow on the front. The caption read I DIED FOR YOUR SINS.

A bit strong, but whatever. Slogan tees were cool in my book.

I smiled and gave Lucy a nod, trying not to appear overly eager yet still interested. Lincoln had told me a bunch of times that girls liked jerks better than nice guys. It didn't make any sense, but girls were harder to figure out than slopes in math. "Hey, Lucy."

"Mercer!" She acted sincerely surprised and, I have to say, really happy to see me. "How's Cinnamon?"

I grinned uncomfortably. "Fine. Great."

Charlie elbowed me in the ribs. "Who's Cinnamon?"

Lucy looked confused. "You didn't tell them about your new pet mouse?"

Reed laughed. "You mean the mice he uses for—"

I kicked Reed under the table and finished his sentence. "Companionship? Nah, I didn't get a chance yet." I shot Reed a look, hoping he wouldn't blow my cover.

"Mercer's always such a loner. Those mice bring him such comfort." Charlie patted my shoulder, back in preacher mode.

"What's with the clipboard?" I asked Lucy, deliberately changing the topic.

She opened her mouth to answer when the redhead cut her off. "Let me explain. I'm Haley, and this is Jeanette and Lucy." She pointed as she said their names. "We've started a Woodley High chapter of HALT and we're looking for new members. Our mission is to speak for the millions of animals who suffer horrible deaths at the hand of humans. We want to put a stop to it with your help. The first step is making this cafeteria meatless, and we want you to sign our petition."

Lucy touched Haley's arm. "This is the guy I was telling you about, Haley." She handed me the shiny pink clipboard and pen with such admiration in her eyes, you'd think she was handing me an Oscar. "Sign your name right after ours, Mercer."

Reed held up his hand. "Wait. Did you say *meatless?* You mean, like only vegetables?" Lucy turned and stared at him, making my chances go up in flames. One look at Reed, and she'd think I was as handsome as a potato sack.

"I'll take that, thanks." I shot Reed a conspiratorial glance, hoping he'd take my cue that I liked this girl and to keep his mouth shut about my carnivorous ways. I took the pen from Lucy, letting my hand slide across hers. I scrawled my name on the line.

Haley snatched the clipboard from me and held it out to Charlie. "How about you? Are you interested in fighting for an animal's right to remain whole and alive?"

Charlie smiled at Haley. "Why, yes. I'd love to, my little hot tamale."

Jeanette giggled at his remark, tucking a few green-streaked strands behind her ear. Haley visibly winced, glaring at Charlie. "Just Haley is fine, thanks."

"Haley *is* fine." Charlie chuckled, one sinister eyebrow arched. "I'll call you anything you want, my paprika-haired angel. And I'll sign your petition just as soon as you agree to have dinner with me tonight."

Haley exhaled loudly. "Never mind." She shot Lucy a look as if she'd known that coming to our table would be a waste of time. "How about you?" She poked Reed's shoulder with her pen. "You want to be the big man and fight for animals' rights, like your friend over there?"

Reed looked up at her, his forehead creased with confusion, the burger grease still evident on the corners of his mouth. "You're kidding, right? I just ate half a cow here."

Haley made a face, her top lip curling up into a sneer. "That cow was in a field minding her own business a week ago. Eating animals is cruel and should be outlawed."

"Outlawing meat is cruel, if you ask me." Reed tossed his used napkin on the table.

Haley rolled her eyes. "Forget these guys. Let's go."

She started to walk away when Charlie called out, "Wait, my little veggie girls! Don't leave yet. You haven't heard the menu I have planned: Green Bean Mishmash with a side of Tofu Schmofu Salad, but I'm open to skipping that and going right to making out if you prefer."

"Gross," Haley said, scrunching her face.

I had no idea how Charlie had kept a straight face while saying all that stuff. I worried that his act would frighten Miss Lucy away, but she shrugged. "Sorry. I have plans."

"Same," Jeanette said, but not as convincingly. She looked more amused than horrified.

Lucy stared directly into my eyes. "Since you're an official HALT member now, Mercer, do you want to walk around with us and get more signatures?"

The choking feeling I'd felt a few minutes earlier returned —but this time there was no potato chip to blame. I definitely wanted the girl but most definitely did *not* want to walk around asking guys to give up meat. Could be dangerous come gym time.

Reed nodded at my untouched second dog. "Are you going to eat this, Mercer?"

Lucy gripped the clipboard tightly to her chest. "Is that a *beef* hot dog?"

I swallowed hard. "Uh, I'm not sure."

Lucy looked disappointed. "Well, it is, but since you didn't know, I can forgive you this time. But the good news is that if we collect enough signatures, we can get some vegetarian dogs here instead. You want that too, right, Mercer?

Reed shook his head but Charlie burst out laughing. "Yeah. Right, Mercer?"

I knew this was my chance to back out—to say that though I thought she was awesome, I loved hot dogs and hamburgers. But one look at Lucy's luscious, meat-free lips, and I knew kissing her would be worth a million meatless lunches. "Definitely."

ELEVEN

THE NEXT DAY AT SCHOOL WAS THE BEST YET. IN the hall between periods, Lucy waved to me and called out, "See you at lunch, Mercer!" A swarm of guys nearby shot me dirty looks.

At lunch, I bought a salad and a bag of Cheese Puffs in case Lucy asked me to sit with her — and was rewarded for my brilliance. As I sauntered toward my regular table, she waved me over. Did I want to join the HALT team for lunch? Hmm . . . sit with the girl who had a padlock on my heart, or sit with Reed and Charlie?

I was seated next to Lucy so fast you'd think I had superpowers.

Then Reed and Charlie carried their overflowing lunch trays over to us. Charlie slid his tray next to mine. "Move over. The men have arrived."

Lucy and I started to scooch over when Haley waved her half-eaten banana in the air. "Sorry, but you're only welcome to join us if you have meat-free lunches."

One look at their trays had them slinking back to our old table. Whenever I glanced over there, Charlie flaunted today's special at me — a barbecue pork chop sandwich on a steamed sesame seed bun. My stomach growled and my mouth watered, but sitting next to Lucy and listening to her excited chitchat made it all worthwhile—even if there was more drool than balsamic vinaigrette on my chef's salad. Whether the drool was over her or over the pork chop sandwich was anybody's guess.

When the topic of the meatless cafeteria petition came up again, I quickly pointed out that they'd gotten only four signatures, hoping to persuade them to discontinue that drive. The thought of walking around the cafeteria asking other teens not to eat meat was not only pointless but also risky. If I got too close to someone's meatloaf, my resistance could crumble and I might scarf down the person's lunch.

Lucy nodded. "I think you're right. What else could we do to help local animals?"

"We can leave Cheese Puffs on the floor for all the mice to munch on during the night," I suggested, tossing one over my shoulder. Lucy obliged me with a hearty laugh.

"Are you sure you want to be part of the club, Mercer?" Haley narrowed her eyes at me, immediately stifling Lucy's giggle. Haley was obviously the heavy in this organization, which was ironic, since she was thinner and shorter than my fifth-grade sister. Maybe I'd joined this club too hastily. Could I have won Lucy's heart without all of this deception?

"He already said he did, Haley," Lucy argued on my behalf, surprising me. "He has a funny sense of humor, that's all. You're glad you signed up, right, Mercer?" Lucy licked her lips, her sage green eyes wide and hopeful, making a blast of heat race through my body.

As much as I wanted to back out, I wasn't positive Lucy would stick with me if I did. "I didn't eat meat, did I?" I lifted my empty Cheese Puffs bag and salad container as proof, one soggy radish slice swimming in balsamic vinegar dressing. "I'm still starving, though."

I gazed longingly toward the kitchen, wondering whether my parents would care if I bought two lunches in one day on their dollar. Not even two blinks later, food appeared in front of me as if I had rubbed a genie's lamp. Jeanette gave me half of one of her cream cheese and jelly sandwiches, and Lucy gave me a cupcake.

Yep, Lucy was right. All of this attention being showered on me as the only male member of the group was a huge downer. Too bad everything in my life couldn't be this terrible.

Haley bit her apple, munching loudly. "By the way, there's a big HALT rally on Saturday morning at Wool-Mart on Main. Can you guys go?"

Jeanette frowned. "I can't. It's my grandma's seventieth birthday party."

"Too bad." Lucy shrugged. "I'm going. How about you, Mercer?"

Hang out in front of a store protesting wool wearers? How could shearing sheep be considered cruel to animals? It's not as if it killed them. I was about to ask for a clarification when the bell rang, signaling the end of lunch. Everyone shot out of their seats and headed toward the door, but Lucy was still looking at me, waiting for my answer.

I ignored the warning in my head. "Count me in." When she clapped her approval, I knew I'd made the right decision. My parents, however, might not be so happy. But, hey, they didn't tell me everything that was going on in their lives, so why should I tell them everything in mine?

Besides, maybe there was something I didn't know about the wool industry — something painful to the sheep. Though HALT protesters could be over the top, I knew that some people really were cruel to animals and needed to be stopped. I'd heard of farm animals starving to death, circus animals being beaten into submission, and horses becoming lame because they hadn't been shod properly.

As I tossed my tray onto the stack by the cafeteria door, I figured out a plan. I'd have Lincoln drop me off at the mall on his way to his job. This could work. A few minutes later, Reed and Charlie caught up with me at my locker.

Charlie elbowed me. "So tell us . . . how was your salad, Mercer? Feeling bloated from all those croutons?"

Reed added, "Stuffed to the gills with carrots and sprouts?"

"Keep laughing, boys, because any day now, Lucy and I will be sharing some *French* dressing while you'll be alone, licking your forks."

Reed made a face. "Ha, in your dreams."

Charlie's eyes widened. "Man, that's it. Tomorrow I'm buy-ing a salad and getting me a Veggie Girl too. That Jeanette is mighty tasty looking." He rubbed his hands together.

"I'll believe it when I see it, Chubs." I had never seen Charlie eat a salad in the entire time I'd known him. Hell, I wasn't sure how long I could continue this no-meat charade myself. Starting tomorrow, I'd load up at breakfast—maybe some steak and eggs with a side of roast beef and chicken.

The next day, Charlie stayed true to his word. He brought his two grilled cheese sandwiches to the HALT table, and then asked Jeanette if this was the spot where all the models sat. She giggled and he sat next to her, and the two started chatting up a storm. Haley didn't seem too pleased, especially after Reed joined our table when he was done eating—a deep-fried chicken patty still in his gut. She told him that he'd have to stop eating meat al-together if he wanted to sit at her table. I heard him tell her, "That'll never happen. Deal with it."

Haley looked annoyed but didn't say anything more, making me cringe at how much of a wimp I truly was.

The rest of the week flew by. My classes were okay, but lunch was amazing. Reed inhaled his carnivorous delights with some other guys before joining us, but Charlie and I maintained our meatless lunch bid and ate with the girls. It worried me that Reed kept sitting right next to Lucy on her other side when he joined us, even though he knew I liked her. It kind of pissed me off even more because, every time he spoke, Lucy had to turn her head toward him, which left me out of the conversation. I know I was being irrational, but when it came to Lucy, I couldn't think straight.

Haley cleared her throat. "So are you guys coming to the protest on Saturday or what?"

"Can't," Reed stated. "The three of us always go off-roading Saturday mornings."

"'Tis a long-standing tradition, lass," Charlie said, using an Irish brogue.

"But Mercer's coming with us." Lucy's head spun toward me. "Aren't you, Mercer?"

All eyes were on me. I swallowed hard. "Yep. Sorry guys. I can't go with you Saturday."

Reed looked disgusted, maybe even angry, but Charlie winked at me. "We'll manage without you . . . this time."

By Friday, things were starting to go really well between Lucy and me. When I leaned my leg against hers, she didn't move away. She even offered me a bite of her bean sprout and spicy tofu sandwich, which I foolishly accepted. I lasted only two seconds before spitting it into my napkin. "That stuff tastes like crap!"

"Oh, really? You eat crap regularly?" Lucy raised her eyebrows.

"Only on Wednesdays, but enough to know good crap from bad." Then an amazing thing happened. She bit the same part of the bread that my mouth had just touched. That had to be a sign that she was secretly craving my germs. At least that's what I told myself.

At home, things weren't as great. Cleaning the entire mews every day was time-consuming and tiring. And even though I worked with Flip for at least an hour, solid, every night after cleaning, it wasn't as much fun as I had hoped. Not because I'd lost interest, but because Flip hated me. Hard as it was to believe, he was lazier than I was. Never wanted to fly to me, just sat on his perch and looked the other way.

Too bad Monocle couldn't hunt with her one eye, or she'd be the best hunting partner ever.

That night, Lincoln went out with Lauren, and I went out with Flip. Yep, Friday night with my hawk. As I brought Flip to the training area, scores of birds flew out of the stand of pines along our property line, alerting every mouse, squirrel, and chipmunk that a hawk was in the house. Flip tried to take off after them, and would have too if I hadn't been holding on to the jesses attached to his legs.

"Are you hungry, Flip?" I asked him. "I've got just the thing."

Flip stepped onto the perch, and I pulled out a small piece of rabbit meat, thinking he'd bowl me over trying to get to it, but he didn't. He groomed himself, as if he had already eaten that day and was now "fed up," a falconer's term that meant your bird was too full and wasn't interested in hunting anymore. Watching Flip ignore me made *me* fed up—with him. I thought about sending him back to the woods and forgetting about becoming a falconer altogether, since I clearly sucked at this.

I knew I was being stupid. Even though Dad's falcon, Troy, responded to his hand signals as if Dad were the Pied Piper, and Lincoln's goshawk, Bella, was already within a few ounces of her hunting weight, I'd had Flip for only a week. I sighed, hating the whole idea about having patience and wishing I could hurry things up and have him fully trained by tomorrow.

"Hey, Skinny. Where's your dad?" Weasel asked, making me jump. That was one thing about falconers—we learned to cross a field soundlessly, careful not to step on sticks or shuffle our feet. If we did, we'd scare the quarry into hiding before our birds were close enough to nab the prey. Guess I would've been eaten if Weasel had been a hawk and I a rabbit because I hadn't heard a thing.

I explained that Dad had gone to train some volunteers who were interested in working in the bird sanctuary out in Sleepy Hollow. He nodded, asking how things were going with Flip. "He's living up to his name," I joked, even though when Dad had said it I hadn't thought it was very funny. "He keeps flipping his middle talon at me and ignoring me."

"Nonsense." Weasel scratched his chin. At least I assumed there was chin under that thick beard, although I'd never actually seen it. "How's he doing on the creance line?"

I shrugged. "We haven't started that yet. Dad said we'd try this weekend." Dad probably had sensed I would suck at that as well and was trying to delay my inevitable failure.

"I see. Well, I've got a hunch your friend Flip is bored with flying only five feet and wants more of a challenge." He took a deep breath and narrowed his eyes. "I don't suppose your father would mind if I stepped in for a session, since he's busy and all. Want to give it a shot?"

I had my doubts that Flip could do anything besides eat and mute, but I said, "Sure! That'd be cool."

Weasel retrieved a self-winding 270-foot creance line from the rehab center. After he attached the swivel clip to Flip's jesses on his ankle, he walked with me and had me stand what seemed like miles away from Flip.

"Just so you're not disappointed, Flip's probably too dumb to catch on to this," I warned him.

"No such thing as a dumb hawk, Mercer. Only dumb falconers—remember that."

"Hey!"

"You'll see what I mean in a second." Weasel stood behind me, his hand on my shoulder. He pointed to the piece of raw rabbit meat I had in my fingers. "Put that dry turd you're holding back into your pouch and pull me out a piece of meat that's got some spit on it."

I dug into my waist pouch and pulled out a wet chunk of meat. "Much better. But turn your hand like this." He twisted my hand so that the last of the sunlight glinted off the wet piece of meat. "Now hold still and wait." I did as instructed, but Flip remained on the perch, motionless.

"See?" I said sourly. "You've met your first stupid hawk."

Weasel whispered, "Shhh. Don't move. See how he's turning his head a bit? He sees it. Just give him a few more seconds and—" Before he had finished his sentence, Flip flew across the field and landed on my fist.

"Boo-ya!" I grinned at the hawk tearing at the meat I held between my thumb and forefinger, and then back at Weasel. "That was great."

"It's all about finesse." Weasel gave me a few more tips that Dad had never shared, and then had Flip fly back and forth several times. Weasel said that Flip would be ready to fly without the creance soon enough, but timing was everything. Waiting too long might make a bird lose interest, but moving too fast might confuse him and he would fly off into the woods.

"Does the same thing apply to girls?" I joked.

Weasel laughed. "You know it. And to prove my point, I've got to get my butt home before Jenny kills me. I've been gone just long enough for her to miss me, but not long enough to tick her off. It's all about the timing." He messed my hair before turning to leave. Why did people always do that to me?

I unhooked Flip and headed into the mews to put him away and say good night to Monocle. If timing was everything, then things needed to change. I had to stop acting so sheepish and officially ask Lucy out tomorrow at the rally.

TWELVE

I GOT UP EARLY SATURDAY MORNING TO TAKE CARE of my falconer chores, much to Dad's delight, but I had my own private agenda. It was a crisp fall morning, the kind that makes you shiver and wonder when the parentals would put the heat on in the house. I cleaned the mews in record time. Even Monocle was happy when I spent a few minutes telling her how pretty she was. She looked a bit alarmed when I told her that if everything went well today, I might have a new woman in my life. She herked at me as I walked away, but, hey, that was the price she paid for loving a blazing-hot GQ model–slash–hit man.

I ran to the house to clean up before heading off to meet Lucy. I shaved, ever so carefully, put on my cleanest jeans, and tossed on my PEOPLE TELL ME I'M TALL LIKE I'M UNAWARE T-shirt.

I hurried out to the rehab center to tell Dad I was leaving.

"You're going shopping?" he asked disbelievingly. He tore his eyes from Rusty, a small kestrel with a permanently disabled wing. "You need new shoes or something?"

"Nah. There's this band playing in the parking lot that I want to see." I had come up with that alibi last night and thought it sounded decent.

"A band? This early?" He checked his watch.

I shrugged. "Some promotional thing, I think." I wanted this conversation to be over with before he dug any deeper for details.

"How are you getting there?" Dad rubbed his cheek with the back of his wrist to avoid getting his skin oils on his fingertips, which wasn't good for birds' wings.

"Lincoln said he'd drop me off, and then I'll just walk home afterward." As if on cue, a loud honk blasted from the front of the house. "Later!" I jogged off to catch my ride.

"Call me if you need me to pick you up!" Dad yelled.

"Okay!" I shouted back, knowing there was no way I ever would. I didn't want either of my parents to see me within a mile of the protest. Not only because they might find out what I was up to, but also because everyone knew that having your parents pick you up or take you anywhere once you got past eighth grade was social suicide.

A three-mile walk was nothing compared to *that* humiliation.

As I got closer to Lincoln's old silver Caddy, he barked, "Hurry up!"

I sprinted to the car and got in, but he pulled away before I had even slammed the rusty door. His car guzzled gas the way my dad downs coffee, but it had smooth gray leather seats and an awesome music system. Lincoln wasn't a gearhead like Reed, but he did okay. Kept it pretty clean in there too. Knowing my brother, that probably had something to do with having the back seat ready for action at a moment's notice, just like the minutemen.

He sped down Pine Road toward town. "Why are you going to the mall, anyway? You hate shopping." He eyed me suspiciously.

"I'm meeting that girl I told you about." I was sort of unable to believe it myself.

Lincoln's head jerked toward me, and he punched my thigh. "Way to go, little bro! So you got some balls and asked her out."

I resisted the urge to rub away the painful spot on my leg. "Today's a group thing, but I'm planning to ask her to the movies later on. Got any tips?"

He smiled, and I could tell he was proud that I was asking. "Depends. Is she hot?"

"Exceptionally hot, but in a cute way."

"Nice. And you're sure she's not blind or anything?" he joked.

"Ha-ha. Yes, she knows what I look like, you jerk."

Then I prattled on about how funny and sweet Lucy was and how I'd been sitting with her at lunch every day. That she was originally from Wisconsin too, and that she loved it there, just like we did. I even told him how Charlie offered his stain removal services to the girls.

Lincoln laughed. "Chubs is one weird dude."

I quickly mentioned my worries about Reed maybe liking

Lucy too, and Weasel's advice about timing being everything. "So what do you think my chances are?"

"Her picking you over Reed? Slim, but hey, what have you got to lose? The worst that could happen is that she'll say no." He turned onto Main Street, now only a block from Woodley Town Centre.

I widened my eyes. "Which would totally suck! It's fun sitting with her at lunch, and I don't want to screw that up."

"Okay, wuss boy. So you'd rather eat lunch with her and let Reed make his move?"

"No."

"Then ask her out. Grow a pair already, will you?"

I simmered at my brother's assessment of me but knew he was right. "Okay, fine. But there's one small problem." I bit off part of my fingernail and spat it out, dying to ask his opinion on the whole animal rights thing.

"Uh-oh. That doesn't sound good." He pulled into the first open spot in the mall's parking lot, but kept the engine running. "What's wrong with her?"

"Nothing. She's just"—I took a deep breath—"part of that HALT group."

Lincoln whacked my chest super hard with the back of his hand. "HALT? Those animal freaks? Are you insane? After what they did to Mom?"

I poked at a small rip in the leather seat. "Chill out. It's not like *she* did anything."

"Stop pulling on that!" he ordered. "I don't know, Mercer. Nothing like picking the wrong girl." Lincoln stared at me with contempt, shaking his head.

"It's not like I picked her off a tree or anything. We just started talking and we clicked. What did you want me to do? Walk away?"

"Maybe. If you have to change who you are." He rubbed his clean-shaven jaw. "But I know what you mean. A hot girl who is into you is hard to resist—even if she doesn't meet *all* the requirements."

"I'm not changing who I am," I argued, wondering if I was kidding myself.

Lincoln shifted to face me. "What did she say when you told her that you hunt?" He glanced out through the front windshield, where I saw people carrying posters and walking toward Wool-Mart. He leaned forward, trying to get a better look.

Whoa. I needed to distract him before he'd figured out what was going on. "I didn't tell her yet. What time you have to be at work?"

He sat up in a hurry. "Crap! I start in six minutes. Okay, listen. Do what you want, but don't tell her you hunt until you're solid." He held up crossed fingers, I guess as a sign of being a couple. He pointed toward the door. "Now get out."

I scrambled out of the car, relieved my brother had given me the green light. Not that I needed his permission, but if he hadn't, I would've had to add him to the list of people I was lying to. The list was getting longer by the minute. As I was about to shut the door, Lincoln yelled, "Hey!"

I poked my head back into the car. "Yeah?"

"Good luck, bro. Hope she says yes."

I grinned. "Thanks. Me too. Which reminds me—if she does say yes, can you give us a ride to the movies tonight?" I made my most desperate, pleading face.

"You dork." He shook his head, but was smirking. "God, it sucks to be you. Yeah, I can drive you. Now shut the door before I get fired."

I slammed the door and he sped away, leaving me to wander toward the throngs of people hanging around in front of Wool-Mart. The heaviness in my chest made me feel like a lying sneak. I couldn't shake the feeling that I was doing something wrong by being there. Like when you're a little kid and you wait for your mom to go to work so you can eat some of the Halloween candy she'd bought to hand out to trick-or-treaters.

Okay, so two entire bags were excessive. But at least I hadn't ralphed.

I went over my plan—fake an interest in the people blathering on about wool, make Lucy laugh, and maybe throw in a compliment or two. If things went well, then at some point, I'd get her alone and ask her if she wanted to go to the movies. I'd ask casually; that way if she said no, I'd say, "Yeah, well maybe next time." I'd walk away, pretending she hadn't just crushed my total universe.

If she said yes . . . I already had a plan for that too. I'd looked up the movie listings and found a romantic comedy. Girls love those. Figured it would get her in the right mood for a good-night kiss after it was over. Maybe even sneak one *during* the movie if things were going really well. When we got to the theater, I'd buy us a bucket of buttered popcorn, whatever kind of candy she wanted along with a box of Junior Mints for me, and a large pop with two straws. And then, when the lights went down in the theater, I'd wait ten minutes and slide my arm around her shoulders. It'd be awesome. Only one small yes stood in my way.

"Mercer?"

I spun around to see Lucy walking toward me with two older people I assumed were her parents. As they got closer, my stomach dropped. Not only was her mom the frizzy-haired woman in the purple skydiving suit, but her father was Ugly Ponytail Guy.

"Hi, Lucy." I smiled at her, and then nodded at her parents, immediately uncomfortable. I quickly deliberated whether to remind them that we'd met already, or pretend I was someone new.

Her dad stuck out his hand. "I'm Lucy's father, Jerry, and this here's her mom, Frieda."

"I'm Mercer. Nice to meet you." I shook his hand, his grip nearly breaking mine in two. But I hung on, trying to match my strength with his. "Lucy's told me a lot about you two," I lied. I might stink at impressing girls, but was king of sucking up to parents. In fact, they often ended up liking me more than they liked their own kid. Yeah, I was that good.

"It's a beautiful day today, isn't it?" her mom chirped, rubbing her hands together. "And lookie here at all these people! Lucy told us you joined her club at school. It's so wonderful that she's making new friends." She smiled warmly, her large front teeth glinting in the sun as she touched my forearm. She didn't seem crazy anymore.

"It sure is," I said, noticing her father staring at me curiously. "Lucy's a really nice girl."

Her mom chuckled, her shoulders bobbing up and down. "I think so too. Oh, dear me. I almost forgot!" She dug in her purse, pulling out two red stickers on a wax paper strip. "I got you kids something." She peeled off two stickers and stuck them on our shirts. "Aren't they darling?"

I read my sticker upside down: SHEEP NEED CLOTHES TOO — WEAR COTTON! I glanced at Lucy's sticker: WOOL. IT'S NOT FOR EWE. Catchy slogans, even if the concept was lame. I came up with my own: WOOL — IT KEEPS YOU WARM WHEN YOU'RE COLD; but then I figured they might ask me to leave if I shared it with them.

A man on a loudspeaker announced, "Welcome one and all to our fourth annual Cotton Round-Up. We've got a lot in store for you today."

Lucy's father scratched his head. "You know, Mercer, you look familiar to me for some reason, but I can't place it. What did you say your last name was?"

A pain hit my gut like a karate kick. Did they know my

mom's last name? Before I could say a word, Lucy snapped, "It's Budson, Dad. And would you two stop pestering him now? I told you I'd introduce him and I did. Let's go, Mercer." She jerked her head toward the stage, and I followed like a lost puppy. I felt a little weird not correcting her, but I doubted they would let their daughter hang out with the son of the evil lab director, so I stayed mum.

"Don't forget," her father said sternly. "Meet us at the car at eleven."

"You told me three times already," Lucy answered, surprising me somewhat with her attitude. At school she was more like Glinda the Good Witch than the mean one. "I got it."

"Nice to meet you, Mercer!" her mom called out. "Have fun, you two!"

I turned and waved before Lucy grabbed my arm and pulled me away. "God, they're so annoying. Sorry about that." She let go of me as we approached the crowd.

"No problem." I sort of wished she'd kept her hand on my forearm a bit longer. I'd done quite a lot of bird and barbell lifting that week and hoped it showed.

We wound our way through the crowd as the man on the loudspeaker introduced someone named Jess Hibbard, the president of Cotton Mills, Incorporated. There was a rush of applause, and the man climbed the four stairs to the portable platform that had been erected in front of Wool-Mart. People with shopping bags stood watching from the safety of the walkways in front of the stores they had just exited, shielding their eyes from the sun.

We ended up near the front, by a group of townies, a few of whom I vaguely recognized from the rare occasions our family had gone to church. I relaxed, glad no one there knew me well enough that this might get back to my folks. I tried not to think about the wool protest and instead concentrated on impressing Lucy. I couldn't believe we were there together, almost like a date. When she smiled at me, I smiled back but quickly looked away before she thought I was a freak for staring at her.

"Welcome, animal lovers and members of HALT!" Jess Hibbard's voice boomed through the speakers as he raised his hands to a round of cheers. He wore blue khakis and a golf shirt, which I'm sure were both 100 percent cotton. I was surprised they didn't get upset about the mean, nasty humans ripping cotton from the parent stem, the poor helpless cotton bolls.

"We're here to celebrate our solidarity in choosing cotton over wool. As you know, cotton's my business, but it hasn't always been my passion. But about ten years ago, I found out about a barbaric practice called mulesing, and I've been a changed man ever since."

I leaned over to Lucy. "Did Haley come today?" I asked so I'd know exactly how much alone time I had with Lucy before Haley came along and ruined it for me.

Lucy nodded, pointing. "She's running the refreshment stand. The man who introduced the speaker is her dad. We'll go say hi to her later, okay?"

"No-kay," I replied, hoping Lucy would get the hint but not be offended that I wasn't a big fan of her friend.

She gave me a knowing smile and a shake of her head. But she didn't try to change my mind.

The speaker continued, "Thousands of sheep are mutilated when a farmer cuts off the unanesthetized skin around the sheep's genital areas, removing whole chunks of flesh, leaving open, bleeding sores."

Ouch. Mulesing did sound extremely painful. Just an accidental bump in the balls would send me to the ground, so I couldn't imagine what hacking off hunks of skin from the sides of my inner thighs would feel like. I looked down, and to my embarrassment discovered that I had my hand over my crotch, instinctively protecting myself from getting mulesinged, if that's a word. I jerked my hand away, hoping Lucy hadn't noticed.

A woman yelled something about Wool-Mart being monsters. A girl shrieked and called out, "Mutilators!" But when a man from the back shouted, "Raising animals for profit is an abomination!" it went a little overboard.

Jess Hibbard raised his fist in the air to emphasize his point. "Mutilating sheep so we can wear their wool is inhumane and unnecessary and must be stopped. So I'm asking all of you to boycott wool and wear cotton."

A balding man wearing the traditional navy Wool-Mart vest walked halfway between the store and the crowd. "What's the alternative to mulesing, tough guy? You're not giving them the whole picture. Tell them about fly strike."

People started booing so loudly, I couldn't hear what the manager was saying. I did think it was kind of douchey for a cotton grower to speak out against wool, and while I had originally agreed with Cotton Man's message, I wanted to learn what fly strike was. Could there be a legitimate reason for mulesing?

Something else confused me too. I could swear two guys had leather belts around their waists, and the chick next to me had on a leather bracelet. So killing a cow to wear it was okay, but eating it was inhumane? It seemed to me that if you were going to take issue with something, at least you should know what you were doing. Unless . . . maybe some of these people were there only to bleep for the sheep but didn't give a pow about cow.

Since I was a big faker myself, I figured I wasn't the person to criticize. Besides, I felt that people had the right to do what they wanted—eat meat or not, boxers or briefs, protest or partake, straight or gay. Who cares? The only thing I did care about today was asking Lucy out, and if I didn't do it soon, she'd be heading home and I'd have done this whole dumb protest thing for nothing.

No more mouse for me—I was finally going to be the man.

The Wool-Mart manager eventually went back inside to boisterous cheers, and Haley's dad got back onstage. He thanked people for coming, asking everyone to please place their donations to HALT inside the red plastic buckets on the tables. People rooted around in their pockets and purses for money, but all I had was a ten-dollar bill. No way was I giving that up. I had better plans for that money.

"Want to get something to drink?" Lucy shielded her eyes as she squinted in the sun. "We can say hi to Haley."

I faked disappointment. "Only thing is I'm dying of thirst, and look at that line." I nodded toward Haley's table, where dozens of protesters were lined up to get drinks. "How about we head to McDonald's instead?"

"McDonald's?" She gasped, a horrified look on her face. "With my parents here? I'd be shot if I even went near any of those places."

Duh. How stupid could I be? I spun around, scanning for someplace that didn't serve meat. "Is Starbucks okay?" I hoped ten bucks would be enough to cover two drinks there. I'd order water if I had to, so long as Lucy and I could be alone for a while.

"Sure. Let me go get some money from my dad."

"I got you covered," I offered, trying to sound casual.

"Okay, thanks." Lucy looked at me with those gorgeous green eyes, sucking me in like a rip current. I was pretty sure I didn't want to swim out of this one, though.

I had to force myself not to stare. "I only offered because you're wearing a cool shirt." I looked down at her green KISS

ME, I'M VEGETARIAN T-shirt with giant lips on it, imagining she wore it to send me a cryptic message. If things went well, I'd enact that slogan tonight.

"Yours is funny too." She poked my chest, giving me a brief moment of joy.

We went inside and bought our drinks, and I was relieved that I had enough to cover the bill. We sat down in the comfy chairs by the window and talked. I loved how Lucy sipped her caramel Frappuccino, made a comment, crossed her legs, and then asked me a question, with barely a breath between. I was so thrilled to be there, just the two of us, that I forgot to listen for a second. I tuned back in when I heard, "Lord knows my parents didn't have any friends in Green Lake."

"Seemed liked they made a lot of friends here." I motioned out the window. "An entire parking lot full of BFFs, in fact."

Another giggle. "I wish." Lucy swirled her straw through the whipped cream and licked it off. "To be honest, though, my parents are kind of weird. Because we're vegetarian, they check food labels constantly for hidden ingredients, buy all the bruised and about-to-rot produce at the grocery store, and grow things like organic bean sprouts on the kitchen window ledge." Her eyes lit up with a hint of a smirk. "Remember the ones you were so fond of the other day?"

"Oh, you mean the crap sprouts?"

"Yeah, those. Also, they'll only buy things made by companies on the cruelty-free list, vote for politicians who support animal rights, and even only play eco-friendly music from bands like Harvest Time and Father Earth."

I grimaced. "What and who?"

"Exactly. Trust me, the music sucks. It's all nature sounds, like crickets and waterfalls."

I didn't want to diss Lucy's parents, but based on my limited knowledge of them, they did seem odd. Like Aliens-Took-Me-to-Their-Spaceship-and-All-I-Have-Is-This-Lousy-T-Shirt odd.

"Maybe a *little* strange," I admitted.

"You haven't heard strange. Strange is never allowing me to go anyplace with animals on exhibit—zoos, circuses, petting farms—not even horseback riding. Strange is lecturing me when I accidentally bought new mascara from a company on the banned list. Worst of all are the embarrassing arguments they get into with people over animal rights stuff any time we're out in public. It was so bad in the last place we lived that my parents decided to move."

"Really? We moved because my mom got a big promotion, and my parents said we couldn't pass up the money."

Lucy sipped her drink. "Where does your mom work?"

Idiot! If I could have kicked myself in the shin, I would have. Why had I brought up my mother? I blurted out, "At a college. How about your mom?"

"She doesn't work." Lucy swirled her drink around in her

cup. "Which college does your mom work at, and what does she do there?"

I took a sip of my hot chocolate and launched into a fake coughing fit, holding up my hand as if I needed a moment. I grabbed a few napkins from the serving counter, hoping that if I stalled long enough, I could sidetrack her. I sat back down, patting my chest and clearing my throat. "Whew! Sorry about that."

Lucy tilted her head and smiled. "Aw . . . you got all choked up when you talked about your mother. Is she a professor?"

So much for diversion. "I'm not exactly sure what she does," I said, which wasn't really lying because I never did find out exactly what she did with those dogs.

I was desperately scrambling to think of another topic when I heard, "I can't believe they let any old riffraff in here!" Weasel grabbed my shoulders from behind and shook me. "What brings you here today, Mercer?"

"Hot chocolate." I held up my cup, glad he hadn't called me Skinny but praying that Lucy wouldn't bring up the other reason we were there. I had to steer this conversation exactly to where I wanted it to go.

"Sounds tasty." He held up his bag. "I got me one of them big fat blueberry muffins and a pumpkin scone for Jenny." He glanced at Lucy, smacking my shoulder with the back of his hand at the same time. "Don't be an oaf, Mercer. Introduce me to this pretty gal."

"Lucy, this is Weasel. Weasel, this is Lucy."

He took her hand and shook it vigorously. "Nice to meet you, young lady." And that's when he cocked his head and peered at the sticker on her shirt. "'Wool. It's not for ewe,'" he read aloud. "Were you here for that Wool-Mart protest?"

I panicked. *Please don't say my name.*

She nodded, smiling broadly. "Yep. Mercer joined us too."

Dang it! My face heated up and my heart fluttered as fast as when Flip was flipping out. I sat up quickly, realizing too late that I still had the sticker Lucy's mom had given me on my shirt.

"He did, did he?" Weasel narrowed his eyes and tapped my chest, right where the sticker was. "Interesting, Mercer. I'd love to hear more about that sometime." He turned to Lucy. "Well, real nice meeting you."

"You too!" Lucy waved to Weasel, who didn't say another word to me as he walked off.

I did my best not to show I was freaking out, but I couldn't help wondering what he'd tell my dad. I discreetly bit off a piece of my nail, imagining his response. I didn't know exactly what Dad would do when he found out, but I knew at the minimum he'd tell Mom. That lecture would be a long one. Maybe they'd even ground me, or take away my phone. But I couldn't think about that now — I had one final task for that day, and I promised I'd punch myself in the face if I lost my nerve.

I took a deep breath. It was now or never. "So . . . have you seen any good movies lately?"

Before she could answer, a rush of wind blew my hair into my eyes as someone opened the door behind me.

"There you are, Lucy!" Her mother appeared next to me. "Ready to go now, sweetie?"

A ball of anger as big and as fat as the blueberry muffin in Weasel's bag formed in my throat. *Not now! Go away! I need to ask your daughter out.*

Lucy pleaded with her mom, "It's not eleven yet. Can't I have a little more time?"

Her mom shook her head. "Afraid not. Daddy needs to get home. His boss called."

Lucy sighed as she stood up. "That sucks. Well, thanks for the drink, Mercer. Sorry I have to go so soon." She squeezed my shoulder as she walked by. "See you Monday!"

I managed to squeak out, "Yep. Monday it is."

The moment I heard the door clang shut, I slumped back in my chair. So much for being the man. I'd had my opportunity and I'd blown it. Watching the barista pour a brown stream of coffee down the sink, I realized that my chance to be with Lucy was running out too.

THIRTEEN ·····➤

AFTER DOWNING THE REST OF MY HOT CHOCOLATE
at Starbucks, I tossed my anti-wool sticker in the trash and
went outside to look for Weasel. I didn't see him or his truck
anywhere. Not only did I have to walk home, but, even worse, he
was probably calling my father right this very minute. I started
the three-mile trek to my house, filled with worries about what
I'd tell my parents. At least I had a lot of time to think about it.

I walked east on Main Street, and then north along Pine
Road, stomping on the piles of fallen leaves that had collected
along the fence line. But the crackling sound that normally made
me smile failed to elevate my mood.

I was sunk, no question about it. What was it I'd heard someone say once, that lies were like angry geese — they always came
back to bite you? This lie was nipping at my heels, that's for sure.
I decided if my parents went wild on me, asking questions and
demanding answers, I'd just tell them the truth: that I liked Lucy
a lot and had joined HALT only temporarily until I found out
whether or not she liked me back. If she did like me and we
started hanging out, I would confess that HALT wasn't quite
right for me and that I was going to quit. If she wasn't interested
in me, I'd just halt HALT immediately. A win-win situation.

When I walked into the house, I was both surprised and

relieved to find it empty. There was a note: "Went grocery shopping with Madison. Back later, Dad." My spirits brightened when I saw his cell lying on the counter with no announcement about missed calls in the viewing window. Had Weasel gotten too busy and forgotten to call? I rolled my eyes at my own stupidity. No, a more likely scenario was that he came here after seeing me and broke the news to Dad in person, and now Dad was out shopping for a rope to tie me up with so I couldn't leave the house again.

My cell rang. It was Charlie asking if he and Reed could stop by to see Flip. Talk about a perfect coincidence! I told him that they should come quickly. Not only because I was thrilled to finally show off Flip, but also because my father was less likely to strangle me with witnesses around. While I waited, I made two thick ham sandwiches and washed them down with a can of Mountain Dew. I checked the clock, praying my friends would arrive before Dad did. My prayers were answered when, ten minutes later, they drove up on their ATVs, completely covered in dirt and sweat.

"Where'd you go today?" I asked, a bit jealous. "You guys are caked in mud."

"Mount Trashmore," Charlie said, referring to one of our regular spots, a nearby landfill that had tons of hilly areas and natural ramps. "It was muddy; I got bloody." He lifted his elbow to show me a cut. "Definitely not for fuddy-duddies." He chuckled. "So where's the Flipmeister?"

"Follow me." I walked them to the outside of Flip's mews and told them to watch me through the bars. Inside the rehab center, I put on my gear and went to fetch my bird. The second Flip saw me, he started up his crazy windmill routine, flapping his wings like he was taking off for Florida.

"Lord have Mercer!" Charlie cried. "His wingspan is huge."

"And you know huge better than anyone else," Reed joked, elbowing Charlie.

"Hey, there's just more of me to love." Charlie hiked up the waistband of his pants.

I thought it was cool that Charlie never took offense to comments about his size, how expertly he turned things around in his favor. Maybe I could try that the next time Dad complained about my room. *Check it out, Pops. They say a messy room is a sign of genius.*

I shoved some choice raw meat tidbits into my waist pouch before heading to Flip's mews, managing to get him up and on my fist without too much of a struggle. I brought Flip outside and introduced him to Charlie and Reed, pointing out all his features: his razor-sharp talons, his gorgeous weatherproof feathers in ten thousand shades of browns and whites, his powerful beak. I wondered if this was how champion hockey players feel when they hold the Stanley Cup. "Not only that, but his eyesight is so good, he can spot a mouse a football field away."

"Cool," Reed said, keeping his distance. "But very scary, dude." He pulled out his phone and thumbed through a few screens. Guess his Grand Theft Auto app was more interesting than real life.

"Speaking of scary, how'd that protest rally go today?" Charlie asked. "Did you get to beat up any wool wearers?"

"Only a couple," I joked, using my right fist to jab the air. "Actually, I'm a little worried because my dad's friend Weasel saw me there. If he tells my parents, I'm dead."

"Ya think?" Charlie asked sarcastically. "Maybe your dad will even have you stuffed and hung on the wall above your fireplace to show what happens to traitors."

"Don't laugh. It could happen." Flip flapped his wings, so I waited until he'd calmed down. "That wasn't the only part that sucked. Just when I was about to ask Lucy if she wanted to go with the movies with me tonight, her mom walked in and dragged her home."

"You were going to ask her out?" Reed looked up from his phone, waiting for an answer.

"Yeah. I told you guys yesterday, remember?" I replied with a shrug. Why was Reed acting as though this was the first he'd heard I liked her?

"Too bad you wimped out. Better luck next time, Merman." Charlie thumped me on the back.

"I didn't wimp out," I protested. "Her mom was there."

"Well, it doesn't matter, anyway," Charlie said, "because once she finds out about ol' Flip here, she'll dump your scrawny butt. And then, my friend, she can have herself a wool-free dog lover." He patted his chest.

"You never told her that you hunt?" Reed pinched his lips in disapproval. Apparently he hadn't caught on to the whole belief system of HALT. Perhaps he needed some remedial tutoring in Social Dynamics 101 in addition to Algebra.

I made a face. "I'm pretty sure a girl who loves animals as much as Lucy does wouldn't dig hunting. Duh."

Reed turned his attention back to his phone. "So you're just going to keep on lying to her? That's dumb. I'd never give up working on cars just because a girl didn't like it."

"Not your problem, I guess," I retorted, unsettled by his comments. "And technically, I haven't lied to her because she never asked if I hunt." Having this conversation made me want to put Flip back and send Reed home, but they were here and so was Flip, so I'd just have to hope Reed would shut up.

"Let's move on, ladies." Charlie rolled his hand in a circle. "C'mon Mercer. Show us how Flip does his tricks."

Thank God for Charlie. Although I was glad he acted as a buffer, apparently I hadn't explained the process of falconry very well to him. "He doesn't do tricks. But I can show you the training routine I do so we'll be able to work together when we hunt."

"Whatever. Show us," Reed said, glancing up from his phone.

Ignoring his jerk-off behavior, I asked them to move back before tossing the swing lure with a bit of quail attached to it in a circle overhead. "Watch this," I instructed. Flip swooped down and snatched the bait in midair. Well, on two of the five tries, anyway.

"Cool." Charlie dug a peanut out of his pocket and shelled it. "What else does he do?"

"I'll show you." I placed Flip on the standing bow perch and walked about seventy feet away — just as Weasel and I had practiced. Flip waited patiently until I pulled out a small piece of quail, and then he flew right to me. *Yes!* I held him up, walking back toward my friends. "Wasn't that awesome?"

Reed didn't seem all that impressed, but at least his phone wasn't in front of his nose. "It's great and all, but you've got a line connected to his leg. Not much free will, is it? No offense, but it doesn't look that hard to do."

"Yeah, sorry ol' chum, but he's right," Charlie said. "What happens if you take that thing off? Would he fly away?"

My Stanley Cup took a tumble, getting dented and tarnished. "I'm not sure what he'd do," I admitted. "He only learned how to use the creance line yesterday. Weasel said that once they're on the creance line, it doesn't take long to progress to flying free. Flip should be ready real soon."

"Today's real soon," Reed said, elbowing Charlie. "Don't you think?"

"That *would* be cool," Charlie agreed. "Can you do it?"

I hesitated. What would happen? Flip did seem to be responding to me in the last two days, as if he had finally figured out I wasn't going to hurt him. I mean, I'd fed him and cleaned his crap for over a week. That should count for something.

"He's probably afraid he'll take off," Reed said.

"I'm not *afraid*." Not enough to admit it, anyway, but Reed was pissing me off. I reasoned that since I hadn't fed Flip yet, once I produced some juicy rabbit chunks, he'd fly right to me. "Fine. Let's try it. You guys can witness his first flight flying free." I laughed. "Try saying that ten times fast."

While Charlie and Reed gave my tongue twister a couple of tries, I removed the creance line from Flip's leg but still held on to his foot for assurance. I noticed my fingers quivering a bit. Should I do this? I looked at the guys, waiting and watching. Now or later—it had to happen eventually. I hesitated a second before letting go of Flip's foot, freeing him from all his attachments. Holding my breath, I backed away from the bow perch.

Flip eyed the wet hunk of rabbit meat I held in my hand. *Please don't fly away,* I begged silently. He stared at it for a second, tilting his head slightly, and then took off at full speed—in the opposite direction!

"Damn it! Flip! Flip!" I shouted, my words catching in my throat. What was the command to bring your bird back? In my panic, I couldn't remember anything. I took off running after him.

"Get him, Mercer!" Charlie yelled, pointing. "He's flying away!"

"I can see that!" I screamed, nearly losing it. All that time to trap him, to man him, and in three seconds, he was gone? I bolted after Flip, almost in tears. Why had I let Reed get under my skin? Flip suddenly took a sharp turn, and in one fierce swoop dove toward me. I stopped running and froze. Three seconds later, he landed back on my fist, earning himself a juicy chunk of meat as a reward. Score one for the underdogs! A small tear leaked out, this one of happiness, but I wiped it away before the guys caught up to me.

Charlie bellowed, "You did it! That was so cool!"

"Thanks. Sorry about yelling before," I said to Charlie. "I thought I lost him. But flying free is what is so cool about falconry. Once you've gained the hawk's trust, he always flies back to you. Until you release him back in the wild at the end of hunting season, of course." That idea was beginning to bother me —letting Flip go and never seeing him again after all this work —but I'd worry about it when the time came.

My arm a bit tired, I brought my foot up to rest on a rotting tree trunk so I could prop my elbow on my knee. A second later, a chipmunk came zipping out from the opposite end. Before I knew what was happening, Flip flew off my fist, swooping into action. Flapping his wings rapidly, zigzagging back and forth following the chipmunk's movements, he skimmed across the field, heading toward the pond. The chipmunk ran like, well, like a hawk was chasing him.

I screamed, "Go chipmunk! Go Flip! May the best man win!"

Flip pulled his wings in tightly and extended his talons as

a high-pitched squeal pierced the air. Had my bird caught his breakfast? When I got closer, I saw Flip standing proudly on his catch, holding the chipmunk tightly in his talons.

"Atta boy, Flip!" I cheered, my heart beating as rapidly as I knew Flip's probably was. I knelt down, ready to dispatch the prey if it was still alive, although I hoped it wasn't. I didn't know how to break a chipmunk's neck without the thing biting me. It would be only a tiny bite, but still. Maybe chipmunks had rabies. Or carried diseased fleas that could jump on me.

Okay, fine. I didn't like getting bitten by things, no matter how small they were.

"That was so frickin' cool!" Reed yelled, showing excitement for the first time since he'd arrived.

"Totally sick!" Charlie galloped over, hitching up his pants.

Flip spread his wings out to hide his catch, bobbing his head up and down excitedly in anticipation of a good meal. Before I had a chance to figure out what to do next, Flip ripped a chunk of flesh from the chipmunk's side.

"Oh man! He's tearing it to shreds, Mercer!" Reed smacked my arm as if to alert me to something I wasn't aware of. Or had control over. Wasn't like I could train a hawk to use a knife and a fork.

"This is better than a National Geographic special," Charlie declared. And then switching to a British accent, he added, "And a lot more bloody fun!"

"You knuckleheads." I laughed, pleased they didn't think it

was lame or, worse, cruel to hunt with a hawk. But watching nature in action—live and with sound effects—couldn't be beat.

I knew that on an actual hunt, I would have to distract Flip and remove the prey quickly before he ate it and became fed up, which would make him lose his desire to hunt any more that day. But hunting season didn't start for two more weeks —which technically made this catch illegal. I wasn't sure about the proper protocol, but decided to try to remove the chipmunk from his grasp, now that the little guy no longer posed a threat to me.

I grabbed a chunk of meat out of my waist pouch and distracted Flip by waving it and calling his name, making him leap to my fist to retrieve his reward. I gently kicked the lifeless chipmunk out of Flip's sight. Now what? Usually we picked up all the downed prey—either for our birds or for our family to eat, because that was the main purpose of hunting, after all —but if your bird killed something that wasn't in season, the rule was that you had to "leave-it-lay." I didn't think that applied to chipmunks, though, because, well, there was no season for chipmunks. None that I'd ever heard of anyway, but who knew? People ate squirrels, raccoons, bears, snakes—all sorts of animals, so why not chipmunks?

I discreetly scooped up the chipmunk and slipped it into my waist pouch without Flip noticing. The chipmunk was small enough that I wouldn't have to cut it into parts like with a rabbit or a pheasant. One cool thing about raptors is that you could give them the whole animal to eat, bones and all. They used what they needed and then, presto chango!, barfed up the inedible parts in a little gray ball, like a mini trash compactor.

The guys waited outside for me while I returned Flip to the mews and washed up, and then the three of us went into the house. On the way in, I told them that this chipmunk incident needed to stay our little secret, as did my joining HALT. Oh, and going to the protest rally too. Looked like I had a virtual warehouse of secrets.

The guys sat on the kitchen stools while I tossed two bagel dogs into the microwave, opting to leave mine in the freezer, my appetite gone. All of these clandestine activities must have given me a bellyful of indigestion. While we waited for the food to cook, the door banged open and Lincoln strutted in with a girl I'd never seen before. She wore a ton of makeup, had bleached blond hair with dark roots, and a huge chest that even a pirate would envy. Her skimpy, low-cut shirt made sure everyone noticed her set of twins, which I'd bet ten bucks were adopted. Who was this bimbo, and more important, where was Lauren?

"Hey, guys, this is Zola. Zola, this is my little brother, Mercer, along with his two girlfriends, Charlie and Reed."

I rolled my eyes at his introduction and forced a smile. "Hey, how's it going?"

Zola giggled, waving. "Hi, Linky's little brother and his friends."

Linky? Was this chick for real? Charlie scrambled out of his chair to shake her hand. "I'm Charlie. You ever get sick of this dude," he said, pointing at Lincoln, "I'm the man for you."

Lincoln pushed Charlie's shoulder. "Down, boy. Go take a cold shower."

I stupidly hoped that Zola was one of Lauren's friends, and that Lauren would be walking in the door any second. But then Lincoln grabbed Zola around the waist, pulling her close, and mumbled something in her ear. Guess not.

"Stop it, silly." Zola giggled again, smacking his chest playfully. "Not in front of your brother and his friends."

Shaking my head, I brought the bagel dogs and a few cans of pop to the kitchen island. Charlie and Reed pounced on those hot dogs the way I would have if I hadn't been "fed up" with all of my lies. Guess Flip and I had more in common than either of us knew.

Lincoln slid a bag of popcorn into the microwave and faced us, leaning back against the counter. "What are you guys doing here? Why don't you go scope out some hot babes like Zola?" He looked at her and raised his eyebrows twice, as if he had something in mind other than eating popcorn.

"Aw . . . thanks, sweetkins." Zola smiled, squeezing Lincoln's forearm.

Didn't she see that he was treating her like a piece of raw meat? Why would she want to be with him?

"Mercer showed us Flip today," Charlie explained, his mouth bulging with food. "And it was flippin' cool."

I picked up a pen off the table and started clicking it nervously. "Glad you liked him."

"Me too," Reed agreed. "I had no idea you could let him fly away and he would come back on his own like that."

I swallowed a ball of worry, glancing toward Lincoln to see if he had heard.

"What do you mean 'on his own'?" Lincoln managed to pry his eyes away from feasting on Zola's bounty for a moment.

Lie again or brag my ass off? I decided I'd had enough deception for one day. "Uh, well I took him out for a training session, and guess what? I flew him free today."

"You *what*?" Lincoln glared at me. "Did Dad say you could?"

I leaped off my bragging perch in a hurry, worried by his accusatory tone. "No, but Weasel said I could," I lied. Looked like I was an expert at something, after all.

"Bull." Lincoln narrowed his eyes. "Weasel would never overstep his bounds. Only the sponsor makes decisions like that, you liar."

Zola patted his arm. "Be nice, Linky."

"Yeah," I agreed, although I thought that "Linky" was an idiot for being attracted to this girl. Lauren was way prettier than Zola, and she didn't giggle after every sentence. After spending only two minutes with Zola, I'd guess her IQ matched her bra size, a 40 Double Dumb.

"Whatever. Where is Dad, anyway?" Lincoln popped open the microwave door, handing Zola the popcorn bag.

"Shopping with Maddie."

"What time are they coming home?" He grabbed two Cokes out of the fridge with one hand and placed his other on Zola's back.

I was about to ask why he wanted to know so badly, but when I saw him heading for the basement, I was pretty sure I knew the answer. "How the heck should I know?"

Lincoln opened the basement door. "Catch you ladies later."

As much as I loathed being a whiny tattletale, the thought of my brother ruining things with Lauren for some alone time with Zola irked me. "You're not allowed to bring people downstairs when Mom and Dad aren't home, you know."

"Thanks for the news flash, Grandma," Lincoln said. Right before he closed the door, he added, "And don't bother us."

As the door clicked shut, I heard Zola ask, "Your grandma's here?"

I rolled my eyes. "Let's get out of here. I don't think I can take much of Zola, Girl Genius, any longer."

As we walked outside, Reed whistled. "That was quite a show. The craziest thing is, Zola looks a lot like Patty Piston, this month's Garage Girl."

"That's why she looked so familiar!" Charlie shook his head. "Man, your bro is one lucky dude, Mercer."

"You guys think being with Zola is lucky? She's dumber than a rock. What's so great about that?"

Charlie laughed. "Well, for one, she'd think Reed was the smartest guy she knew."

Reed shoved Charlie hard, but playfully. "Shut up."

"Besides, I wouldn't be making out with her brains, anyway," Charlie added.

"I guess . . ." I shrugged, feeling unsettled. Was it wrong to want a girl who was smart or funny, not just pretty? Why couldn't I just go for the thrill of victory the way Lincoln did without overanalyzing things? I decided to drop it for now. "You guys want to take the paddleboat out?"

"Nah. I got to get going." Reed lifted his helmet off his ATV.

"Me too," Charlie agreed. "Dinner's at six. Can't miss that."

"But you just ate a bagel dog," I pointed out.

Charlie put his arm around my shoulder. "Mercer, Mercer, Mercer. I eat when it's *time* to eat." He hoisted himself onto his ATV with a grunt and looked at his watch. "You see, four o'clock was snack time; six o'clock, it'll be dinner time. Got it?" He situated his butt cheeks on the seat and pulled his T-shirt down in back. "Thanks for the dog, though."

"Same." Reed cranked up his ATV.

After Charlie had started his bike, the two of them lowered the visors on their helmets and rode across my lawn—just as Dad's pickup pulled into the driveway.

I stood on the blacktop, torn between running into the house to alert Lincoln and letting Dad walk in and catch my brother with his pants down, so to speak.

As much as I wanted to realign Dad's image of Lincoln being the perfect son, I did the brotherly thing: I ran my butt off trying to get into the house before Dad.

FOURTEEN ⋯⋯🦅

I **BURST INTO THE HOUSE AND SPRINTED TO THE** basement door. I whipped it open, yelling, "Lincoln! Dad's home!"

I listened at the head of the stairs. Quiet whisperings and a flurry of footsteps meant that Lincoln had gotten the message. Moments later, Busybody Maddie arrived at the house, out of breath.

"Mercer, why'd you run into the house like that?"

"'Cause I felt like it," I replied casually, breezing past her into the kitchen. Dad came in through the side door, arms loaded with groceries.

Lincoln and Zola tromped up the stairs, carrying their Cokes and the popcorn bag.

"Lincoln?" Dad spun around. "I thought you said you were working today."

Lincoln shook his head. "Nope. My mistake."

"Were you just downstairs?" Dad asked. No doubt he expected Lincoln to produce a hammer and nails that he had retrieved from the workroom, thereby giving him a valid reason for being in the basement with a female guest.

"He was, Dad, I saw him," Maddie said, her tattletale antennae erupting out of her head.

"Chill out a second, Maddie," Lincoln said coolly. "Dad, this is Zola. Zola, this is Dad."

"Hi, Dad." Zola giggled, giving a little wave. Was she joking, or had she actually forgotten what her own dad looked like since she'd left her house this morning, and she thought this might be the guy?

Dad forced a smile. "Nice to meet you, Zola."

Maddie's mouth kicked into second gear. "Dad, I thought you said he couldn't have girls downstairs in the family room. Zola's a girl and she was downstairs." Besides having a knack for pointing out the obvious, I realized that every single thought that went into Maddie's brain instantly spewed out her mouth like liquid gray matter.

Lincoln chuckled and put his arm around Maddie. "Hey, Bratison, take it easy. Zola had to use the bathroom, and since Mercer over here stank up the main one, I offered her a nicer smelling bathroom to use downstairs, that's all."

My brother was smoother than freshly ironed pants. If Zola hadn't known the truth, I would have been embarrassed. Still, Lincoln was a weasel for saying I stank up the bathroom. I'd get him for that later.

Dad nodded. "I see. Well, I'd better get back to unpacking the groceries, then."

That was it? End of conversation? That was the equivalent of giving Lincoln the green light to have Woodley High's all-female swim team downstairs next week. I hated that Lincoln could do anything he wanted and still make Dad happy, while all I had to do was sneeze when a red-tail was nearby to get reamed out.

I ran upstairs to play video games and avoid being asked to help put away the groceries. I had just picked up the controller when Maddie strolled into my room.

"Why does Lincoln—"

"Get out of my room. You didn't knock."

Maddie sighed. "But I just wanted—"

"Just nothing . . . knock." I pointed to the door.

I waited for Maddie to go back out in the hall and knock. This was fun.

"Yes?" I asked pleasantly. "Who is it?"

"Mercer, you can see it's me standing here. Can I come in?"

"Yes, Tattleson, you may enter. What do you wanteth?"

"Why is Zola here? Did Lincoln break up with Lauren?" She picked up my bottle of Intimidate cologne off my dresser and unscrewed the lid. Apparently she wasn't intimidated enough to leave it alone. A strong piney scent wafted through the room, making me wonder whether Lucy would like it if I wore that stuff. I made a mental note to splash some on tomorrow.

She lifted the bottle to her nose and sniffed deeply.

"Don't touch my stuff," I ordered. "Or smell it either."

Maddie set the bottle back on my dresser with a sigh and plopped down on my bed—uninvited, I might point out. "Did Lincoln bring her home just because she's got big boobs?"

I had to laugh at that one. "Maybe."

"Well, I hope when you date someone, it won't be just because of *that*."

"Hey, I'd be happy with any girl who liked me back."

Okay, I'll admit it. I'm not quite as upstanding as all that. Big boobs would be a bonus. Make that two bonuses. But I wouldn't tell that to my little sister.

"And I know he didn't go downstairs because it stank in the bathroom by the kitchen." Maddie folded her arms across her chest. "Because I went in there and took a big whiff, and it smelled just fine."

I faked a grimace. "You weirdo bathroom sniffer."

She ignored me. "He went downstairs to make out with Zola, didn't he?"

"You're crazy." I turned back to my game so as not to give anything away with my expression.

Her mouth dropped open. "Oh my gosh! That's why you ran in the house, isn't it? To tell Lincoln that Dad and I were home?"

I got distracted by Maddie's comments, and an army guy on the screen nailed me. I paused my game. "No, that's not why, Miss Know-It-All. I was in a hurry to play *Common Enemy*. Which you just made me lose, by the way."

"Come on, Mercer, tell me the truth. I won't tell anyone, I promise." She bit her bottom lip and raised her eyebrows expectantly.

I laughed out loud. "Ha! You'd be downstairs so fast blabbing the news, you'd leave burn marks on the carpet."

"That's not true! I can keep a secret. Pleeease?"

The way she begged me made me think she meant it. I looked at her face, all sweet and innocent like her stinky little hamster, Peanut. "If I tell you, and you say something to Mom and Dad, I'll never tell you anything again. Ever. I mean it."

She rolled her eyes. "You think I'm such a baby."

"You are a baby. You're always tattling."

Maddie's eyes widened. "I only tattle on you because you're so mean to me!"

"And I'm only mean to you because you tattle on me. Like this morning, when I left the cereal box open in the pantry, you told Mom about it."

"But that's because the cereal gets all stale when you do that!"

"So? Is stale cereal going to ruin your life? Just close the box and move on."

Maddie grabbed the fringe from the edge of my blue bedspread and ran it through her fingers. "Okay, fine. I promise not to tell on you anymore if you promise not to be mean to me. Like not pulling my hair and not calling me Tattleson. I hate that."

"Fine. No more tattling on me — no more Tattleson for you. Deal?" I held out my hand and she shook it.

"Deal," she said, grinning. I hoped she'd forget to ask what she came in here for, since I'd so deviously detoured from talking about Lincoln's field trip to the basement, but I must have underestimated Maddie's thirst for gossip. If she had the ability to grow gills and swim in the stuff, she would.

146

"Soooo . . . tell me. What really happened with Lincoln?"

I hesitated a second before answering. "All I know is that he didn't go down there because I stank up the bathroom."

"I knew it!" She stood to leave, but caught sight of herself in the mirror. She picked up my brush, which was lying on the dresser, turned to see if I was watching, and wisely put it back. "Well, thanks for trusting me, Mercer. You're a great brother — sometimes."

That shocked me a little. Did she really think I was great, considering how I treated her?

An hour later, Dad called me down to dinner; everyone was already seated at the table. Mom was home from work, pouring a glass of wine. Lincoln was riding solo, so I figured Zola must have gotten tired and went home to take a nappy poo.

"Hi, Mercer," Mom said, placing a napkin over her lap. "How was your concert?"

I almost said, "What concert?" when I remembered my first lie of the day — explaining why I was going to the mall. "Oh, it was all right." I shrugged, slinking into my seat. "Nothing great."

The delicious aroma of Italian food made my stomach growl and my mouth water. Dad dished out a big plate of fettuccini with marinara sauce, placing two nice-size meatballs on top before handing it to me.

"Look familiar, Lincoln?" I jabbed my elbow into his side.

"You know it, bro." Lincoln elbowed me back.

The phone rang and Mom warned us to let the answering machine pick up. She tried to divert our attention away from the phone with talk about the weather, but it was useless. All of us stopped chewing, straining to hear who was calling.

It was Lauren. "Hey, Buddie family! I tried calling Linc's cell, but it went right to voicemail. When I went to Home Depot today to see him, they said he called in sick. I just wanted to see how he's feeling. Have him call me when you see him. Thanks!"

Dad stopped chewing. "I thought you said you didn't have to work today."

"Uh, well. I didn't feel like it, so I called in sick." Lincoln sniffed, indifferent. "Big deal."

"It is a big deal, Lincoln," Dad argued, shaking his head. "Not so much about lying to your employer, but lying to me."

"And calling in sick all the time *is* a big deal." Mom put down her fork and wiped her mouth. "How would I keep a job if I didn't go in whenever I didn't feel like it?"

Lincoln let out a chuckle. "Good one, Mom. I mean, have you ever called in sick? Seems to me you're always at work."

"That's not fair, Lincoln. I'm the director. People expect me to be there." Mom took a sip of her wine. "I can't call in sick without good reason."

I grabbed a piece of garlic bread from the basket. "Well . . . you could probably stand to call in sick once in a while, though. I needed to look at your picture on the piano yesterday to remember what you looked like."

Okay, so it was a bit of an exaggeration, but not much. I did look at her picture to ask if I could borrow the five-dollar bill that was on her nightstand. For the record, she said yes.

"Ha-ha." Mom smiled. "Have you forgotten that Dad and I are going away for our anniversary next weekend? And I'm taking that Monday off, so there." She picked up her fork and twirled some noodles around it.

I had a vague recollection of Mom telling me about this anniversary trip a while back. I was glad they were going — it seemed rare that they went anywhere alone together.

Dad patted the table. "Oh! Which reminds me." He looked at my brother. "I need you to work with Mercer next weekend. He can't miss a day of practice. Not with this bird."

My fork stopped halfway to my mouth. "Really, Dad? For your information, Weasel had me fly him on the creance line yesterday, and today I flew him free."

"You *what*? Who told you to do that?" He stared, mouth ajar, waiting for an answer.

"I did it on my own," I replied quietly. "But it worked."

"I knew it." Lincoln sneered. "Liar."

Dad took a deep breath as he raked a hand through his hair. "You were very lucky. Frankly, I'm shocked. Most birds need at least two weeks before they're ready for that."

"Where are you two going on your trip, anyway?" Lincoln

asked, expertly veering the topic away from me. I'd have to thank him for that later.

"Milwaukee," Mom said. "There's that nice art museum on the lake I've heard so much about." She cut a meatball in half. "Dad's going to bring Grandma Buddie here to come and stay with you kids while we're gone."

Lincoln and I both jumped in at the same time, protesting. "We don't need a babysitter," I argued. Lincoln said, "You're going to drive all the way to Brown Deer, bring her back here, and then go back up to Milwaukee? Why?"

We loved our gram, but she came up with all these "fun ideas!" and then was offended if we said no. Last year's anniversary trip started off with her asking Linc and me to pick up "a few things" for her at the grocery store (nearly eighty bucks' worth) while she and Maddie got their nails done on Friday night, woke us all up for a surprise big breakfast at the crack of dawn on Saturday morning, followed by a mandated visit to the haircut place "just for trims," and then treated us all to a Disney movie Saturday night. Maddie loved it all, of course, but Lincoln and I ended up tired, aggravated, and sporting hairstyles we didn't want.

"Spending time with your grandmother is important. You shouldn't begrudge doing a few things with her or for her," Dad said, his eyebrows pinched together in disappointment.

I could tell right away that complaining wasn't going to cut it. "It's not about us, Dad. We're worried about her. I think we wore her out last time."

"Mercer's right," Lincoln agreed, quickly tuning in to my line of reasoning. "Gram had a hard time getting up the stairs, and she had to sleep on the couch."

"Stress isn't good for someone her age," I added as backup for our cause. Guess I had learned something from those Wool-Mart demonstrators, after all.

Dad smoothed his mustache. "She did say she had a backache for a week afterward. And Mercer's right about the stress." He glanced at Mom, as if looking for her input.

"It is a lot of driving back and forth," Mom said, setting her fork down. "Regardless of whether Gram comes or not, Maddie has a birthday party at the bowling alley on Sunday at one o'clock, so Lincoln, you'll need to give her a ride."

"Can't." Lincoln downed his milk. "I work Sundays, eight to three."

"If you don't call in sick, that is," Dad added sarcastically.

"I have to go to the party," Maddie complained. "It's Joanna's birthday, and she's going to have cosmic bowling and everything!"

"That presents a problem," Mom said to Dad. "Who can you call to carpool?"

Since Mom wasn't home after school, Dad did most of the driving whenever Maddie or I needed to be chauffeured somewhere. He cleared his throat. "I'd give Susan Jenkins a call, but she's going out of town too." Dad looked at Maddie. "I'm really sorry, honey. Not sure it's going to work out this time."

"You'll live, Tattleson," Lincoln told her. "There'll be other parties."

"Shut up, Lincoln." Maddie took a sip of her milk, setting the cup down loudly. "Mom, did you know Lincoln hung out with Zola today *in the basement?*"

I was in mid-chew when she asked that, causing me to bite my tongue hard. The unmistakable taste of blood filled my mouth. I popped my eyeballs wide at Maddie, sending her a telepathic message: *Shut your big mouth before you get Lincoln in major trouble with Mom and Dad and, worse, me in major trouble with Lincoln—which could have adverse side effects.*

"Dad already knows that." Lincoln pointed to the basket next to me. "Can you pass me the garlic bread?"

Another great diversion ploy on Lincoln's part. I played along, figuring I owed him one. "Sure thing. Great dinner, Dad." After handing him the basket, I pressed a napkin against my bleeding tongue.

Maddie continued, "Yeah, but do you know they went down there to make out? That's why Mercer ran into the house, to warn him that we were home. Tell them what you told me, Mercer."

Four sets of eyes turned to me.

"I neva thaid that!" I argued, hiding behind the blood-spotted napkin.

"You're *dating* Zola?" Dad asked, looking confused. "I thought she was Lauren's friend. What happened to Lauren?"

"Nothing happened," Lincoln said. "We're just taking a break, that's all."

"Didn't sound like it on the machine," Maddie retorted.

"Mind your own business," Lincoln told her.

Mom shook her head, reaching for her wine. "We have rules in this house about where we entertain guests of the opposite sex, Lincoln. The kitchen and the living room are fine, *not* upstairs or downstairs. We've discussed this."

"I know, but seriously. I'm eighteen. Don't you think I deserve some privacy?" Lincoln glanced at our parents, but gave me a dirty look along with it.

I knew that look. It said I was dead meat. My stomach lurched. I swallowed a ball of guilt and gave the same dead meat glare to Maddie.

"If you don't like our rules, don't bring girls here." Mom stared at Lincoln a moment. "End of discussion."

"Fine." Lincoln stood abruptly, his chair falling onto the floor with a loud thwack. He lifted it up, elbowing me in the head in the process. It hurt like hell but I didn't say a word. "But don't ask me to drive Maddie and Mercer around anymore. Favors work both ways." He deposited his dishes in the sink with a loud clank and headed toward the stairs.

Dad and Mom exchanged glances. Mom shrugged. "He's got a point."

"Not budging on this," Dad said firmly. "We'll talk later."

My appetite gone, I cleared off my place and hurried upstairs, needing to set Lincoln straight on what really had happened earlier with Maddie to avoid any backlash on his end. When I got upstairs, I knocked on his door softly. "Lincoln, let me in," I whisper-yelled through the door. "I want to explain."

"Go away, snitch."

I cringed, turning the handle. It was locked. "Come on. Open up."

He bellowed, "Go away before I beat the crap out of you!"

He didn't need to tell me twice. That's when I saw Maddie stroll to her room. I decided to give her a piece of my mind — the piece that was steaming mad right now.

I found her sitting on her frilly pink comforter watching TV and smiling, as if she hadn't just announced the secret that she clearly swore she'd never tell only an hour before.

"Out of my room. You didn't knock," she said, imitating me.

I ignored her and stood in front of the TV, blocking her view. "You begged me to tell you what happened, promising you'd keep it a secret. Now Lincoln's pissed, and you know he's going to find a way to get even with me."

"Lincoln's always mad about something." Maddie rolled her eyes. "Besides, Mom and Dad needed to know what he was doing."

Her way of butting in to everything made my face heat up. "No, they didn't! If it doesn't involve you, stay out of it! Grow up and stop your whiny-ass tattling already!"

She got up from her bed and rushed toward the door.

"Where are you going? Downstairs to tell Mom and Dad I yelled at you? That I swore?" I stepped toward her, pushing her toward the stairs. "Hurry! Run and tattle, just like always!"

She froze two feet from the door, like she was contemplating whether to stay or go. Suddenly, she burst into tears. "I'm sorry, Mercer. I do have a big mouth—I can't help myself. I got mad when Lincoln called me Tattleson, and it slipped out." She plopped face-down on the bed, sobbing. With her voice muffled, she wailed, "I won't tell your secrets ever again, I promise."

"Like I'll ever tell you one again?" I stalked off, wondering what made me think I could trust a ten-year-old anyway.

At least I didn't have to worry about how and when Lincoln would strike back. On Sunday morning, I saw a mute pile as big as Mount Zola underneath Flip's perch, which could mean only one thing—Lincoln had snuck Flip a double helping of dinner last night. I swear, lazy old Flip laughed when I put him on the scale, knowing full well that he'd be too heavy for me to fly him, the same way I'm unmotivated to do anything after I eat on Thanksgiving. And to think that all through grade school I wanted to grow up and be like Lincoln. Now I thought he was an egocentric loser.

My only hope was that he couldn't read minds or I'd be in big trouble.

FIFTEEN ····⟍

ON SUNDAY AFTERNOON, MOM AND DAD TOOK THE whole family to the Johnny Appleseed Festival over in Crystal Lake. The whole family sans Lincoln, of course. Mom and Dad never make him go with us anymore. At first I declined as well—until Dad dangled the promise of waffle fries, funnel cakes with cherries and whipped cream, and my favorite, corn dogs on sticks. Since Reed was working on his future car with his dad and Charlie wasn't answering his cell, I figured I'd go.

Corn dogs have that kind of power over me.

When we got there, Mom and Maddie headed to the Craft Barn, while Dad and I made our way to the motocross track. We decided we'd all meet back at the Corn Dog Hut in an hour. Five races later, I had learned a ton of new tricks to show Reed and Charlie the next time we took our dirt bikes out, and was ready to chow down.

Mom and Maddie waved to us from one end of a partially occupied picnic table. Dad and I bought six corn dogs and three orders of onion rings—all on sticks. The smell of those foods nearly sent me running to the table. After handing Mom her freshly squeezed lemonade, I slid in next to Dad and dove for my first corn dog. I took a bite, and savoring the deep-fried cornmeal coating outside and the juicy hot dog inside, I confirmed what I already knew: everything's better on a stick.

"Maddie and I had fun, didn't we?" Mom patted a large bag on the bench between them.

Maddie glowed, grinning widely. "I love all the stuff you bought me, Mom. Thank you sooo much. You want to see the necklace and earrings I got, Dad?"

"Sure!" Dad grabbed an onion ring.

"Let me guess. You bought something pink," I said, my mouth full. A small chunk of corn dog slipped out.

Dad flicked it off the table with his napkin and a shake of his head.

"Sorry," I managed, before biting into a crispy brown onion ring. That's when I heard a man behind me say, "Frieda, isn't that the woman who's the director of that research lab?"

I froze, the onion ring still dangling from my lips. I'd heard that voice before.

The woman answered, "Oh Lord. I believe it is, Jerry."

Oh no. Please be a coincidence. I risked a peek behind me, and sure enough, Lucy's parents were a mere six feet away. Crap! Both of them wore bright red HALT sweatshirts and carried handmade protest signs attached to yardsticks. One sign read MEAT IS MURDER and the other ANIMALS ARE NOT ENTERTAINMENT.

Guess I was wrong about everything being better on a stick.

I spun and faced my mom and sister, contemplating what to

do — run to the john, keep my back turned the whole time, or confront the situation head-on, saying, "Oh, hi there, Mr. and Mrs. Wendel. Fancy meeting you here." Yeah, definitely not *that*.

I groaned when I heard Lucy's father say, "How do you live with yourself, lady?"

My mother set her corn dog down on her napkin. "Not this again."

Dad stood up, awkwardly straddling the picnic bench. "Mind your own business. We're here with our family."

Lucy's father raised his voice so that everyone within thirty feet could hear him. "I'll mind my own business when your wife stops killing innocent animals. Hey, everyone! Did you know that the woman in the maroon shirt injects dogs with poison and watches them die, just so that the Illinois University of Rockford can profit from the development of new drugs? Hundreds of dogs are slaughtered each year, all for corporate greed."

The people sharing our picnic table gasped, craning their necks to see who was speaking. Dad scrambled to get his other leg over the bench too, pointing his finger. "Walk away, pal. This is not the time, nor the place."

"That's it. I'm getting security," Mom told me, tucking her hair behind her ears, which she does whenever she means business. She slid to the end of the bench and stood up.

Lucy's father yelled out, "Are you going to run away now? I'd run too if I tortured animals for a living and didn't want my neighbors to know."

Lucy's mom pulled on her husband's sleeve. "That's enough now, Jerry. Remember what happened last time."

Maddie clutched at my hand from across the table. "What's going on, Mercer?"

"Shhh," I told her, pulling my hand away. "It'll be fine. Stay here and watch our stuff." I stood up, not sure if I should get involved or keep my back turned, since the Wendels hadn't noticed me yet.

Mom had only walked ten feet toward the main building before she spun and faced her attacker. "You know what? Perhaps you should find out what clinical research is all about before you spout any more of your false accusations."

Dad put his hand up like a stop sign. "Quiet, Shalene. Don't even talk to these people."

That's when Lucy appeared out of nowhere, carrying a cone of blue cotton candy. "Who are you guys talking to?" She looked over at the table and broke into a huge grin. "Hey, Mercer!" She took two steps toward me when her father grabbed her shoulder.

"Stay here," he spat.

My meal became a gnarled mess in my stomach watching Lucy pluck uselessly at her father's grip. "Let go of me, Dad," she argued. "That's Mercer. The boy who came to the Wool-Mart protest with me yesterday, remember?"

Uh-oh.

"That's him?" her dad asked. At the same time my father barked, "He did *what*?"

"Is that true, Mercer?" Mom's tone was so sharp, it could break glass.

I swallowed a lump of guilt and shrugged noncommittally.

Jerry herded his wife and Lucy away from us. "Let's leave. These people make me sick. And you stay away from him, Lucy, you hear me?"

Before Lucy got dragged off, our eyes met briefly. She didn't say anything, but I could tell that she was confused and worried. I knew that by the time they reached the parking lot, her parents would have filled her in about my mom's job, and that would be the end of Lucy and me. No movie date, no first kiss, and no more sitting at her table at lunch.

If my parents ever let me leave the house again, that was.

My mother started in on me first, her arms flailing as she spoke. "You want to explain what you were doing at a wool protest with the daughter of those HALT fanatics? Didn't you know who she was?" The cheerful music of the Ferris wheel was a weird accompaniment to this conversation. A funeral dirge would have been more fitting.

"He knew," Dad, the betrayer, said. "He spoke to that girl outside the lab last week."

Mom squinted at me. "Why, Mercer? I don't understand."

"I like her, all right?" I stared at my half-eaten corn dog, wondering how things could have gone from appetizing to appalling in a matter of minutes. "I did it so I could spend time with her."

160

"We don't spend time with people like that." Mom swiped her palms together the way people do when they have crumbs on their hands, as if signaling the end of my relationship with Lucy. "There are a million other girls, Mercer. Find one who doesn't destroy property and break the law."

"Or throw fake blood on people," Maddie added.

I responded angrily to the only person I could. "Shut up, Maddie."

I shot a dirty look at the woman gawking at us from the next bench until she turned away. Dad gathered the remaining food and walked it to the trash. Another perfect lunch ruined by HALT. Dad balled up his napkin, throwing it on the table in disgust. "Let's go."

Following behind my family like a convicted felon being led to the electric chair, I jammed my hands in my pockets, no longer interested in being at the fair.

We dodged in and around the other carnival-goers until we finally made it through the exit. As our feet crunched the gravel parking lot, Mom spoke over her shoulder. "I'm still in shock over this, Mercer. Needless to say, there are going to be consequences for your actions."

Wasn't losing the girl of my dreams consequence enough? "Consequences?" I met her eyes for the first time, incredulous. "Because I went to a protest you don't believe in?"

"No," Mom answered matter-of-factly, "because you lied to your father about where you were going." That was what she *said,* but I knew the protest had her way madder than the lying part.

"I didn't lie about where I was going," I pointed out. "I did go to Woodley Town Centre."

"You lied about why," she replied.

"Yeah, but if I told him the real reason I was going, he wouldn't have let me!" I argued, exasperated with this Catch-22 situation I found myself in.

Dad said, "Enough! There are always consequences when you don't do the right thing."

Normally when Dad uses his angry voice, I back down, but not this time. This black-and-white moralizing didn't sit right with me. "Don't do the right thing? Are you saying that fighting for animal rights is wrong? Am I not allowed an opinion here?" I wasn't even sure how I felt about this complicated issue, but I knew that my parents couldn't dictate my beliefs. Doing that would be communistic or fascist, or some other corrupt form of ruling I had learned about in World Political Systems, which I'd obviously forgotten. Still . . . it didn't matter what it was called; they were wrong.

Mom slid her purse onto her shoulder. "Mercer, stop arguing. I told you not to speak to that girl again and that's that. End of story."

I couldn't believe my ears. Rules were one thing, but this was tyrannical.

"Not quite." Dad pulled his keys out as we neared Mom's

car. "Apparently Mercer isn't sure whether falconry is right or wrong, Shalene."

"I never said that!" I insisted, but Dad continued as if he hadn't heard me. "And as his sponsor, I'm afraid his apprenticeship is now in jeopardy."

I slammed the door as I got in, getting another dirty look from Maddie. I stared out the window, amazed that ten minutes ago I was the happiest guy in Woodley — I had a chance with the girl I liked, I had a hawk who had his first kill under my command, and I had a belly full of onion rings and corn dogs. And now all I had was indigestion. And Flip, of course.

Oh yeah, maybe not even that.

SIXTEEN

THE SECOND WE GOT HOME FROM THE FESTIVAL, I flung open the car door, eager to get away.

Before I could make it five feet, Dad said, "Mercer, meet me in the rehab center in fifteen minutes. We need to talk."

There was nothing that sent the fear of God through my system more than hearing Dad utter those four little words. He headed off toward his bird sanctuary while I retreated to my room to think about what I would say if he told me I had to quit falconry over this.

Lying on my bed bouncing a tennis ball against the far wall over and over, I told myself that Dad was a reasonable man. If I could endure his little speech about lying and keep my mouth shut, everything would be fine. As I trudged toward the rehab center fifteen minutes later, each step closer made my gut tighten.

I took a deep breath before pulling open the door.

To my great relief, Maddie sat on the wooden worktable, balancing the small kestrel leather hoods on her fingertips like miniature puppets. This was one time I was thankful for her nosiness, as Dad wouldn't let himself get too worked up with her around.

He had our latest patient, a prairie falcon, in the raptor restraint. We called him Bullet because the duck hunter who brought him to us said he mistook him for a duck and shot him, blowing off two of his toes in the process. The same way I mistook that guy for someone with a brain. If all went well, we'd release Bullet back to the wild in a few weeks.

"How's Bullet doing?" Although I hoped the diversion might help lessen the anger in his lecture, watching Dad work his magic with these birds never ceased to fascinate me.

"His foot's healing nicely, but something's not right." Bullet's head was hooded, allowing Dad to examine every inch of him before placing him on the scale.

"What's wrong?"

Dad eyed the scale before checking his notes. "He's weighing in light. The thing is, he ate everything I gave him this morning." Dad stroked his mustache, thinking. He looked at me and frowned. "You've kept his mews clean and given him fresh food and water every day, haven't you?"

I thought back to Thursday, when I wanted to play some video games before I did my homework. Lying could jeopardize Bullet's health even more, so I decided to gloss over my explanation and hoped it'd fly.

I squinted, looking up into the air as if thinking. "Well, I gave him fresh water Thursday night, but he had so much food left in his dish, I didn't replace it." I hastily added, "I didn't want to waste our supplies."

"Didn't want to waste our supplies," he echoed, his tone drenched with sarcasm, "or you didn't want to waste time getting him fresh food so you could go play your video games?"

The man obviously knew me well. "I didn't think he needed it, that's all." Which wasn't exactly a lie. Sometimes I skip a meal when I'm sick. Rarely, but it happens.

"We went over this, Mercer! That piece of meat was probably spoiled, which is why he didn't eat it. But then he got so hungry, he ate it anyway. I'll bet you Bullet's got coccidiosis now, damn it!" He strode over to his medicine cabinet and began combing through the dozens of little bottles of liquids and powders.

I knew I shouldn't challenge him, but if I was going to learn anything, I had to ask. "Sorry, Dad, but the only thing I don't get is that I read online that the average falconer cleans his mews once a week." I shrugged, hoping he wouldn't get too mad when I asked the next part. "So there must always be bits of leftover food hanging around. How can it be my fault that Bullet got sick from only one time?"

Spit flew out of Dad's mouth like liquid exclamation points. "Once a week if you've got strong, healthy birds, not rehabbers! We've got to keep our mews pristine. Bullet could very well die from this!" He reached into the medicine cabinet, selecting a small glass bottle filled with reddish liquid. "Not that it's going to be your concern anymore after today."

An icy chill ran all the way up my spine, the same way it does when I'm at the top of the Giant Drop at Six Flags, waiting for the ride to begin. "No, wait! I'm really, really sorry about Bullet, and I promise I won't do that ever again. But I don't think you should take away my apprenticeship for going to that protest."

Dad came back to the table and rested his hand on Maddie's knee. "I need you to go in the house now, okay? Mercer and I have to talk."

"Okay, sure." Maddie plucked the leather hoods off her fingers, leaving them in a pile on the table. I'd have to clean those up later, but I wasn't about to speak up. Not with the biggest lecture of my life looming seconds away.

Dad turned his attention to administering Bullet's meds. The falcon flapped and protested, but Dad managed to get the medication down his throat. After several painstaking minutes, he finally faced me. "Are you having second thoughts about being a falconer, Mercer?"

"Me? No, not at all," I said emphatically. "And I don't know how you could possibly have asked me that. I love it as much as you do."

"Are you sure?" He took the medicine bottle back to the cabinet. "Because your allegiances seem to be a bit shaky lately, especially after what you said at the carnival today about wanting to explore being an animal rights activist." He eyed me a second before setting to work changing the dressings on Bullet's toe.

I took a deep breath, hoping to rid myself of the heaviness in my chest. "Okay, honestly, I was mad because it seemed that you and Mom were dictating how I should feel, so I just said those things to get back at you." I expected some sort of rebuttal, but Dad stayed silent. "But even when Flip doesn't do what I want him to do, I never once thought about giving up." Okay, so maybe I had once, for about a minute, but I wasn't about to admit that now. I looked Dad square in the eye, needing him to hear my plea. "Being a falconer and having my own bird is something I've looked forward to my whole life. Ever since I was little." I flicked a leather hood against another, watching them spin. "I just wish I didn't suck at it."

Dad's expression softened. "C'mon, Mercer. Don't say that. You don't suck at it. In fact, if you keep at it, you're going to be one heck of a falconer. You have a special knack with birds. Take Monocle, for example. I've never seen such an amazing relationship between raptor and human before, and neither has Weasel."

"Thanks," I mumbled, feeling a drip of sweat roll down my back.

"I'm not done." He briefly glanced at Bullet, who seemed to have received the medicine without any problem, not regurgitating it as some of our birds had done in the past. "I have to admit that Flip is the feistiest, most stubborn hawk I've ever seen. I've never told you that before because I didn't want to scare you. You've done an outstanding job so far of convincing that hawk that you two can work together. Trust me when I say that wasn't an easy feat."

The lump in my throat returned. Dad had never spoken to me like that before. "Thanks, Dad. So, uh, does that mean I can still be your apprentice?" I held my breath, waiting for his answer.

He shrugged. "I guess that depends."

"On what?" More sweat dripped down my back, making me rethink getting a haircut. I'd never be caught dead in a ponytail.

"On you." He tossed the used syringe into the trash before returning to extricate Bullet from the raptor restraint. He set him on his fist. "Follow me and I'll explain. I need to put him back in the mews so he can heal in peace." Normally the birds protested a bit when being handled, but Bullet seemed somewhat complacent. Dad had told me that the sicker the bird, the quieter he became. I prayed Bullet would be okay. Seeing him like this made me feel even worse about abandoning my duties so I could play *Wreckage Warrior*.

I held the door open as we proceeded down the hall to Bullet's mews. Dad said, "What I was trying to say was that, in my opinion, a person can't be a falconer and a member of HALT. Those two ideals are in conflict with each other."

"But why can't—"

Dad held up his free hand. "Let me explain why before you jump in. I support freedom of speech, and I'm doing my best to raise you kids to think and act on your own system of beliefs. That's part of becoming an adult. Talking about differences between what you believe and what I believe is important. It helps the other person see things from a new perspective." As we passed Monocle's mews, she started herking like crazy.

I sensed he was done, so I gave my opinion a shot. "I get that, but I don't understand why someone couldn't do both — be in HALT and be a falconer. Protest against some things, like people who hurt animals for fun, but then stay home for other things, like when they protest clinical research."

When we got to Bullet's mews, Dad tethered him to the lowest perch to minimize his chance of injuring himself further. Monocle's cries for attention continued to echo across the rehab center.

Dad scratched his face, leathery from being outside so much during hunting season. October through March isn't the best weather in the Midwest, let's put it that way. He smiled. "Let's go see Monocle before she wakes the neighbors."

"Or the dead," I joked, glad for the reprieve on Dad's lecture. He still hadn't answered my question, so I hoped maybe he was considering what I'd said. As I opened Monocle's door, the volume of her herking increased and she moved around on her perch excitedly. I rushed toward her before my eardrums split. "Hey, Mon. How's it going?" I rubbed her chest and she tilted her head in pleasure.

"Hello, Monocle." Dad stroked her back, but she edged away from him.

"She only likes her head and chest scratched."

He laughed, scratching next to her ear, and Monocle relented.

"You know, Mercer, I'm not so old that I don't understand liking a cute girl and wanting to do things together. The ironic thing is, falconers and many animal rights activist groups do have something in common—we both want birds of prey to thrive. What many protesters don't know is that hawks raised in the wild have only a thirty percent chance of surviving their first year, but in captivity, they have a ninety-seven percent chance of making it."

I nodded, having heard him say that at his public awareness talks.

He continued, "HALT is a specific group of animal rights activists who believe that *any* form of interacting with animals other than through observance is cruel. Hunting is cruel, eating meat is cruel, even owning a pet is cruel. Which is fine by me —to each his own. My only objection is when HALT members break the law to get their point across."

I thought about the way the protesters had harassed the Wool-Mart manager until he left, and how they had thrown rotten tomato soup on my mom, ruining her suit. And my lunch at Elliot's Pine Log. "I see your point. I promise that if I'm out protesting something, I won't break the law."

"Apparently I'm not making myself clear. Lucy and her family are not your average animal lovers. While there are many less extreme groups out there who fight for animal rights without infringing on others' rights, HALT isn't one of them. This particular group acts with a vengeance to prove their point."

As much as I wanted him to be wrong about this, I couldn't

deny that Lucy's parents were fanatical about their beliefs. I sighed, despair creeping over me slowly but steadily, like a fog rolling through a cemetery. "Yeah. I get that."

Dad stopped scratching Monocle and looked at me. "So in order to protect our family and the birds I've sworn to safeguard, you're going to have to choose one or the other."

A thought occurred to me, one that could save me from having to sever ties with Lucy. "I understand what you're saying, but do you seriously think they'd be against you helping injured birds? They can't be *that* crazy."

"But they are," he said sternly. "Falconers have been the target of this group for years. You being in HALT is a conflict of interest to my profession, and I'm not going to jeopardize my business. I'm sorry, but I can't make an exception because you're my son either. If you want to be my apprentice, you can't be a part of HALT—as simple as that. Decide what you want to do and let me know by tomorrow." He gave Monocle one last pat. "I've got a few more things to take care of tonight. I'll meet you inside."

After he walked away, I stood there numbly, wondering what to do, when Monocle dumped a juicy mute right on my shoe. It looked like I had even more crap to deal with on my already crappy agenda.

SEVENTEEN

AS I PLODDED ACROSS THE YARD BACK TO THE house, I ruminated over my options, which basically boiled down to choosing Lucy or falconry. While I'd had my heart set on being a falconer, having Lucy as my girlfriend ranked pretty high too. Not that she'd even speak to me again after finding out about my mom. Although, now that I thought about it, if Lucy hated me, that would make my decision easier.

Suddenly I had an idea. What if I *told* my Dad I quit, but then snuck out to rallies when I felt like it? That could work — if I had a car. It wasn't as though I could ask Dad to drive me to a HALT protest, and I wasn't sure Lincoln would cover for me. Not to mention that I didn't want to be a big fat liar who had to sneak around all the time.

And even though Flip wasn't exactly a star pupil, the first hunt of the season was in less than two weeks. There was nothing I wanted more than to show up at the meet with my own bird under my command. Outside of my birthday and Christmas, the annual Midwest Falconers' Club hunt was my favorite event of the whole year. I couldn't give that up. But I wasn't willing to ditch Lucy either.

That's when I thought up a possible solution — one that would make everyone happy. I could tell Lucy that my parents freaked out about my being in HALT, so I couldn't officially belong, but that I would still help out in some small ways—like eating vegetarian food or handing out pamphlets. God, did that sound wimpy. Lincoln would never do this to impress a girl.

Or, what if I told Lucy the truth—that HALT was a conflict with my parents' work, so I'd have to quit, but that I really liked her and still wanted to hang out with her? Then, if by some miracle we started going out, I'd invite her over and show her around the mews, explaining how we were both on the same side. Give her the statistics that Dad had shared with me about saving more raptors by having falconers raise them rather than letting them grow up in the wild. Then she'd see that HALT was wrong and we were right.

That was the plan. That was exactly what I would do.

Before I went to bed Sunday night, I wanted to tell my parents the good news. I found them lying in bed, the nightstand lamps on both sides lit. Dad was watching sports highlights on TV, and my mom was next to him reading a stapled packet of papers.

"Hey guys." I stood at the foot of their bed. "I just wanted to tell you—"

"Hold on a second." Dad leveled the clicker at the TV and muted the sound. Mom glanced up, putting her research materials to the side. "Okay, go ahead."

I took a deep breath. "I decided to quit HALT and continue my apprenticeship."

"You had actually joined HALT?" Mom looked at me, alarmed. "Did you sign something?"

"No, Mom. There was a club at school, but I'm quitting tomorrow, so don't worry."

She sighed and pulled her reading materials back onto her lap. "I'm glad to hear it, Mercer. I can't believe you even considered it."

Dad held his hand up to give me a high-five, which seemed kind of lame, but I high-fived him back. "Excellent choice, Mercer." He seemed genuinely happy, a giant smile lighting up his face. "There are times in a man's life when he has to take a stand. It may not be the same choice another man would make, but if he's true to himself, that's all that matters."

My eyes started to glaze over a bit at his statement. I felt guilty that I wasn't mentioning I still wanted to go out with Lucy but decided that I was taking a stand on going out with her. "Thanks, Dad. I'm going to bed now." I headed back to my room and flung myself across my bed. All this deception was too much for me. Was this what it was like to be a spy? My stomach contents churned thinking about what Lucy would say to me at school tomorrow.

When I went downstairs the next morning, Maddie informed me that Lincoln had left without me, the impatient little butthead, so I had to take the stupid school bus. I waited outside on the corner with two other kids for about fifteen minutes before the bus came. The second I got on, I made my way to the back. That's when the curtain opened and the real drama began.

Haley stood up from her aisle seat. "Oh, look. Son of the canine killer."

"Lay off, Haley," I told her, looking for Lucy. "For your information, my mom does heart attack research."

I caught a glimpse of Lucy's blond head, scrunched way down in the seat next to Haley. She had her knees up, wedged against the seat in front of her, and wasn't looking at me. I sat down kitty-corner from her.

I slid my knees sideways into the aisle, leaning toward Lucy. "Crazy day yesterday, huh?"

She stared straight ahead, and I could tell making small talk wasn't going to work, so I got right to it. "Look, I'm sorry about what went down at the carnival. I want to explain my side of things."

"A little late for an explanation, don't you think?" Haley snapped. "We kicked you out of our club, F-Y-I."

Although I planned to quit anyway, I didn't like being told what I could or couldn't do. "Why is that? Because you don't like my mom?" My mother might not be Betty Crocker in the kitchen, but she works hard and is super smart. If Haley continued to diss her, I'd tell her to stick it and worry about the consequences later.

Lucy finally turned my way. "Liking your mom has nothing

to do with it. 'Do you like what she does for a living?' is the question I'm interested in."

I knew this was my test, but luckily, I'd already read the *CliffsNotes*. "That's what I wanted to explain. She's a scientist conducting research to save people from dying of heart attacks. She doesn't do plastic surgery on pigs like you thought. To tell you the truth, I didn't even know what she did at work until the day I saw you guys protesting at the university."

Haley rolled her eyes. "You live with the woman, so how could you *not* know?"

Lucy looked at me with a furrowed brow. "I guess I can believe that. A lot of kids don't know what their parents really do at work. But is it true that she kills dogs?"

The bus's wheels screeched as the driver braked to pick up our next passengers. I flicked the hair out of my eyes. "You know what? Does it really matter what my mom does or doesn't do at her work? We're two different people, with our own opinions and beliefs, and you shouldn't judge me because of her."

"That's true. I wouldn't want anyone judging me because of my crazy parents." Lucy seemed satisfied with my response. "Let's give him another chance, Haley. I think it's great that Mercer still wants to be in HALT even if his mother doesn't like it." She smiled at me. "Welcome back."

My face heated as panic clawed its way up my throat. I wanted out of the club and into her heart. She stared at me, waiting for an answer, so I blurted out the first thing that came to mind. "That's cool. I, uh, just can't go to protests, if that's okay."

As soon as the words left my lips, I hated myself. Why didn't I just tell her I quit but wanted to still hang out? I made myself a promise right then and there that I'd get out of this mess as soon as I had a chance to speak to Lucy privately. Just not this second. Not with Haley the Hater in the seat next to her.

Lucy's pretty eyes stared down at her hands. "Well . . . that kind of works out because my parents said I couldn't hang out with you anymore."

My heart sank. "Oh."

Lucy fiddled with her gold heart necklace. "But I'm sure once I tell them you don't feel the same way as your mom, they won't mind." She looked at me with a mixture of emotions. Like relief and something else, but I couldn't quite pin it. Confusion? Disbelief? What was that?

I wasn't sure until she sighed and blessed me with the most incredible smile, one that transformed the roar of the rowdy students and the rumbling of the bus motor into a mellow buzz. And that was when I knew she liked me as much as I liked her. All I had left to do was go in for the kill, so to speak. If I handled things the way hawks did — with ferocity, skill, and courage — perhaps Lucy would be as helpless as a chipmunk when I turned on my charm and finally asked her out.

And this time, nothing was going to stop me.

EIGHTEEN

I STOOD NEAR CHARLIE'S AND REED'S LOCKERS, recounting the horrible scene at the Johnny Appleseed festival, my dad's ultimatum, and ended with my fast-talking on the bus to smooth everything over. "Today at lunch, I'm taking the plunge and asking Lucy if she wants to hang out with me on Friday night."

"Whoa! Is this the same meek Mercer who needed help asking Marcy Feldman to the graduation dance last year?" Charlie threw his books on the floor, and then used his foot to stuff his coat and mounds of gym clothes and other crap into his locker, before slamming it shut.

I rolled my eyes, both at his comment and the disgust level of his locker. "I didn't need help, just advice."

Charlie raised one eyebrow. "Advice in the form of me walking over there with you, and starting up a conversation with her that ended with 'Mercer wants to know what you're doing for the dance.'"

I pushed his shoulder, laughing. "Shut up. I wasn't that bad."

Reed grabbed a spiral notebook and his algebra book from his locker. "I've got some advice for you. Go out with someone you don't have to lie to."

"Oh, burn." Charlie grinned, watching my reaction.

"Shut up, Reed. I did tell Lucy that I couldn't go to any more protests."

"Wait. So you're still staying in HALT?" Charlie stuck a pen behind his ear.

I shrugged. "Not exactly. Things are still sort of up in the air."

The bell rang and Reed slammed his locker. "Did you tell her about Flip?"

"Not yet, but soon," I snapped, not liking his tone.

"Sure you will." He shook his head as he walked away.

"Back off, Reed," I called out, but he didn't turn around.

I balled up my fists, settling for a weak fist pound on the locker. "Did you hear that? What a douche."

Charlie pinched my shirtsleeve and pulled me the opposite way, toward our classes. "Eh, what does he know? He changes girlfriends faster than he changes oil. He's like Lincoln—loves 'em and leaves 'em."

"Yeah, I guess," I mumbled. Was that what Lincoln was doing to Lauren? Or was Zola the one who'd be leaving? I didn't want to think about that now. "So wait, are you saying Reed likes Lucy too?"

"Not that I know of. But like you told Flip the other day, 'May the best man win.' Go get her, Merky." Before we parted ways, Charlie gave my upper arm a little punch. Seeing as it hurt only a little, I figured I must be getting stronger from all of my apprentice duties.

As I walked to the gym, I thought about Reed's comment. Since when had he become Mr. Honest? He had copied my algebra homework before class tons of times. Did he tell every girl he liked the truth — that he spent every spare moment restoring old cars and dirt biking around Mount Trashmore? Did he mention that he got mostly C minuses and Ds on his report cards, and that was *with* tutoring help? I doubted it.

Besides, all this lying would end if Lucy and I started going out — which is exactly why I needed to ask her today. If she wasn't interested in me, I'd come clean and these little lies would become one innocent little blip on my integrity radar. The thing that bothered me most, though, was the idea that Reed might like Lucy too. What happened to the bro code? Wasn't he supposed to back down? I'm positive I made it clear I liked her way before he did.

When fifth period came, I nearly knocked people over in the halls trying to get to lunch. I needed to get there before Lucy took her seat with the Veggie Girls. I buzzed through the cafeteria line and bought two soft pretzels with cheese and a large Coke, not even bothering to grab a tray. I stood by the entrance to the cafeteria, balancing my two Styrofoam plates on top of each other, eyeing the swarms of students streaming past me. I must have looked like a dope standing there, but then Lucy walked right up to me and instantly upped my reputation.

"Hey, Mercer. What're you standing here for?"

"I was waiting for you." I motioned with my chin toward the

courtyard. "You want to eat outside today? The weather's nice for a change and . . ." I looked down at my feet and thought, *And what? I want to ask you out when no one's around in case you say no?* "And the leaves are at their peak."

The leaves are at their peak? That was something a grandmother would say, not a cool guy about to ask out the cutest girl in school. Not only that, but my statement was another lie. The leaves wouldn't peak until mid-October. I knew because it was my job to rake the front lawn after the peak took a nosedive.

She gazed at me as if I were an adorable puppy — her eyes wide open, her lips puffed out in a cute way. "Aw, that's sweet. I love it when the leaves change colors too. Should I go invite everyone else to come out with us?"

Here's where I had to play it cool, or all could be lost. "Nah. Charlie and Reed said they wanted to entertain your friends, so I thought I'd let them go at it awhile. What do you think?"

She tilted her head ever so slightly, as if assessing me. I could tell by her expression she was quickly comprehending that I wanted us to be alone. I waited for her reply, my mouth contorted into an awkward, frozen smile. If she declined, I'd feel as miserable as my stomach did at that very moment, but at least I'd know where we stood.

She held up a purple lunch bag. "Sure, why not? Let's go."

Yes! First hurdle over. We went through the double doors and out into the courtyard. It was quadruple the size of our family room and had a red maple in the center surrounded by a sitting wall. On the outskirts of the courtyard, there were benches, interspersed with prickly yellow and red bushes. Groups of twos and threes lounged around eating their lunches. I steered us to a sunny bench off by ourselves.

As we sat down, Lucy admired the massive maple tree. "The leaves didn't turn out as pretty this year."

I wanted to add, *but you did,* and then held back. It was way too cheesy, even though it was true. Her lips were shiny with lip gloss, and her gorgeous blond hair was draped over one shoulder, catching the sunlight every time she moved. I wondered what Lincoln would say if he were me right now: *You look so hot, I might burn up if you don't kiss me,* or something equally lame. He'd told me that girls eat flattery up like chocolate and I should dispense it as if I owned a candy store. I decided I'd at least try to give her a compliment if I got another chance.

Lucy set her lunch bag on her lap and pulled out a pita sandwich. She took a bite and then sat sideways to face me. "When you lived in Wisconsin, did your family make huge mountains of leaves and burn them up in the yard?"

I nearly choked on my bite of pretzel in an effort to answer quickly. "All the time! Burning leaves is one of my favorite smells. You'd drive around the neighborhood, and everyone had huge smoldering piles of leaves. Not being able to do it in Illinois is another thing that sucks about being a FIB, huh?"

She nodded enthusiastically. "Totally! Not to mention all the traffic here. Ugh!" She grimaced and crossed her eyes, making me laugh. "I start Driver's Ed next semester. How about you?"

"Me too. But since my dad has a huge pick-up truck that looks impossible to drive, and my mom . . ." I paused, worried about bringing up my mother. But if I was going to be more honest, I couldn't avoid talking about her. "My mom babies her sports car, so I probably won't get to use it much."

"Bummer. My mom doesn't drive, but I'm pretty sure my dad is going to go all 'commander general' on me behind the wheel. He's intense."

We took bites of our sandwiches—Lucy thinking about driving and me wondering how I could drive this conversation toward going out on Friday. I peeked at my cell. Another fifteen minutes before the period ended. I didn't want to ask her out until right before the bell, though. If she said no, this lunch would get awkward quickly.

Before I could find out what else she missed about Wisconsin, Lucy asked, "Did you hear that we're planning a 'HALT the Killing of Our Furry Friends Car Wash' to raise money for that no-kill shelter—Joy's Animal Salvation?" She bit into a celery stalk, crunching loudly.

"No, I hadn't. When is it?" A huge blast of guilt pressed against my chest. If Dad found out . . . I swallowed hard. Wait a second. How could he be mad at me for raising money to help orphaned dogs and cats in an animal shelter? In my mind, it more or less made up for the ones my mom euthanized at work.

Reed's advice leaked into my brain. Was all this conniving worth it? One glance at how cute Lucy looked in her skinny black T-shirt with a cartoon frog on it that read DON'T FROGGIN' DISSECT ME, and I thought, *oh yeah. She is totally worth it.*

She paused a second. "Aren't you worried your dad would get mad if he knew?"

As if she had read my mind! Her question so surprised me that the sip of Coke in my mouth went down the wrong pipe, making me cough. Lucy patted me on the back. Her gentle touch sent an awesome sensation through my body. "A little, I guess."

She nodded. "I was nervous when I told my dad that you might come. Sorry to say, he went ballistic, yelling that the apple didn't fall far from the tree." She took a bite of her sandwich, not looking me in the eye.

"Oh." My stomach felt as if a professional wrestler had not only flipped me to the mat but kicked me in the gut to boot. Asking her out now would be futile.

She swallowed fast and wiped her mouth with her napkin. "But then, in the middle of this long drawn-out lecture, I got so mad that I finally told him I could hang out with who I wanted and he couldn't stop me."

Holy crap. That had to mean something. I held back a smile. "Whoa. What'd he say when you told him that?"

Three dark-haired girls walked by, talking in Spanish so loudly that we both looked up. I wished they'd hurry past us so I could hear her answer.

Lucy shrugged, fiddling with her lunch bag. "He said I'd be grounded for a month if I ever talked to him like that again, and that if I knew what was good for me, I'd listen to his advice. So . . . maybe skip this event and only do the ones my father doesn't come to?" She studied me, waiting for my response. Her message was as obvious as if written in spray paint on the bench we were sitting on: if we went out, our parents couldn't know about it. Which definitely worked for me as well.

"Looks like we're kind of in the same boat then." I smiled at her and placed my hand on her knee, testing the waters to see if she moved her leg away. She didn't. "But don't worry. I'll get you some pretty pink pillows to sit on or something so our boat will be comfy."

Lucy laughed, easing the tension. "I prefer blue, actually."

"Blue it is." I squeezed her knee twice and let go, not wanting to push things too quickly. I grinned at her, thinking that if I did have to be on a sinking boat, there would be no one I'd rather be with. When she bit into her sandwich, I said, "I'm afraid to ask what you're eating."

"Cucumbers with cilantro and hummus. Want a bite?" She held it out to me.

I made a face. "Uh, no, thanks. I'll stick to my pretzels and cheese. You want some?" I held out my mostly uneaten second pretzel.

"Sure. Thanks." She pulled off a small section and dabbed it into my cheese. No, *our* cheese, which I thought was a rather cheesy thing to think.

"This was a great idea, Mercer. It's really nice out here." We both turned when the Hispanic girls screamed ten feet from us, swatting at some yellow jackets that had taken a liking to their lunches.

"I hate bees!" Lucy said, visibly shuddering. "My dad says that at this time of year, they get drunk on all the fermented apples lying around and freak out."

I wanted to ask if her dad felt swatting a yellow jacket was abusive, but decided it might ruin the mood. When I saw some kids tossing their lunch bags into the trash, I knew the period was almost over. I glanced at the time. Three minutes left. Was that enough time?

Just do it already! my brain screamed.

I took a deep breath. "Speaking of freaky things, have you seen that movie, *Flight of the Living Dead,* yet? The reviews say it's the scariest, goriest undead movie in ten years. Anyway, I was planning to check it out on Friday. You want to come with?"

For several unbearably long seconds, I detected a crazy look of dread on her face. Had I made a huge mistake? *Reverse, back up. Pretend I didn't ask.*

Then she wiggled her fingers up by her face, repeating the tag line from the trailer using a spooky voice, "Come aboard the flight to hell."

I laughed out loud, as much from relief as from humor. "I think you'd be the perfect flight attendant. So how about it? You want to go?"

She nodded. "I'd love to! That would be fun. Let's see who else wants to go from our group, and maybe we can all go out for pizza after or something."

My heart fell out of my chest and landed with a splat on the sidewalk. That was her way of telling me she didn't want it to be just us. I clenched my teeth while keeping a smile on my face so as not to appear disappointed. I managed to nod. "Cool. I'll ask Reed and Charlie if they want to go too."

"And I'll see what Haley and Jeanette are doing. It'll be awesome!" She zipped up her lunch bag and stood, waiting, while I tossed my trash. As we walked toward the door, she said, "I hope you all wear ear plugs, though, because I scream my head off at scary movies."

"I'll be screaming too," I joked, adding, "but in a manly way, of course. It'll be much more of an *aaahhh!* than an *eeekkk!*"

She laughed as the bell sounded. "Good, because I'll need someone manly to hold my hand if I get *too* scared." She bit her lip and shot me a coy look, waiting for my reaction.

I wanted to howl with joy. "As long as you don't mind a tough guy with super-buttery popcorn fingers. Or maybe even . . . a dead guy." I made a scary face, turning my hands into claws and trudging toward her as if I were a zombie. She ran toward school, laughing and screaming.

Life was froggin' great.

NINETEEN

I BUZZED ALONG ON A LUCY HIGH ALL AFTERNOON.
I couldn't wait until Friday night. I'd already mentioned the movie to Charlie and Reed, and they had both agreed to go. Although Reed seemed skeptical, he didn't ask if I talked to Lucy about Flip. My only hope was that Lucy's friends could come too, or she might change her mind if it was only me and two other guys. Or maybe she'd like that. Who knew? Girls were so hard to figure out.

On another great note, Dad made an amazing dinner: marinated venison with a side of mashed potatoes. Oh, and some creamed spinach that I pretty much ignored. When dinner was over, Dad picked up his plate and brought it to the sink. "Maddie, it's your night to load the dishwasher. Mercer, let's get outside. We only have about two hours before dark. Tonight we're adding whistles to the plan. I'm interested to see how Flip does with this."

"He's going to rock," I said, not entirely believing it myself.

"It can go either way," Dad explained. "All birds have their own unique blend of personality quirks. You have to find out what works with each one to get them to cooperate."

"Just like girls?" I joked, walking to the sink with my plate and cup.

Dad slid the patio door open. "Just worry about your bird right now, and forget about girls until *after* the Midwest Falconers' meet." He stopped and looked at me. "You're not thinking about that HALT girl, are you?"

I chose my words carefully. "Her name's Lucy, and you can stop asking me about HALT. I told her today that I quit."

"Good." He nodded at me and stepped outside.

As I walked down the long expanse of yard toward Buddie Waters, I caught an incredible whiff of our white pines. Talk about aromatherapy. The massive maples on the far end had begun to change into a brilliant yellow, and the sky was a giant swirl of blues, whites, and pinks. All of this beauty was reflected in the pond, making my heart fill with pride. As much as I had hated moving here, I had to admit that our property in Illinois was ten times nicer than what we had left behind.

When I got to the training area, Dad surprised me with a brand-new whistle on a maroon leather strap. I placed it around my neck, feeling as if we had performed some ancient ceremonial rite. "Thanks, Dad. It's cool."

He immediately switched into Joe Falconer mode. "When Flip flies toward you, blow a two-second whistle blast. That way he'll associate that sound with coming to you. Give him a treat the first few times and then only sporadically. He needs to want to come to you with or without food, or you'll have trouble retrieving him in the field."

He made it sound so simple, but after several attempts, Flip was as confused about the whistle commands as I would be in the women's lingerie department. He flew to the perch when he was supposed to fly to the fist, and came to me when he was supposed to go after the lure.

Dad rubbed his chin. "He doesn't seem to like the whistles. Let's forget about it for now."

But I didn't want to forget about it. Using whistle commands was a great way to retrieve your bird. Out in the field, your hawk flew from tree to tree, while down below, you scared up quarry with your stick. I knew it didn't matter so much now —Flip had flown only to the perch and back, never up to the trees, but he needed to learn this. "Let me try one more thing." I dug out a wet tidbit from my waist pouch and held it in my fist.

"What are you doing?" Dad asked. "You don't want to scare him."

"I won't." I gave the whistle one long blast, showing Dad that I knew what I was doing.

Flip took off from the perch and landed in a pine tree about fifty yards away.

"For gosh sakes, Mercer," Dad said tersely.

"Sorry! How was I supposed to know he'd freak?" I let the whistle fall to my chest, hoping Dad had a simple solution. "What do we do now?"

"*We* do nothing. *You* sit and wait." Dad shook his head, his hands on his hips. "You scared him big time. He could be up there for hours, and if he likes it too much, you could lose him."

"Lose him? But he's wearing his telemetry device on his tail." Was Dad just trying to scare me to make his point?

"Come on, Mercer. You should know this. The telemetry device helps us locate our birds — it doesn't force them to fly back to us. The bird has to want to do that on his own."

I sighed. "Oh yeah."

He pointed in the direction Flip had gone. "Well? Better go after him."

I hurried toward the tree that Flip had flown to, hoping wildly that he'd come back. I held out my tidbit and yelled, "Hup!" which was falconer for "come here." Flip stared at me for a full minute before deciding to groom himself, exactly like the day I had trapped him.

After forty minutes of beckoning to him, my throat was sore and my arm exhausted. I sat on a stump to take a break, pissed at myself for being so pigheaded. Moments later, I heard fluttering. Flip was on my fist.

Grabbing his jesses so he couldn't take off again, I greeted him with enthusiasm. "Welcome back, Flip! Sorry the whistle scared you. I won't do it again, I promise."

Flip seemed to sense he had won our little contest of wills, but Dad's words hadn't been lost on me — listen first, act second. As I stood, a beam of sunlight flitted through two branches, illuminating Flip's chest. He looked like a diamond on display in a fancy jewelry store. His beak was closed and he didn't seem jittery in the least. As if he actually liked being with me. As if we were a team. I grinned at him. "You and me are going to win that pin, huh, boy?"

As I strolled into the mews, Lincoln was coming out with Bella on his fist.

"Heard you had a close call." He frowned. "Dad said you made a bonehead move."

"What else is new? He probably says stuff like that all the time."

Dad coughed loudly in the rehab center. Lincoln and I exchanged guilty glances. I wandered past Rusty, Dad's colorful little kestrel who had a wing that had healed crookedly in the wild, before peeking in on Liberty, our one-winged bald eagle with her own enormous mews. Because Liberty couldn't fly, she waddled around the floor like a toddler, albeit a feathered toddler with talons long and strong enough to yank a ten-pound northern pike out of the Mississippi.

I said good night to Flip before scratching behind Monocle's ear tufts for several minutes. When I got outside, Weasel was there in his familiar red flannel shirt and jeans. He stood next to Dad, both of them with bottles of beer in hand. Normally I'd be thrilled to see Weasel, but I hadn't seen him since Starbucks and wondered what he thought of me.

"Hey, how's the caveman doing?" Weasel asked, acting friendly enough.

"Okay, I guess." I shrugged, not in the mood to act it out. "Tried the whistle. Freaked Flip out."

"Your dad told me." The wind blew then, making Weasel's beard waffle in the breeze. *"Hoo-wee!"* He lifted his pant leg to show me a pair of thick gray socks with a red stripe across the top. "Good thing I put this warm pair of wool socks on tonight, huh, Mercer?"

What the heck was he doing!? My eyes shot toward Dad, trying to gauge his reaction.

Dad turned to Weasel, who was glancing down at his socks. "Wait. You knew about that?"

"Knew about what?" Weasel tilted his head slightly, acting innocent.

"I'm talking about Mercer going to that wool protest." Dad shook his head, staring at his oldest buddy. "When were you going to tell me that my son was parading around the mall like a wolf in sheep's clothing?"

"Wasn't my place to tell." Weasel took a swig of his beer, looking out toward the pond. "Things have a way of working themselves out without me butting my big nose in."

Dad replied, "Sometimes a big nose is welcome."

"Not this nose." Weasel reached up and gave his nose a tweak. "It's staying right where it belongs—here on this handsome face of mine."

Lincoln stood six feet away, twirling the swing lure over his head while Bella waited on the perch. He blew two short blasts on his whistle, and Bella swooped down, instantly grabbing it in her claws. Lincoln yelled out, "Is *that* why you met that HALT girl at the mall? To protest people wearing wool?" He stroked Bella's chest. "My God, get a spine."

"*You* knew about it too?" Dad ran a hand through his hair. "Geez!"

Maybe now Dad could see that other people felt I was entitled to act on my own beliefs. "It's okay, Dad," I told him. "It's not like I was out robbing a bank."

"Robbing a bank I could deal with," Dad sniped. "Joining HALT is what's criminal." His response was so unexpected that we all burst out laughing. Dad added, "Luckily, that's all over with, so everything's good on the home front." He held up his empty beer bottle. "Except that I'm out of beer. You need another?"

Lincoln answered, "Boy, could I ever. I'm dying of thirst."

"I wasn't speaking to you, Lincoln," Dad said, pride slipping into his reprimand again. "How about it, Weasel? You thirsty?"

"Always." Weasel downed the last quarter of his beer and handed the bottle to Dad.

Dad said, "I've got to check on Bullet, but then I'll be back with two cold ones."

After Dad was out of earshot, Weasel clapped his hand on my shoulder. "Close call. Sorry about that, Mercer. I was just having fun with you. I didn't think he knew."

I nodded, shrugging it off. "No problem. Thanks for not saying anything earlier."

"You can count on that," Weasel affirmed. "If not telling your dad something won't kill you or hurt your bird, I keep my mouth shut."

Lincoln called out, "I'm heading to the woods on the far side of the pond. Bella's getting her groove back, but she needs to shed those last few ounces."

Compared to Flip, Bella looked like a giant, almost as if she could shed a few pounds instead of ounces. Her dark gray back and snowy white chest and face made her appear regal, like a queen.

Weasel reached into his pocket and popped a toothpick into his mouth. "What's her weight now?"

"Fifty-six ounces," Lincoln replied without missing a beat. Instantly I became aware of how well he knew his stuff. He stroked Bella's chest and she didn't seem to mind. He knew the proper falconer lingo and when to use it, and he always appeared confident. "Her hunting weight's fifty-two, so we're getting close."

"Good news. Tessa's within three ounces," Weasel said, referring to his own female northern goshawk. "Go get started. Skinny and I will watch from the pier." He turned to me as we walked toward Buddie Waters. "Sorry I missed your training session. Your dad told me you flew Flip free when he wasn't home. That's amazing."

"It is?" I had expected him to tell me how foolish I was to attempt something new without my sponsor around to guide me.

"Flying free in less than a week?" He looked surprised that I asked. "Most birds need at least ten to twelve days of manning to do that. You must be spending a lot of time with him to get him to take a shine to you so quickly."

"Pretty much, I guess."

We tromped along the weeds, getting closer to the pier, as the setting sun reflected across the surface of the water. There was barely a ripple except for a few water bugs making lazy circles. "So what's happening with that HALT girl you were with on Saturday?" The toothpick moved to the opposite corner of his mouth. "Did your dad make you quit her too?"

I ran my fingers up through my hair, not sure how much to tell Weasel. After what he'd said about not telling Dad things unless they hurt a bird or me, I decided I could trust him— maybe even feel him out about a few things that I couldn't ask my father. "Dad didn't forbid me to hang out with her, but he said I had to choose between being in HALT and being a falconer. He said it's impossible to be both, but I'm thinking people don't have to be all one thing and not another." I wasn't sure if I was making sense, but Weasel nodded anyway.

He stepped over a log in his path. "So I take it that means you're dating her?"

I took a quick check over my shoulder to see if Dad was coming. "Nothing official yet."

"I see." He pulled at his beard, and I half expected a confused squirrel to dash out. "And you're sure she's on the up and up? Not trying to coerce you into anything you don't want to do, right? You're standing by your own principles?"

"Definitely." I wasn't sure if I had any principles, but if I did, I could stand by them all day long if it meant I could see Lucy.

Weasel chomped on his toothpick, making me think Goat might have been a better nickname for him. "Well, I hope it works out for you better than it did for me. I wasn't exactly honest about how much time I spent with my hawks before I married my first wife, and, eventually, it's what killed our relationship. That's why I married me a lady hawker the second time around." He looked across the pond, distracted, watching. After several seconds, he yelled, "Bella looks great, Lincoln. After she drops those last few ounces, she's going to be mighty fierce at the hunt."

"Thanks!" Lincoln called back. Bella soared out across the pond, skimming the reeds along the edge, before landing high in a pine tree off in the distance. Lincoln blew one long blast and Bella came flying right back to him, no problem.

I looked at Weasel, shaking my head in disbelief. "Bella does everything Lincoln asks. Too bad they don't sell whistles like that for girls. Can you imagine? One long blast means 'come here,' and two blasts means 'kiss me.'"

Weasel grinned, a thin line of pink lips between two hairy

face nests. "If you're lucky, you won't need a whistle to fetch the right girl, Skinny. The good ones will want to kiss you all on their own."

As I watched Bella effortlessly navigate between two trees, I wondered if there was any chance Lucy would kiss me on Friday. The possibility kept me smiling all night long.

TWENTY ·····✦

THE REST OF THE WEEK FLEW BY. I SAT NEXT TO
Lucy every day and we talked about a million things. Best
of all, we made each other laugh. I rested my knee against hers
and flirted like crazy, alternately complimenting her and teasing her. On Thursday, Haley brought HALT news articles about
various animal cruelty acts around the world. Some were petty,
like feeling bad for goats in petting zoos, but others were valid
—widespread random killing of dogs by clubbing them over the
head because of a rabies infestation in that country, even dogs
that had been immunized. Pretty gruesome. It made what my
Mom did pale in comparison.

Little by little, Charlie made his move on Jeanette as well,
telling her dirty jokes and buying one of those giant chocolate
chip cookies at lunch for them to share. Reed pretty much went
with the flow, nodding to girls who floated past our table to flirt
with him and joining in the conversation when it suited him,
which wasn't all that often.

On Friday morning, Lincoln, Maddie, and I stood in the driveway, saying goodbye to our parents. Mom and Dad had decided
that Gram's services weren't needed, seeing as how Weasel said

201

he'd come by and check on us. Dad told him to drive by and make sure that we—meaning Lincoln—weren't throwing any parties.

Mom leaned forward from the passenger seat to make eye contact with us. "Call us if there are any problems. And Lincoln, don't forget you agreed to take Maddie to her party on your lunch break tomorrow."

"For ten bucks," he reminded her.

"Yes, I left it on your dresser," Mom told him. "And Mercer, you're in charge when Lincoln's not home."

Maddie argued, "Mercer? In charge?"

I kneed her behind her knees, making her legs collapse. "You got a problem with that?"

Maddie straightened up, bending sideways to rub her leg. "Stop it. That hurt."

"It did not," I told her.

Mom dug in her purse and handed me twenty bucks. "And how about you get a haircut? I'm starting to think I have two daughters."

"Ha-ha," I said, pocketing the money. If I had time, I'd go to one of those cheap haircut places and use the rest to pay for the movies tonight. Sometimes I amazed myself with my brilliance.

Dad slid the car into drive, but kept his foot on the brake. "Mercer, it's imperative that you give Bullet his medicine at the scheduled times, like I showed you. Ask Lincoln if you need help." He turned to Lincoln. "I'm counting on you to take care of your brother and sister."

"That's right." I poked Lincoln's chest. "And don't forget that I prefer to have my diaper changed hourly."

Lincoln pushed my shoulder, laughing. "I'm not getting paid enough for that. Sorry."

Dad shook his head, smiling. "Keep out of trouble. We'll be back late Monday afternoon."

"I got it under control, Dad." Lincoln thumped the roof of the car a couple of times. "Have fun."

I put my head down so I could see my mom. "Just make sure you two don't come home with a kid named Milwaukee, okay?"

Dad chuckled. "Very funny. But that reminds me: no friends in the house this weekend—girl, boy, or otherwise—for any of you."

"Girl, boy, or *otherwise?*" I repeated. "Dang. Looks like I'll have to cancel my date with that hot Vulcan chick."

"Guess you won't be able to 'live long and propagate,'" Lincoln joked.

Our parents finally took off down the driveway. We waved goodbye until we heard a distant toot-toot, and Mom's Camaro turned the corner toward the highway.

"Paaar-tay, little brother." Lincoln high-fived me.

"You got that right," I said, ecstatic to have the weekend to ourselves.

Maddie frowned. "Are you guys really having a party?"

"What if we do?" I asked her, raising my eyebrows. "You going to run and call Mom?"

"Nope." Maddie shook her head violently. "I'm not saying a word."

"Glad to hear it, little sis." Lincoln patted her on the head. "Hope Mercer over here can do the same. Likes to blab my business." He smacked my arm hard with the back of his hand.

"Drop it already, will you?" I rubbed the spot he'd hit. "I trusted Tattleson when I shouldn't have. End of story."

"Don't say that!" Maddie ran to keep up, tagging along behind us. "I learned my lesson. You can trust me now, guys."

"Okay, Maddie. Whatever you say." Lincoln and I exchanged eye rolls before going into the house to grab our backpacks. "But don't worry. We're not having any parties."

Twenty minutes later, Lincoln dropped Maddie off at her school before heading to ours. On the way, I told him I had plans to go to the movies with Lucy that night. "Said she'd hold my hand if she got too scared."

Lincoln smiled, bopping his head to the music. "Sounds like you got this girl in the bag. But definitely keep it on the down low around Dad."

"Yeah, like in the dungeon low." I laughed, glad we were on the same page.

"Lauren's coming over tonight, but we'll just watch a movie with Maddie, so relax."

I shrugged. "I don't care what you do. Hopefully Maddie won't babble through the whole thing."

I got out of the car, expecting Lincoln to follow, but instead he said, "Later, dude. Catch your own ride home."

"You're cutting?" I asked, jealous. "But they'll call Mom and Dad to ask where you are."

"I got it covered. Just keep your mouth shut and I'll be fine." I slammed the door and he peeled out, tires squealing. I didn't ask where he was going. I didn't want to know, especially if it involved spending time with a certain bimbo named Zola.

When I saw Lucy during a passing period, I rested my hand on her back a second while I said hello. She turned and gave me one of those blue ribbon smiles. I cruised along on happy mode for a good two hours.

At lunch, though, I still hadn't the courage to talk to her about the whole no-meat thing. Every day, Reed and Charlie bought whatever meat product they wanted, ate at the table next to ours, and then joined us when they were done eating, despite Haley's decree. I'd actually become a Veggie Girl, I realized with disgust.

"Hello, friends." Charlie set his rump on the bench between Haley and Jeanette, opposite Lucy and me. Reed sat down next to me. I'd gotten smart, figuring out that if I sat in the middle of the bench, Reed couldn't make a move on my girl.

Haley moved over, making space between her and Charlie. "Gross. I can smell roast beef on your breath. I think we should take a vote about kicking out members who don't follow our rules."

Charlie raised his hand. "Sounds good. I vote no."

Haley shot Charlie a look of exasperation. "Your vote doesn't count."

"Okay then. I vote no," I said, deciding that if things went well with Lucy that night, I'd be joining the MEAT (Men Eat All Types) crew on Monday.

Jeanette tossed a potato chip at Haley. "Come on. Don't kick them out, Haley. They both said they'd help us at the car wash next week. We need some guys too, you know."

"I suppose . . ." Haley picked up the chip and placed it in her brown lunch bag.

"Really?" I asked, surprised by this news. I knew Charlie liked Jeanette and would happily spend time with her, but Reed volunteered to help too? I glanced at the two of them, looking for some sort of response.

Charlie grinned wickedly, raising his one evil eyebrow. "They said if it was nice out, they'd wear bikini tops. What can I say?"

Reed cleared his throat. "My family got both of our dogs at that animal shelter. Seems like a nice place."

Knowing that Lucy would be there with Reed made me clench my fists under the table. I hoped the weather for the car wash would be fifty degrees with a chance of thunderstorms so Lucy would have to wear a raincoat and waders. Better yet, a blizzard. Then it'd be canceled altogether and save me a lot of grief.

"Not that keeping dogs in cages is cool, but at least they don't murder them after a week," Haley said in her usual Little Miss Sunshine way. "So how's everyone getting to the movies tonight?"

Jeanette tugged on a green strand of hair, twirling it around her finger. "I could ask my parents if they could drive us girls."

"My parents are out of town for the weekend, but I can ask Lincoln for a lift," I added, knowing he wouldn't be up for driving around and picking up the others, though.

Reed said, "I might be able to drive too. Not sure yet."

All five heads turned toward Reed, shocked by his announcement. "Wait. You're sixteen?" Lucy sounded a little more amazed at that news than I would have liked.

"Yeah. My parents had me repeat kindergarten," he lied, but I didn't call him on it. Probably too embarrassing to say he'd flunked. "Anyway, my dad and I have been working on my birthday present for months." Reed smiled. "If we finish the carb replacement on my Mustang after school today, I'll have my own wheels by tonight."

"You will?" I asked, astonished. I mean, Reed's not the most talkative guy, but I thought he would have told me that. Of course, I had been kind of avoiding him lately.

"A Mustang? Cool! One of my top five muscle cars. What are its stats?" Lucy asked, taking me aback with her grease monkey lingo. She said she hadn't taken Driver's Ed yet, so I would've guessed she wasn't very familiar with automotive stuff.

Reed's head jerked toward her as if he'd been face-masked. "It's a five-year-old midnight black 'Stang with a black leather interior and a twin turbo engine. Only fifty-eight thousand."

"Dollars?" I asked, my mouth open.

"No, stupid. Miles!" Reed said, twisting up his face at me, making me realize I'd said the most ridiculous thing ever.

Lucy laughed. "I'm sure he was kidding, Reed. It'll have a ton of pickup, that's for sure."

I swallowed hard, embarrassed that Lucy knew more about cars than I did. Whenever I had trouble with my ATV, I just told Reed about it and he fixed it. I never paid much attention. "Speaking of pickup, maybe can you pick me up for the movie tonight then, Reed?" I hoped to curtail any more car talk, and even more important, sway things in my favor. If things went well tonight, I'd slide my arm around Lucy's shoulder in the back of his car and try to sneak in a kiss or two.

"Maybe, but don't count on it." Reed shrugged. "Like I said, it depends if we get it done in time."

"It's settled then," Charlie declared. "After you get Mercer, you can pick me up. I'm very good at map reading." He grabbed Jeanette's hand. "Oh, and palm reading too." He examined her palm closely, before closing his eyes and raising her hand to his forehead. "I foretell that you will meet a very handsome stranger in the next two seconds." He opened his eyes. "Oh, will you look at that? My prediction for you came true."

I laughed, turning to Reed. "Text me if your car is fixed before six thirty. The movie starts at seven, so we need to meet outside the theater around six forty-five. Is that okay with everyone?"

"Um, one problem. My dad can't see you there, Mercer, remember?" Lucy frowned, looking at me. "Do you mind if we all meet by the popcorn counter instead?"

Reed sat up straighter, leaning forward to see Lucy. "Why can't your dad see Mercer?"

Why do you care, Reed? Just meet at the popcorn counter and move on. I shifted slightly forward, hoping to block him out a bit.

Lucy tilted her head, as if surprised by Reed's question. "It's because of his mom, you know, being a researcher."

"Oh, *that*." Reed made a face, but at least he didn't mention Flip.

Still. I'd have to tell him to stop his righteous crap. I'd tell Lucy about falconry when I was good and ready.

The rest of the day dragged endlessly while I waited for the bell to ring. When it was over, I rushed home, sprinting to the rehab center to get my apprentice chores done. As I was feeding the birds, I started thinking more about Reed's comment. Was he trying to screw things up between me and Lucy so he could swoop in and steal her away from me — maybe at the car wash? I hoped it wasn't that, because it'd sure be hard to compete with a Greek god.

Still pondering Reed's actions, I sped to Bullet's mews and administered his meds, glad that he seemed to be doing better.

With still two hours to kill before I had to leave, I brought Flip outside, hoping to make the time fly along with my bird. If nature could ease someone's worries, that day would have been the perfect cure. The sky had a pinkish hue with wisps of cotton candy clouds tucked here and there, while a downward breeze crossed the field at a steady clip. I gave Flip the command to take off and he spread his wings, the chocolate brown tips contrasting sharply with the sky. He soared across to the other side of the pond and back, seemingly without effort.

I thought about one of the articles Haley had read to us about the poor mental health of caged animals. Did Flip enjoy our partnership, or would he rather be off in the wilderness without me? I shrugged it off. If Flip didn't like it, he had been given plenty of chances to fly off, and he chose not to.

Flip did so well at snatching the lure that I now felt confident he'd secure my reputation as a talented falconer next weekend at the hunt. I just hoped things would go as smoothly tonight with Lucy. How soon could I safely tell her about my falconry apprenticeship without having her hate me? Was it unreasonable that she might actually think it was cool?

Some desperate herking sounds emanated from Monocle's mews. I yelled, "Sorry, girl, but I've got a hot date. Don't wait up for me." Although Monocle was, by far, my favorite feathered female, I had only forty minutes until I had to leave for my date with destiny. I raced into the house, excited but anxious.

Before hopping into the shower, I texted Charlie and Reed to ask about a ride. By the time I was drying off, Reed hadn't answered, so he was either still under the hood, covered in grease, or getting cleaned up. Charlie had texted to say that his mom was dropping him off, since he hadn't heard from Reed. I guessed I'd have to take Lincoln up on his offer to drive me.

After exhausting every possible grooming technique I could think of, I was ready thirty minutes later. I did a quick mirror check. My hair was still a little damp but was drying just the way I liked it, and both my jeans and black button-down shirt were clean. I even slapped a few drops of Intimidate on my face. When six thirty came and went, still without word from Reed, I grabbed my jacket and ran downstairs to tell Lincoln it was time to go.

Lauren, Lincoln, and Maddie were all sitting on the couch watching TV, cans of pop and a bowl of pretzels spread out on the coffee table in front of them. Lincoln whistled when he saw me. "Trying to take after your big bro, eh?"

"We'll see," I said, wishing I had one-tenth of Lincoln's swagger.

"You look really nice, Mercer," Lauren added. I hoped Lucy would think the same.

"Yeah, Mr. Hottie Pants," Maddie said, giggling.

As we drove toward town, Lincoln changed the radio station while I busied myself with picking lint off my shirt. He asked, "So did you tell her you hunt yet?"

I sighed. "Not yet. I opted for the coward's way out by avoiding the topic altogether. I'm a little worried what'll happen when she finds out."

He laughed. "I hear you. I was too embarrassed to tell Lauren that I was a stock boy until our fourth date." He turned onto Main Street, now only two blocks from the theater. I flipped down the mirror and checked my teeth as a huge fluttering of nerves started up in my gut. He continued, "Well if it ever comes up, don't say you're a hunter, just say you're a falconer. Nine out of ten people have no idea what that is. That way you're not lying."

"Like you never lie to girls?" I teased. "Did you tell Lauren about Zola?"

"No way." He spun to face me. "And I'm not going to either. Neither are you."

"Duh," I said, irritated that he felt the need to tell me that.

Lincoln dropped me off in front of the theater and told me to text him when I wanted to be picked up. I thanked him and hurried to the end of the ticket line, trying to shield my face from any cars that drove up. If Lucy's dad saw me, he'd zoom away with his daughter in tow. I caught a glimpse of headlights turning into the parking lot and risked a peek. An older model black

Mustang — exactly like Reed's dad's old car. He must have gotten it fixed in time, after all!

I watched him drive toward me, thrilled that he had received the ultimate birthday gift for every sixteen-year-old. Man, this was going to be great. He could drive us to school, the ATV shop, the electronics store — heck, anywhere we wanted. When the car got closer, I saw a second head in the front seat. Why hadn't he called me? Disappointment changed to anger when I homed in on the laughing passenger.

Lucy.

TWENTY-ONE ···➤

SO REED HAD GONE BEHIND MY BACK AND PICKED Lucy up? What a backstabbing maggot! The realization that he was trying to steal her right before my eyes hit me like a bucket of cold water to the face. I didn't know if I was angrier at Reed for calling her or at Lucy for saying yes. I felt like punching something.

"Next customer, please," the old man in the ticket window called out.

I stepped forward, flicking the hair out of my eyes, my thoughts racing. *Should I even go now? Is Lucy more interested in Reed than in me?* I stalled, taking my time removing my wallet from my pocket.

"What show, please?" he persisted.

I grumbled, "One for *Flight of the Living Dead*." We exchanged money and I went inside, not bothering to turn around. Had I read Lucy's intentions that badly, or had she simply changed her mind? A horrible thought rushed to my brain, making a chill run through my body.

Had Reed told her I hunted and she decided she wanted nothing to do with me?

I headed straight to the john to sort things out. I washed my hands and then stood at the hand dryer, weighing my options:

214

leave and walk home, or stay and act as if nothing was wrong. Fat chance of pulling that off. If I left now before anyone saw me, I could say I got sick. As the warm air blew over my hands, a voice in my head suggested an alternative. Could there have been a good reason for Reed to bring Lucy here? Maybe her dad's car had broken down on the side of the road and Reed just happened to see them and—*stop!* Reed called her and she said yes, and that was that. This wasn't one of Maddie's teenybopper shows where everyone had good intentions. This was two guys both liking the same amazing girl.

"There you are, dude," Reed said, catching me by surprise. "I saw you in line. Why didn't you come out and see my car?"

"Because I saw Lucy in it, you jagoff," I snapped. "Couldn't you have at least waited until I struck out before trying to hit on her?"

"Hit on her?" Reed's face contorted into an angry mess. "What the hell, Mercer? My dad and I just finished fixing my car a half-hour ago! I called you to see if you wanted a ride, but you didn't answer your cell. When I called your house, Maddie said you'd already left."

"What—so you called Lucy up and asked her if she wanted a ride instead?" I asked, not backing down. He knew I was supposed to be her date. The hand dryer stopped, and I hit the button for a second round so I'd have something to do with my hands that didn't involve choking my friend.

"You know what? Lucy's dad ended up having to work late,

so she didn't have a lift. She told me she tried your cell, but you didn't answer, so she called me, figuring you'd be coming with us anyway. So get it straight—she called and asked me to pick her up, not the other way around. Who's the jagoff now?" He strode toward the door.

I glanced at my phone. Two missed calls from Lucy and one from Reed. Whoops.

"Sorry, Reed. I didn't know, man."

"Eat me." He walked out and I followed, mad at myself for acting so jealously.

I caught up to him and grabbed his arm. "Seriously. I'm sorry, dude."

He wrenched out of my grasp and marched ahead of me into the lobby. Beads of sweat sprouted on my forehead as I replayed my mistake. I knew eventually he'd forgive me—I just hoped it was before we all went out to eat after the movie. Sitting across the table from someone who is pissed at you is no fun.

Charlie, Haley, Jeanette, and Lucy stood in the concession line chatting as I edged toward them, feeling out of sorts. But when Lucy smiled and waved me over, the black cloud lifted. "Mercer! There you are! You want to go in on some popcorn?"

"Nope," I told her. When she looked confused, I announced, "Because it's my treat."

"Aw . . . thanks!" She grinned at me, smoothing her hair as if worried it was out of place. Like that mattered? Not only was her summer-blond hair straight and shiny, her jeans fit tight in all the right places, and she wore a pretty blue top that showed some cleavage. Was all of this for me? I couldn't stop smiling at the possibility.

I listened as she told me the story that Reed had already explained. I glanced over at him, but he avoided eye contact. Haley chatted about a few HALT protests coming up while I paid for Value Package Number 3 for Lucy and me to split: a bucket of popcorn with extra butter, two large drinks, and a box of Junior Mints.

Some value — it cost me seventeen bucks.

By the time we walked into the theater, the previews had already started, so we had to scramble to find six seats together. I wished Lucy and I could sneak off to our own row, but short of dragging her by the hair like the caveman that I was, there was no way I could ask her to do that. Jeanette and Charlie went into the aisle first, followed by Reed, Haley, Lucy, and then me.

The beginning of the movie was slow, like most horror movies, setting you up for the scary parts later on. I had fun screaming, "Don't get on the plane!" and "He's hiding a knife inside his artificial limb!" which made Lucy crack up. Who cared if the usher came over and told me that I had to quiet down or leave? I was having the best night of my life.

At one point our hands touched reaching into the bag at the same time, so I slapped her hand away. She forced it into the bag and threw popcorn at my face.

Haley hissed, "Shhh!"

"Yeah, Lucy. Shhh!" I joked. "Keep it down, will ya?"

She hit me and I laughed, and the tension in the movie increased as the plane finally got in the air with a mass murderer aboard. I set the popcorn on the floor next to my feet and reached across Lucy, grabbing a napkin from the other cup holder. That's when she leaned forward and gave me an unexpected kiss on my cheek.

I grinned at her, happier than the serial killer on his plane full of victims. "I think I'm going to need a *lot* of napkins tonight," I whispered in her ear, making her giggle. I wiped my hands before sliding my arm around her shoulders. When she snuggled in closer, the rest of the movie became a blur. It was official — she really did want to be with me, not with Reed. Within the next two hours, I discovered a lot of things about Lucy that I didn't know before — that her earlobes flared out a teeny bit at the bottom, that her hair smelled like newly bloomed lilacs, and that she sucked on the edge of her thumbnail when she got nervous.

When the zombie killer lopped off the head of the pilot, Lucy scrunched her face into my chest and screamed, so I did the only manly thing — I imitated her, screaming and holding my free hand to my mouth, making her laugh so hard, she choked on her Sprite. I patted her back until she recovered, and she put her hand on my knee when she thanked me. I never knew having a girlfriend was so much fun.

After the movie ended, I couldn't tell you which passengers

had survived the zombie attack and which ones bit the dust, but I did make up my mind to kiss Lucy before the evening was over. As we stood up and made our way to the exit, I thought of a great opportunity I couldn't let pass me by. I purposely waited for the rest of our group to file out ahead of us by grabbing Lucy around the waist, tickling her, dawdling. When we reached the door, I casually pulled her to the side in the darkness.

She laughed quietly. "Hey! What are you doing?"

"This." I leaned her against the wall in the dark and put my mouth on hers, and she gently kissed me back. Her lips were soft and buttery and I loved all ten seconds of it. The kiss was so amazing, I didn't even bother checking to see if her eyes were closed. Who cared, anyway? I felt proud that I had found the guts to put myself out there and was rewarded for my efforts. "I was dying to do that all night," I said, and then, thinking of the movie, I quickly added, "but I mean that in a healthy, alive way."

She laughed again. "I liked it in a healthy, alive way too."

We shared another mind-blowing kiss before heading out of the theater. I was so completely happy, I worried my heart would burst. No wonder Lincoln spent so much time trying to win over girls. This was exhilarating.

We caught up to the rest of the gang hand in hand, and Charlie spun around. "Goodness golly! I turn my back for a minute, and you two go sneaking off on us."

"Our deepest apologies. Lucy and I were watching the credits." I grinned and squeezed her hand, and she squeezed back.

"Thanks for making us wait," Reed grumbled under his breath, cranky as an old man.

"We didn't mind. Jeanette and I were practicing our dance moves." Charlie grabbed Jeanette's hand and spun her in a circle. She complied, giggling all the while. I noticed he didn't let go of her hand afterward, so things must have been going well between the two of them also. Good for Charlie.

We plodded along behind a mass of people heading toward the lobby, but I didn't care how long it would take. I wanted this night to last as long as possible. Lucy and I swung our hands as we walked, accidentally bumping the couple in front of us. The guy turned around.

"She did it," I told him, pointing to Lucy.

"I did not!" she squealed, hitting me.

Reed shook his head and jammed his hands into his pockets.

So Reed was obviously still mad, even though I had already apologized twice. Couldn't do anything more about it now. Maybe tomorrow I'd buy him lunch after we went off-roading. If that was still on.

When we got to the lobby, we stood in a circle off to the side, deciding what to do next. I couldn't care less what we did as long as I could stay out with Lucy, so I spent my time amusing her by trying to beat her at thumb wars.

Reed zipped his hoodie. "Where are we going to eat?"

"Nowhere that I'm going to have to watch you guys hork down meat, or I'll be sick." Haley hugged her purse to her chest.

After I victoriously pinned Lucy's thumb down, I asked Haley, "You mean watching all those people eat humans didn't bother you, but having someone eat chicken will?"

Lucy slapped my arm playfully. "Be nice, Mercer."

Haley scowled at me. "One's real, one's not."

Talk about no sense of humor. Haley probably enjoyed attending wakes. I wasn't even sure why Lucy and Jeanette hung out with her.

Lucy attempted to lighten the mood. "I thought the sickest part was when the lifeguard zombie ripped off the pilot's arm and started chewing on it."

Charlie imitated the Australian pilot flailing around, holding one arm behind his back. "Aaaaah! My arm. Don't eat my arm, dude!" He started hobbling toward Jeanette, dragging a leg and swaying from side to side. She squealed in mock horror, dashing out of his way.

Reed laughed. "Ha! That kind of reminds me of what your hawk did to that chipmunk the other day, huh, Mercer?" He paused, holding a hand to his mouth. "Whoops."

I froze, a bullet to my gut. Reed challenged me with his eyes. Clearly his statement was no accident. The little baby was tattling on me because he was angry — the same way Maddie had, but she was only ten years old. "Yeah, yeah. Whatever you say, Reed."

"Wait. A hawk?" Lucy looked at him and then at me. "What does that mean?"

I answered before Reed could. "Who knows? Reed gets confused easily, just like in school. I mean, flunking kindergarten? How dumb can you be?" I knew I was being mean, but he had crossed the guy code and he knew it.

"Shut up," Reed said, his voice laced with battery acid. "At least I'm not a liar."

If I could have whipped him to the ground and punched his face in, I would have. But since he had twenty pounds on me, I used my only weapon: sarcasm. "You're right. I lied. You aren't only confused *in* school, you need a tutor *after* school too."

Lucy let go of my hand, but whether it was because of what Reed had said to me or what I'd said to him, I had no idea.

"Screw you, Mercer." The chords in Reed's neck were pulled taut, and the fire in his eyes made me nervous.

I didn't want to have this conversation, not in front of Lucy. "Right back at you." I glared at him. "So how about we just drop this whole thing for now and go eat, okay?" I headed toward the door, glad when I heard the rest of the group following.

As we reached the front of the theater, a dweeby male employee in a red vest cheerily told us, "Have a good night, folks."

I wanted to say that after Reed's little blowout, I wasn't sure we could. We walked outside into the crisp night air. Maybe the chill would cool Reed off and shut him up. Lucy was still looking unsettled so I mouthed to her, "I'll tell you later." She nodded, and I stepped closer, wanting to get us back into the good mood from a few minutes ago.

Jeanette looked at Charlie. "What was all that about?"

"I'm befuddled, darlin'," Charlie said, trying out an Irish brogue. "Boys will be boys."

"It was nothing," I said sharply, hoping my tone would give her the indicator to drop it. "Let's forget about it, okay?" When I glanced at Lucy, I noticed she was shivering. I rubbed the sides of her arms briskly for a few seconds before throwing my arm around her shoulder, the way I'd seen Lincoln do at football games with his dates. "So . . . should we go to Starbucks? No major food complaints there, right?"

"Sounds good to me," Lucy said, smiling. "You might even say I'm *dying* for a hot chocolate."

"I'd kill for one," I added.

"Starbucks?" Charlie wailed, invoking his one-armed pilot shtick. "How can I drink coffee without an arm?" Good old Charlie, trying to help me out by providing a diversion.

"With your other one, dummy," I told him. "Let's go."

We had taken only ten steps toward Starbucks when Haley asked, "So do you really have a hawk, Mercer?" She had to go and bring up the unwanted topic like a regurgitated worm.

Before I could think of a response, Reed said, "Yep. It's a red-tailed hawk named Flip."

His disloyalty was a stab in the heart. "Shut up, Reed." I pulled my arm off Lucy and took a step toward him, my hands in fists. "I can answer for myself."

"Then do it. You've had weeks to fess up. What're you

waiting for?" He spat on the ground, as if drawing the proverbial line in the sand with his saliva.

"Maybe if you shut up, I will." I stepped forward and pushed his shoulder, not hard, but enough for him to know I wasn't screwing around. He slapped my hand away, and shoved me back. I'd braced myself, having been conditioned by Lincoln's retaliations, barely moving an inch. We stood three feet apart, giving each other the eye-to-eye stare-down.

Charlie wedged his body between ours, his gut edging me back a few steps. He chuckled. "You see what happens when I let these guys watch a violent movie?" He shook his head in mock disgust. "That's it. Only G-rated movies from now on for you two."

"So is he right? Do you own a hawk, Mercer?" Lucy asked, the group reclustering in a circle. "I don't get it. Is it like a pet?" Strands of hair blew across her face. But I could still see the confusion in her eyes.

"For God's sake, Lucy. Wake up. People don't have hawks as pets. They use them to do their dirty work, hunting down and killing innocent animals." Haley's superior attitude made me want to jump kick her in the face the way they do in *Commando Force*.

"You go hunting?" Lucy's mouth dropped open.

Frickin' Reed. I couldn't believe he'd do this to me. I watched him taking it all in, his broad shoulders hunched against the breeze inside his navy blue Chicago Bears hoodie. I bet he was loving every minute of it.

224

"Actually I'm learning how to be a falconer," I told Lucy, remembering Lincoln's advice. I flicked the hair back off my face, trying to look casual. "It's a sport."

"Oh? It's a sport?" Lucy sounded relieved.

Jeanette shrugged. "Then what's all the fuss about?"

"Because the sport is watching hawks kill animals," Haley bristled. "Like bullfighting." Her jacket was wide open, but she didn't seem the least bothered by the cold, the ice queen.

"Not true. You got your facts wrong." I dismissed her argument with a frown.

"I actually met Mercer's hawk," Charlie interrupted, "and he was quite a pleasant fellow. Said please and thank you, the whole bit." I would have smiled if I hadn't been under attack.

"I saw what falconers do on a HALT documentary." Haley moved closer to Lucy, looking her in the eye. "They bring the hawk to a field and force it to kill, and then take the dead animal home and eat it. I even went to a falconry protest with my parents once at the forest preserve."

So those had been HALT protesters. Dad and Weasel had told me how crazy people with bullhorns and noisemakers showed up at one of their falconry demonstrations and stood in the parking lot making so much noise, they couldn't risk taking the birds out of the carriers. They had to cancel the whole event, even with a ton of spectators there waiting.

Haley's ignorance made me so mad. *Force* a hawk to kill?" I scoffed. "Like they need coaxing?"

She rolled her eyes. "Whatever. Are you going to stand there and tell us that a hawk would rather be chained up in a cage instead of flying around in the wild?"

I made one last desperate plea before this whole night went up in flames. "Okay, listen. I wondered the same thing. But you've got it all wrong. If Flip hated being with me, he could fly away at any time."

Haley shrugged, Jeanette and Lucy looked nervous, and Reed stood back, probably waiting for Lucy to walk away so he could pounce on my girlfriend of two hours.

I got a crazy idea right then and decided to run with it. "You know what? I can even prove it to you. Why don't we all drive over to my house right now so you can see for yourselves? I live in the last house on County Q, that big white farmhouse next to the highway. We can order pizzas and I can show you Flip, along with all our other birds. I'll even pay for the food. What do you guys say?"

Charlie raised his hand as if he was in class. "If Mertini's buying, I'm eating."

Haley sighed. "No, thanks, Mercer. There's no way I can stomach seeing hawks chained up in tiny cages. Let's just go to Starbucks."

"We don't keep our birds chained up in tiny cages."

Reed shook his head, mumbling, "Yeah. You keep them chained up in big cages."

"Shut up, Reed!" I stepped toward him, this time pushing

him hard with both hands. "I told you to mind your own business!" I didn't even care if he came after me at that point. My shove knocked him backwards a few steps, surprising me. Reed might have been stronger than me, but I was twice as pissed. I felt invincible, as if his fists would bounce off me like rubber balls.

He got his footing quickly, however, and came back toward me, pushing up his sleeves. "I'll say whatever the hell I want."

"So will I!" I unzipped my coat and whipped it to the ground. If Reed wanted to have it out here in the mall, I was ready. I might get the crap kicked out of me, but I figured that the way I felt right now, anger alone could help me hold my own for a while.

"Whoa, whoa! Down boys!" Charlie leaped in front of me, pressing his hands against my chest. "Let's calm down and talk things out at Starbucks. Maybe over a Caramel Moco Loco or Frith-Froth Smoothie?"

I ignored Charlie and stared at Reed, finally realizing the truth. Reed wasn't mad at me for falsely accusing him of trying to steal my girl. He was mad because Lucy liked me instead of liking him. He was trying to sabotage my chances with her — so he could have her for himself. I glared at Reed over Charlie's shoulder. "You suck, you know that, Reed?"

A man and his wife strolled along. They exchanged glances and hurried past us.

Haley looked at me and sneered. "No, you suck, Mercer. Why'd you even join HALT anyway?"

"Haley!" Lucy snapped. "Don't be rude.".

Jeanette backed up, twirling a lock of green-tinged hair around her finger nervously. Haley shrugged off Lucy's rebuke, nodding her head toward Starbucks. "Fine. Let's go then. I told you he was faking his love of animals. You see that now, don't you?"

I touched Lucy's sleeve. "Can I explain?" I pleaded quietly. "Privately?"

"I'm not sure." Lucy bit her bottom lip, her eyes darting from me to Haley and then back to me. I debated grabbing her hand and running away, back to the protective darkness of the movie theater. I'd whisper to her that maybe, if she really, really wanted me to, I'd even give up Flip if only she'd agree to stop looking at me with sadness and kiss me again.

"You want to know why I joined HALT?" I turned my back to the others and spoke only to Lucy. I knew they were eavesdropping, but I didn't care. "I'll admit that at first I only joined because I thought you were pretty and funny and I wanted to talk to you some more."

"See? What did I tell you?" From the corner of my eye, I could see Haley waggle her head in smug satisfaction, her lips pursed.

"Let him talk, Haley-tosis," Charlie said, pointing his finger at her. "You got to say what you wanted, now it's his turn."

Thank God for Charlie. I took a deep breath. "But then you guys made some valid points about animal rights, and you got me thinking about things from a different perspective than my father's. I figured I could pick which activities I wanted to protest against and stay home for things I didn't agree with."

Lucy nodded, but continued staring at her feet.

I faced Haley. "But no one told me HALT was a cult — that you either drank the Kool-Aid or you were out."

Haley huffed. "A cult? Please. No one's making you do anything, Mercer. Why don't you just go home and torture your birds some more?"

"Rarrr!" Charlie growled at Haley, pretending to wield a whip. "Back to your cage." With a sneer, she flipped him the bird. Charlie held out his arms and walked toward Haley, Jeanette, and Reed as if he was a shepherd herding his flock. "I have an idea. Let's walk to Starbucks and give Mercer and Lucy a little space, shall we?"

As they headed away from us, Reed called out over his shoulder, "I can give you a lift home whenever you want, Lucy."

"She doesn't want anything from you!" I yelled back, wondering where Reed had learned his guy code — because it was obvious that someone had given him one that malfunctioned.

Struggling to stay calm, I turned back to Lucy. I needed to get this right. "Look, I know things got all messed up here tonight. This isn't the way I wanted you to find out. Do you think you could come over tomorrow so I can prove that Haley's wrong?" I reached out and grabbed her hand. "So I can show you that I'm not some freak animal killer?"

She pulled her hand out of mine. "It's not that I can't come, Mercer. I don't think I want to anymore." She glanced at the group walking away. "You lied to me about hunting, just like when you said you didn't know what your mom did when I asked you the first time. It makes me wonder what else you lied about. I mean, is your name even Mercer?"

That hurt, but I couldn't blame her for being angry. I stepped closer, ready to spill the truth, to tell her everything I'd been wanting to say but hadn't—that my parents expected me to quit HALT altogether, that falconry was a lot like owning a dog, only different, and also that I thought she was the prettiest, coolest, most awesome girl I had ever met. "Actually I never lied to you —I just never told the full truth. I didn't say who my mom was because I knew you'd hate her, and if you think about it, I never denied being a falconer. I simply never mentioned it."

She tilted her head and looked at me. "That's equally bad and you know it."

I nodded. "Okay, you're right. I should have told you—and seriously, I was planning on it if things worked out between us tonight—but falconry is in my blood. Bird rehab is what my dad does for a living. He only *helps* birds, though, he doesn't hurt them. But I worried you'd think that anything to do with caged animals was horrible, just like Haley." Now it was my turn to look down at my shoes. "So I kept quiet because I like you a lot and didn't want to screw things up between us."

"Pretty ironic, huh?" She zippered her hoodie to her neck

and shoved her hands into her pockets. "Because I don't know how I would have reacted if you'd told me you were a falconer, but you never even gave me a chance to form my own opinion."

"I wanted to tell you about it, but it never seemed like the right time."

She shivered, or maybe it was a shudder. "I've got news for you, Mercer. I didn't like you because you were an activist. I liked you because I thought you were a nice guy—different from anyone I'd ever met before. But now I don't know if that was the real you or if you're like every other guy I've ever met—only interested in video games and making out, so I'm out of here. Goodbye, Mercer. Don't try to call me, because we're done."

I stood there in the cold, wishing there was something I could do to make things right, but all I did was watch while Lucy walked out of my life and into Starbucks.

TWENTY-TWO

AFTER I FELT CONFIDENT I COULD SPEAK WITH-
out having my voice break, I called Lincoln. He came and
retrieved me as if I were a lost puppy. The second I got in the
car, he asked what was wrong, and I unloaded all that had
happened. How I'd found the nerve to kiss Lucy and how everything was going great until Reed opened his big mouth and
ruined it all. Lincoln said I should have punched his face in
when I had the chance and then afterward told Lucy to either
accept that I was a falconer or I'd dump her. That route would
have been easy for him: he had both the muscles required to
cream someone and a ton of replacement girlfriends if one left
him.

"If Lucy doesn't like you because you hunt, forget her. Plenty
of fish in the sea and all that."

"Thanks. I'll keep that in mind." But I didn't want a different fish—I wanted only Lucy. I had stupidly hoped Lincoln
would tell me that come morning, she'd forgive me and all would
be forgotten.

After grabbing a Coke from the fridge, I walked briskly past
Lauren and Maddie without stopping, merely calling out, "Later.
Going to my room." I definitely didn't want to answer ques-
tions about how my night had gone, or I might lose it. I trudged

upstairs and sat on my bed, guzzling soda, wondering how everything could sour so quickly.

I didn't drop off to sleep until sometime after two a.m., and only from pure exhaustion. Dispelling a popular myth, the light of the next day did not bring with it a sense that everything would turn out great. As I got dressed, wishing I owned a SHUT UP AND LEAVE ME ALONE T-shirt, I kept replaying the events of the night before. The thing that made me the angriest was that deep down Lucy had me all wrong. I *was* a nice guy, one who was interested in more than video games and making out. Well, you know, for the most part.

I felt like calling Lucy and telling her that I'd gone through a lot of trouble to be with her. Maybe she'd be surprised, saying she hadn't known how much I'd risked or realized that I'd put her wishes above my own. Maybe she'd say that she had made a huge mistake. I'd tell her it was okay, and then after we hung up, I'd call Reed and tell him what I thought of him. That he had no integrity, that he had some nerve throwing me under the bus to make himself look good. But as always, I chickened out.

While I was in the rehab center doing my chores, Weasel popped over as promised. I was actually glad to see him. Maybe he'd have some advice for me. I called out that I had to weigh Liberty, our biggest mews guest.

"So how's the girl situation?" Weasel asked, following me to Liberty's mews.

While I coaxed our bald eagle out of the mews with a hunk of dried fish, I poured out the whole sloppy tale. Weasel trailed behind Liberty, listening intently as I led her onto the scale. After I finished, I needed to catch my breath. "So . . . what do you think I should do?"

"You're asking *me*? I'm not an expert on anything besides taking naps." He chomped on his toothpick, not saying another word. After a few seconds, he removed the toothpick and held it in his hand. "I've always been a believer of if it's meant to be, it'll be. So maybe I'd just wait and see what pans out."

I typed Liberty's weight into Dad's laptop: 13.2 pounds. "Oh, trust me. It's meant to be."

Weasel lifted his eyebrows. "Really? I always preferred dating women who liked me." He stuck the toothpick back into his mouth, a smirk on his lips. "But that's just me."

"Very funny. The thing is, all this time I was hiding who I really was, and it turns out, I didn't need to. She said she wasn't mad I was a falconer—she was mad that I lied."

"There's a saying that goes, 'Hell hath no fury like a woman scorned.' Describes my first wife perfectly." He chuckled, pulling a dried fish chunk from his flannel shirt pocket. "C'mon, Lib. Let's get you back home." He enticed Liberty off the scale and back to her mews. She had talons as sharp as steak knives, so we avoided carrying her around whenever possible. "I'll tell you one thing, Skinny. Sometimes you just need to move on. You can't fix what doesn't want fixing."

Not from Weasel too. Why didn't anyone say, "Everyone hides things to get the girl; don't worry, she'll forgive you"?

We finished up and I thanked Weasel for his help, but truthfully, I felt as bad as I had before he came. I spent the rest of the afternoon playing video games while alternately thinking about anything I could say or do to get Lucy back. Sadly, my ideas were as lame as my attempts to eradicate the entire horde in *Zombie Apocalypse*.

Around six o'clock, Maddie's voice disengaged me from my Intravenous Video drip, calling, "Mercer! Pizza's here!"

Food. I hadn't eaten since breakfast. I hurried downstairs into the brightly lit kitchen, my stomach rumbling in response to the smell of cheese and garlic. Maddie sat at the island with a plate of steaming pizza in front of her, the TV blasting.

I pulled off a slice of pizza and took three huge bites. "Why is it so loud?" I picked up the remote, looking for the volume control.

"Wait! Keep it loud like that!" she said in alarm. "Otherwise you can hear her laughing."

"Hear who laughing?" I asked, confused.

"Boobzilla." She pointed above us and frowned.

It took me a second, but I got the picture. "Lincoln's up in his room with Zola?"

Maddie bit her lip and glanced behind her, then motioned to me to lean in close. "He told me to stay down here for the next hour. Then he said he'd have some"—she lifted her fingers to produce air quotes—"'Peanut' butter on his toast tomorrow if I said anything to Mom or Dad when they got home."

"He did what?" I couldn't believe my brother was such a scumbag that he'd threaten to harm Maddie's smelly little hamster so he could bring Zola over. Even worse, what kind of guy would sneak a girl to his room with his little sister around?

"And I saw a hickey on his neck. Sick!"

I shook my head, not quite believing what I'd heard. Not because Lincoln was two-timing Lauren again, but because Maddie knew what a hickey was. When had my little sister started growing up? "Let's get out of here." I grabbed two slices of pizza and folded them in half, not sure where we'd go. I figured Lincoln's hot date wouldn't take long, but what did I know? Just last night I'd had my first major make-out session with a girl who had the decency to close her eyes. First and last, at least with Lucy.

"Maddie and I are leaving," I shouted up the stairs. "We'll be back in an hour."

I heard his bedroom door open a crack. "That's great," Lincoln replied. "Thanks!"

Rolling my eyes, I headed outside. I helped Maddie with the chin strap of her helmet before having her hop on the back of my ATV. I cut across the outskirts of the Bakers' soybean field toward Dairy Kitchen, at the far side of town. Ten minutes later, we strolled into the nearly deserted ice cream shop. I had only three bucks and some change in my pocket, which bought us one medium chocolate marshmallow sundae to split. Maddie and I kept trying to match each other bite for bite, and together, we ate the whole thing in under four minutes. So much for taking our time.

I offered to take Maddie for a quick trip to Mount Trashmore before it got dark, and she was all for it. I drove down my favorite two-track path through the woods, pointing out a startled gopher and stopping to check out the fattest tree around— which was actually four trees that had grown together into one. Minutes later, I spotted a few does hidden in the dense brush about twenty yards from us. We lifted our visors and watched for a bit, trying not to make any noise. Being a nature guy at heart, I was beginning to feel a little more like myself.

After the deer trotted away, Maddie said, "Before you drive home, I wanted to say I'm sorry for telling Mom and Dad about Lincoln the other day. That was a bad mistake and it slipped." I almost told her that words don't "slip" out of your mouth, that she had known what she was doing at the time, but before I could, she added, "But I want you to know I really *can* keep a secret. I did it because I was mad, but now I know that if you make a promise, you can't go back on it just because you get angry. So . . . if you ever need to tell someone something, you can trust me. Seriously."

She looked so sweet and had said it so earnestly that I couldn't help smiling. In all honesty, Maddie would be the last person I'd tell anything important to, but I tried to be a nice big brother. "Okay, Maddie, thanks. I'll keep that in mind."

She paused a moment. "Are you going to tell Mom and Dad about Zola being over, because, like, *I'm* not going to tell. No way. My lips are sealed." She pinched her lips tightly together, locked them with an imaginary key, and threw it over her shoulder.

I had to laugh. "No, I'm not saying a word either, but Lincoln's a jerk for dating Zola behind Lauren's back. He shouldn't lie to either of them like that." As soon as the words were out of my mouth, I realized what a hypocrite I was.

"Erm himm," Maddie mumbled, pretending her lips were still stuck together. I tweaked her cheek the way my grandma always did to me when I was little.

I dug into my pocket and handed her an imaginary key. "Here you go. I happen to be a lip smith."

Maddie took it and unlocked her mouth. "Whew, thanks! And I totally agree that Lincoln's a loser for two-timing Lauren. Did you see how much eye makeup Zola wears? And how she giggles at everything Lincoln says, like he's some kind of god?"

"That's unbelievably stupid, and I totally wish girls would do that whenever I spoke."

Maddie chuckled. "They will. As soon as you get some bigger muscles, that is." She squeezed my bicep.

"Hey, wait. Check this out." I had her feel my biceps again, this time as I flexed it.

"Ooh," she purred. "Almost as big as mine."

"Real funny." I flopped her visor down over her face and took off for home.

When we got there, Zola and Lincoln were in the kitchen chowing down pizza. Lincoln was bragging to Zola about how he swore at some wimpy guy at the gas station, and Zola giggled throughout his story. Shocking, really. It must have been the one talent she possessed—laughing and standing upright without falling.

Lincoln wiped his mouth with the back of his hand. "Hey, Mercer. How's it going, bro?"

"It's fine. Now." I shot him a dirty look, hoping to convey how much of a loser he was.

Lincoln ignored me and looked at Maddie. "Hannah called. Wants you to call her back."

"Hannah called? Cool." Maddie ran out of the kitchen.

I didn't want to stand around making small talk, so I went upstairs. I thought of inviting Charlie over but didn't want to re-hash the whole stupid backstabbing thing with him. Thinking of it just made my gut twist, so I grabbed the controller and played *Resident Evil 5* to get my mind off things.

Maddie popped her head in my room a few minutes later, the phone pressed against her chest. "Mercer, can Hannah stay over-night?"

"Why are you asking me? Go ask Lincoln." I was too busy annihilating bad guys in the parking garage I had wandered into to make decisions like that.

"After he said he'd hurt Peanut? No way. I am *not* speaking to him ever again."

I rolled my eyes. Girls. What did I care who she had over? "Fine. Just don't tell Mom and Dad."

"That's one thing you can count on." She put the phone to her ear. "He said yes!"

I lay around on my bed for the rest of the night with no one to answer to but the enemy. I dropped off to sleep mildly numb and relatively calm and stayed that way all night — until Maddie's ear-piercing, spine-splitting screams woke me early Sunday morning.

TWENTY-THREE

WHEN YOU'RE WOKEN UP OUT OF A DEEP SLEEP by your little sister's screams, you know it's not going to be good. The second I heard Maddie and Hannah, I could tell it wasn't the usual "Oh-my-God-he's-so-cute" shrieks. My gut did a flip as I threw back the covers and yanked on my jeans before bounding down the stairs, two at a time.

"What's wrong?" I yelled to Maddie, who stood by the back patio door. "Are you hurt?"

"Look!" she cried, pointing outside.

I followed the direction of her finger and saw something brown hanging upside down from the hose reel handle. I ran outside, my eyes still bleary from sleep. The grass was wet with dew as I sprinted across it. When I got closer and saw what it was, I lost the ability to breathe.

The brown lump was Monocle.

"Oh my God," I whispered. "Please be alive." I gingerly lifted her body and righted it. I called her name, hoping she'd open her eye. Even if she was badly injured, Dad could work his miracle on her. I rubbed her cheek. "Come on, Monocle. Wake up, girl."

Nothing. She felt heavy, lifeless. Desperate, I blew air into her mouth. "C'mon, breathe, Monocle."

No response. I tried a few more times, tears streaming down my face, but still nothing.

I thrust my fingertips under her wing and found it was cold —the hotbed of her body gone. "Nooooooo!" I cried, a searing pain in my chest. Monocle couldn't be dead! Not my sweet, lovable Monocle. That's when I saw the leather jess attached to her right leg hopelessly wrapped around the handle — her poor toes were twisted and bloody.

"How did you get out here?" I dried my tears on her chest feathers as I freed her from her death trap. I sat back on my heels, trying to remember last night's schedule. After Weasel had left, I'd turned on the night-lighting system and gone inside.

Had I been so lost in my thoughts that somehow I had left both Monocle's door and the rehab door open? How else could she have escaped? I smoothed Monocle's feathers, wondering how I could have been so careless when another of Maddie's piercing screams filled the air, jolting my whole body into action.

Maddie wailed, "Liberty's stuck in the bushes!"

What? There was no way she could have escaped too, unless Weasel had left her door open. But he was as skilled a falconer as my dad, so that was completely illogical. My heart pounded in fear and guilt as I gently set Monocle on the ground.

"I'm sorry, Mon. Love you, girl." I sprinted toward the back of the mews, hoping I could fix whatever was wrong. When I arrived, Liberty was wedged solidly in the center of our overgrown burning bush—now an erratic tangle of red-leafed branches due to the onset of fall. Her wing lay outstretched over the top of the dense shrub, clearly stuck in the midst of it. While I watched helplessly, Liberty attempted one limp wing flap, her soft demeanor extremely troubling.

"Go get Lincoln!" I yelled, with no clue what to do.

Maddie wailed, "He went to work already!"

"Damn it!" Liberty opened her mouth in alarm, stressing me out even more.

Maddie began crying. "You've got to do something, Mercer! Don't let Liberty die!"

Hannah burst into tears. "I'm calling my dad."

"Don't!" I warned, not wanting anyone else to be brought into this mess. "I won't let her die. Please don't cry, girls. And don't call your dad yet—I need your help first." My voice cracked as I held back my own panic attack. I needed to be in control. I took a deep breath, trying to imagine what Dad would do. "Go get me two elbow-length gloves and Liberty's hood out of her equipment chest."

"Okay." Maddie ran off, with Hannah close behind.

I spoke quietly to Liberty, trying to assess how badly she was hurt. That's when I noticed that her feet didn't touch the ground. And then to my horror, I followed a path of blood that started under her wing and trickled in a line down her chest, forming a small puddle on the dusty earth. Liberty chittered softly, her cries barely audible. I knew that if I didn't stop the bleeding soon, she too would die.

From inside the rehab center, I heard Maddie scream, "Oh nooooo!"

I couldn't take any more bad news. Dread enveloped my body when I realized that maybe more birds were hurt or dead because of me.

Maybe even Flip, I thought with terror. *Oh God, please, not Flip.*

Why did this have to happen *this* weekend, the one weekend Dad and Mom were away? Any other time, Dad would have checked the rehab center before going to bed, caught my irresponsible butt, and chewed me out. How could I ever face him again? I didn't even deserve to be a falconer after this, but I couldn't think about that now. I had to help Liberty before it was too late.

Maddie and Hannah ran back to me. "The rehab center's totally trashed, Mercer," Maddie said, her voice quivering. "The lock on the door was broken, and there was a bunch of these on the floor."

She handed me a trifold pamphlet similar to the one Lucy had given me at the protest. I read the headline: BIRDS IN A CAGE ARE FILLED WITH RAGE. On the bottom and was an ad to donate money to HALT. My entire core felt as if someone had ripped my heart out of my chest and crammed it down my throat. An explosion of unrivaled anger ripped through me.

"That witch!" I whipped the pamphlet to the ground and kicked it. Haley must have told everyone that my parents were out of town. She was the only one mean enough to do this.

"Don't yell, Mercer. You're scaring me!" Maddie wailed. "Call the police!"

"The police?" Hannah's voice rose in fear. "I want to go home now."

"Sorry, Maddie. And please wait, Hannah. I need your help." I couldn't even think about calling the police yet — I had to rescue Liberty. Now.

"Here." Maddie sniffed, holding out Liberty's hood and two gloves. "I could only find two left ones, though. I hope that's okay."

"It's fine. Perfect. Good job, girls," I said, my voice shaky, not bothering to explain that falconers wore gloves on only one hand. "Now go check and see if any of the other birds are missing or hurt — and then come back and tell me."

Frickin' Haley. It had to be her. I knew Lucy was mad, but she would never have done this to me — not after we'd kissed and everything. Or would she? I guess that no matter how well you know someone, you can't *really* know for sure what they will or won't do. Take myself, for example. Anyone who knew me would never have thought I'd go to an animal rights protest, but I had. For all I knew, even Reed could have been in on this. I just didn't know for sure. About anything.

The girls ran off, leaving me the task of rescuing Liberty on my own. Her chest heaved with each breath, like a runner in last place. I had seen many sick birds before, and to my untrained eye, Liberty looked a lot like the ones who ended up dying.

"*Aargh,* I hate you!" I cursed under my breath. Liberty jerked slightly, and I knew I needed to calm down. I slid on the gloves, the one on my right hand facing backwards, and approached Liberty.

"Shhh, it's okay, Lib. Settle down now." I wasn't sure what to say to calm an eagle. I inched toward her, shushing her with each step. Liberty's eyes widened, and she opened her enormous yellow beak in defense, trying to flap her wing to get away from me. When I got close enough to touch her, I waited for the right moment to place the hood on her snowy white head. My opportunity came a few seconds later when she closed her beak to swallow. In a flash, I slid the hood under her beak and over her head, pulling the knot in back securely.

Liberty calmed down instantly, as if she'd been given a mask of nitrous oxide. I placed my hands around her chest and lifted her ever so gently, being careful not to put pressure on her lungs. She flapped her wing twice, freeing herself from the bush.

I wanted to cry out with joy, but to my horror I saw a fresh stream of blood race down Liberty's chest. I nudged my fist against her breastbone, grateful when she stepped onto my forearm. Fourteen pounds of bird caused my arm to plummet, so I quickly braced my left arm by holding it up with my right and hobbled into the rehab center as fast as I could.

I nearly choked on my own saliva when I saw the garage door wide open on the opposite side of the rehab center. Had HALT opened all the cages and let the birds out through there? And what if the birds had started crabbing—the larger birds attacking the smaller ones? The thought that all of our birds might be gone or dead made me feel like I might pass out. Blurry splotches popped in front of my eyes like camera flashes as dizziness swirled through my brain. Resting my butt on Dad's wooden stool, I took several deep breaths until the out-of-control feeling had passed. *Keep it together, Mercer. You've got to take charge.*

Maddie and Hannah knelt on the ground behind the sink. "Come on, Rusty, stop hopping away," Maddie coaxed.

A sliver of hope slipped in through all the rage. At least Dad's kestrel was still alive.

"He won't come to us, Mercer," Hannah complained. "How do you catch him?"

"Put your fist right up against his chest and he'll hop onto it," I called out, stepping around an overturned scale. "If that doesn't work, grab a little piece of meat out of the fridge."

"I can't do it, Mercer," Maddie cried. "You gotta help me."

"I can't. I have to help Liberty now. You *can* do it, Maddie. Keep trying."

I hurried to the examining table, placing Liberty up on the largest perch. I needed to stop the bleeding under her wing fast. A bird didn't have much blood in its scrawny body, not even one as big as Liberty. If I screwed up and she died, Dad would get blacklisted. That meant the DNR would never give him any more birds to rehabilitate. A shiver ran up my spine. It would devastate Dad. There was only one thing to do: claim full responsibility for this event, even if that meant that the DNR would revoke my falconry license permanently. My stomach acids twisted and roiled, making my gut ache.

I yanked open drawer after drawer looking for gauze pads. Why hadn't I paid more attention to where Dad kept his supplies? My hands trembled as I opened the glass cabinet door, wishing I could hurry up. I finally found gauze pads along with a few other supplies I thought I might need. Pulling the hinged light closer to Liberty's chest, I began my search for the wound.

"Gotcha!" Maddie squealed in delight. "Come on, Rusty, back to your mews."

"Good job, girls!" At least something had gone right. "How are the rest of the birds?"

"I don't know." Maddie held up her hand with Rusty on her fist. "After we chased Sasha back into her mews, we went after Rusty."

Hannah offered, "But we can go look now."

They ran off right as I located the puncture wound under Liberty's wing. Bright red blood still trickled out like juices on a freshly carved turkey. I'm no doctor, but I did know that to stop the bleeding in humans, you had to apply direct pressure. I hoped it was the same for birds. Grabbing a few gauze pads, I held them tight against the hole. Liberty flinched, but I didn't let go. I wiped my sweaty face on my shoulder, waiting. *Please, please, please be okay, Lib.*

After several scary minutes, I peeked underneath. The cloth had a deep red circle on it, but the bleeding appeared to have stopped. Uttering a silent thank-you, I placed a fresh pad over the wound, using surgical tape to keep the cloth in place. I wasn't sure if that was the correct procedure, but it'd have to do for now.

Maddie and Hannah arrived, out of breath and with new tears. "Mercer! Bullet's missing, and so are Bella, Troy, and Flip!"

Flip was gone. It was as if a knight had taken a sword and made a giant X on my chest. I was about to let out a slew of curse words but held back for the girls' sake. All that work for nothing! There went any possibility of my hunting trip—Dad and Lincoln's too. I should have known our hunting birds would be gone—they were the only ones who weren't disabled. When those HALT people came in here and frightened them, of course they'd take off.

"Um, okay. Let me finish here and then we'll go look." Then I remembered Bullet. Without his medication, he was a goner. A third rehabbed bird injured or dead? They'd surely take Dad's license away for that! I had to get out there fast and find Bullet, but not until I'd finished bandaging Liberty.

Maddie's bottom lip trembled. "Let's call Dad now, Mercer. He'll know what to do."

"No!" I quickly softened my tone. "Just give me a little more time to fix this on my own, or Dad will never trust me again. I'll take care of this, Maddie, I promise," I pleaded, sounding more confident than I felt. "All the rest of the birds are in their mews?"

"Yep. All the rest seem okay. What should we do now?" Maddie looked around.

"Go outside and see if you can spot any of our birds sitting on a tree or a post nearby. I'll be out in a minute to check."

After they'd left, I decided to "sock" Liberty, the way Dad does to keep injured birds from moving around. I found a queen-size pantyhose in the drawer, snipped off one leg and then the toes, creating a long hollow tube. Sliding the nylon tube over her chest and wing, I made sure to keep her appendage tight against her body. Taking two pieces of special spongy tape, I secured the nylon around her neck and by her tail. Right or wrong, that was all I knew how to do.

I carried Liberty back to her own mews, electing to keep her hooded so she wouldn't move around and start bleeding again. The scary thing was, she didn't feel as heavy to me this time, which meant either she had lost a lot of blood or my adrenaline was giving me strength. I prayed it was the second reason.

"Relax now, Lib," I said, backing out of her mews. "And please don't die."

I was worried that the other birds, wherever they were, could be in life-threatening circumstances, too. Whoever had done this hadn't removed the birds' mews jesses from their legs and replaced them with field jesses the way we did when we went hunting—a death sentence by itself. The slits in the birds' everyday leather straps could get caught up in trees and chain-link fences, leaving the birds to hang upside down, which is how Monocle had met her demise. Dad had said birds could last only ten minutes before their lungs stopped working and they suffocated. Before I left to find the other birds, I brought Monocle in and gently laid her under her perch. No way was I going to let a scavenger eat her while I was gone.

"Goodbye, Monocle," I told her. "I'll get even with them, I promise."

I grabbed all the supplies I'd need, shoved them into my waist pouch, and ran to see if the girls had been successful in locating any of the birds. Maddie and Hannah had their hands cupped over their eyes, scanning the sky.

"Did you see any of them?" I asked, hoping for a miracle.

Maddie sighed loudly. "No, not yet. Sorry, Mercer." She squinted up at me, her young face full of sadness.

"Here, take these." I handed her a set of binoculars, keeping another pair for myself.

Hannah looked at me, her freckly face streaked with dirt and dried tears. "We saw lots of birds around here, but no big ones."

"Thanks for trying, girls!" I called out, racing toward the garage. "I'll be back soon."

"Where are you going?" Maddie chased after me.

"I'm going to look for the birds. Stay here and keep an eye

out. If you find one, try to get it to come to you by using meat chunks. Wear a glove, though!" I hopped onto Dad's ATV, the one with the bird carrier he'd rigged on the back. I flew down the driveway, searching the sky, a seemingly impossible task ahead of me.

TWENTY-FOUR ⋅⋅⋅⋅🦅

I RODE DOWN TREE-LINED BACKCOUNTRY ROADS INTER-
spersed with an occasional farmhouse, all the while keeping an
eye in the sky for large birds. Nothing but geese and sparrows. I
drove back and forth along County Q, praying they hadn't flown
to the opposite side of the highway. If that had happened, I would
be looking forever.

Thirty minutes later, I still hadn't retrieved any of our birds
and despair was gripping my chest. Because we hadn't planned
on them being set free, none of the birds were wearing the telemetry devices we hooked onto their tails to track them while hunting. Of course not. That would have made my life too easy. And
who knew at what time they'd been released? They could have
been flying around all night, for all I knew. My anger toward
HALT spiked rapidly, making me stomp on the accelerator.

I finally spotted a large bird sitting atop a telephone pole
about a half mile ahead. I grabbed my binoculars and zeroed in.
My hope soared when I saw a juvenile red-tail. Could that be
Flip? My heart beat even faster, matching the speed of the ATV.
I had to get there before the hawk flew away. *Please be Flip.*
Please, please, please.

I sped down Thistle Lane past several residences, the houses closer together here than by my house. Fifty yards farther on the hawk was still there. I put the pedal to the floor, the vibrations in the handlebars increasing under my hands, but I kept watching that bird the whole time. That's when I saw a blond girl out of the corner of my eye.

Lucy.

She stood by her front gate in pink pajama pants and an oversize yellow sweatshirt, newspaper in hand. I stopped the ATV, rage bubbling over inside of me.

"So *this* was how you got back at me for keeping falconry a secret?" I asked her, shouting over the roar of the engine. "Going to my house and releasing all our hawks?"

"What?" Lucy stepped toward me, faking confusion.

I wasn't falling for her innocent act. "You heard me. Someone broke in last night and trashed our rehab center. Released all our birds. And now four are missing, a bald eagle's at home bleeding to death, and my great horned owl's" — my voice cracked, so I swallowed and tried again — "dead."

Her hand flew to her mouth. "Oh my God. They killed your owl?"

I nodded, not trusting myself to speak about Monocle without tearing up again.

A bad taste filled my mouth when I rewound what she had said. "Wait. Who's 'they'?"

"HALT members." Lucy glanced back over her shoulder at her house. "But that doesn't make sense because I know they'd never hurt any animals they were rescuing." She bit the edge of her nail, looking worried, as if she was about to cry.

The stupidity of this statement floored me. "Rescue them? By letting them go?" I threw my hands into the air in frustration. "Freeing disabled birds is like helping a person in a wheelchair by pushing them down the steps! The birds can't make it on their own, which is why we house them permanently!" I yelled, "Who the hell did this, Lucy? Do you know?"

She clutched the newspaper to her chest, her bottom lip trembling. "Stop yelling and I'll tell you."

It took all my energy to not grab her by the shoulders and shake the information out of her. I fought to get my emotions in check. Speaking more calmly but between clenched teeth, I said, "Fine. Talk."

Her eyes darted down to her hands and then back up at me. "Well, Friday night after you left, Haley started saying how all of us should go to your house and let your birds go free. That it was cruel to keep wild birds locked up and all that. At first I went along, thinking she was just talking smack."

"That's just great. Thanks for that," I snapped.

She winced almost imperceptibly and fiddled with one of her rings. "But instead of dropping it, Haley started naming possible times and locations where we could meet up, and I knew she was serious. Reed said no, that it was going too far, and I agreed with him. Trust me on this, Mercer — I seriously thought that was the end of it."

At least Reed had spoken up. Still, he should've called and warned me. "Did Charlie know about this?" If she said yes, I'd have to wonder if I had any true friends.

"No. He was in the restroom when Haley brought it up." She glanced nervously at her house, and then back at me. "But then yesterday afternoon, my parents came home from this big HALT fundraiser, and they asked me what I knew about your dad's business. That's when I realized that Haley told her parents about all of the birds housed at your place, and they must have spread the word."

I started to get the picture. "Wait a second. Are you saying your parents did this?"

Lucy nodded, tears forming in the corners of her eyes. "I think so." She took in gulps of air, speaking between sniffles. "I explained to them that your dad helped sick birds, but they must not have believed me. I saw my dad bring his toolbox into the garage right before my parents left to see the late show, but I just figured he was fixing something. Now I'm guessing that they must have gone to your place instead of to the movies. But I swear I didn't figure it out until just now, Mercer!"

If I were a lizard, blood would've squirted from my eyes. "That's just great! Maybe I should run inside your house and poke sticks under your parents' armpits and hang them from a bush and see how they like it!" Angry as I was, I realized that me and my big mouth had created this whole mess. I had practically handed Haley and her henchmen an invitation to destroy my house, my family, and all that my dad had worked so hard to create. I gripped the sides of my forehead, going over the whole scenario in my mind. "I'm so fricking stupid!"

Tears rolled down Lucy's face. "I'm so sorry, Mercer."

"You know what? I'm sorry too." I looked her straight in the eyes. "Sorry I didn't take a stand for my family and falconry sooner. I love nature and everything in it, but I can't say the same about HALT. Maybe there are some good animal rights' groups out there, but HALT isn't one of them. They are a mentally effed-up organization without any common sense and I quit!" I cranked up the throttle. "I don't know how you can be a part of HALT either, not when they do crap like this." I kicked the front panel. "To hell with all of you!" Switching into drive, I gripped both handlebars, confident that I'd never speak to Lucy or Haley again. Nor Reed, if he'd known about this and hadn't told me.

"Wait!" Lucy clutched my arm, her eyes wild. "Let me get my shoes."

"What? No! You're not—" Before I could say another word, she'd sprinted across her front yard. As I watched the girl who'd consumed all my available brain space for the past two weeks, I doubted my ability to think straight with her around. Why did she want to come with me? She ducked into the house and I waited for her, keeping the ATV in first gear with the brakes on. If she brought her parents out to talk to me, I was out of there. I kept my eyes steady on the house, ready to peel out if anything at all didn't seem right. Seconds later, Lucy came flying out through the front door, still in pajama pants and sweatshirt, but with white sneakers on her feet, racing full speed across the lawn. As she neared the gate, her dad came dashing out of the house in a blue bathrobe, waving his fists.

What was going on? I was about to take off when Lucy shouted, "Make room for me!"

Before I could weigh my options, I scooched my butt forward, and she hopped on behind me, screaming, "Go!!"

Her dad was halfway across the front lawn. "Get back here *now*, Lucy!"

"You sure?" I asked, my hands on the throttle.

"Yes!! Go!" My heart pounded in fear, but Lucy wrapped her arms around me and placed her head against my back, bracing herself for speed. So I opened the throttle and roared off down her street, leaving him standing there, inhaling my exhaust.

TWENTY-FIVE

AS WE SPED AWAY, MY EMOTIONS CHURNED. WHAT was I doing with the girl whose parents had trashed my place? Was I a traitor, or flat-out foolish? I glanced over my shoulder in time to see Lucy's dad racing back toward the house.

It was difficult, not to mention illegal, to drive with a passenger on a single-rider ATV. Luckily, we both had scrawny butts, so it wasn't a huge problem. Now that the immediate danger was over, I had a few things to sort out with my pretty stowaway whom I had vowed not two minutes ago never to speak to again. But I had to get Flip first. My questions could wait.

When I'd ridden far enough out of sight, I stopped my ATV and grabbed my binoculars from around my neck. I scanned the tree line for the hawk I'd seen before, but couldn't spot my Flip look-alike anywhere. "Where are you, buddy?" I continued to scour, extending my field a bit farther this time, but still no luck. "Damn it! He's gone!"

"I'm sorry, Mercer."

I ignored her apology, my anger resurfacing, this time at myself. Why hadn't I just gone after Flip instead of stopping to yell at Lucy? I'd screwed up yet again! Frustration was building up inside me, ready to explode. The pain of losing Flip was so immense, I couldn't believe I had thought, for even one second, about letting him go to get Lucy to kiss me again. Talk about being immature. I finally understood what Weasel and Dad and Lincoln and, yes, even Reed, had been trying to tell me—to find a girl who liked me just the way I was, falconry and all.

If I was lucky enough to find Flip, I would go to that falconry meet next weekend and win that Best Apprentice pin. But I'd do it for me—not to prove anything to anyone else.

Now that the red-tailed hawk I'd spotted was nowhere to be found, I needed to find out what Lucy was doing here with me. I slid my butt off the seat enough so I could look at her face to face. "Why are you here, Lucy?"

A horrible thought occurred to me after I'd asked my question and she struggled to meet my eyes—could this be some sort of trap? "I have lots of reasons, but . . ." She looked back toward her house and then back at me, both fear and despair woven inseparably through those sage green eyes I'd once fantasized about. "Can you please keep driving? I'm scared my Dad's going to come after me."

"No, not until I know that you're not screwing with me. Like I'm out driving around with you while your parents and their buddies are off burning down my house or something."

She shook her head violently. "God, no! They'd never do that! My parents might be a little fanatical, but he'd never do anything horrible like that. Seriously."

"You call breaking and entering someone's property a *little* fanatical?" I slid off the seat more now, half standing. This conversation needed my full attention.

Lucy held a trembling hand over her mouth, tears streaming out. "Okay, yes. They're crazy, but I know they would never have done what they did if they thought for a second that any of the birds could get hurt."

"You're *defending* them now?" I asked, incredulous. I was about to tell her to get the hell off my bike, when she gripped my arm, hard.

"No, I'm not! Please, Mercer. Just like you said to me on the bus, you are not your mom, and I'm not my dad. You love them because they're your parents, but you can have different beliefs. That's exactly how I am." She swallowed hard, with tears dripping out of her eyes faster than she could wipe them away. But this time, she kept my gaze.

I sighed seeing how much pain she was in, and relaxed a bit. I believed in my gut that she was telling me the truth, and prayed she was right about her father's limits. "All right, fine, but what about you? Why'd you come with me? Are you planning to try to get me to change my mind about rescuing the birds or something? Because if that's the case, you can walk home now. It's not happening."

She shook her head, staring at me intently. "No, please. That's not it. That's not it at all." She glanced down at her hands briefly and took a deep breath. "Look. After my big speech on

Friday night about honesty, I feel compelled to tell you something about me."

That didn't sound good. My heart pounded. I wondered what horrible truth she'd reveal. Had she been faking her interest in me all along so she could find out about my father? Had Reed asked her out at Starbucks after I'd left? The scenarios got worse the longer I conjured them up, so I decided to let her put me out of my misery. "All right, shoot."

She picked at her chipped nail polish, not making eye contact. "You probably think I love everything about HALT, but I don't." She glanced at me briefly before turning back to her nails. "I mean, I do love animals and enjoy going to protests whenever I think we can make a difference. And sometimes we do. We've made companies — whole industries, even — change the way they do things so animals are treated humanely. I'm proud I helped. That's the part I love."

"Go on," I said warily. I didn't really want to hear any more HALT propaganda, and yet, I couldn't help connecting with what she said. It was exactly what I had tried to communicate to my father.

She paused, as if agonizing over what she was going to say. "But I absolutely *hate* when HALT does kamikaze protest stuff — like destroying science labs worth millions of dollars or freeing minks from a mink farm, only to have them creamed by cars on the highway a mile later. That's the kind of thing that makes me angry — when HALT goes too far and makes things worse, like what they did to you." She looked at me and shrugged, wiping away a tear on her shoulder. "So that's why I'm here. I can't erase what my parents did, but I'll feel better if I help you rescue your birds."

I looked away, wondering what to do. The question was, Would *I* feel better if I let her help me? And if I let her help, would she think I'd changed my mind about HALT and what they had done to my family? I hated making decisions like this because I seemed to always make the wrong one, at least in my dad's eyes. I tilted my head back, taking a deep breath. "I don't know, Lucy. I can't—"

She put her hand on my thigh. "*Please,* Mercer. Let me help. It's not my fault my parents have such strong beliefs. They'll do these crazy things to make themselves feel good. Please. I want to help rescue those disabled birds."

My heart melted a little against my will, not to mention that the hand-on-thigh placement was making me feel good too—albeit in a very different way. I coughed, conjured up the image of Monocle, and things quickly settled down. Though I wanted to hate Lucy and her family for everything they stood for, the truth was, her family and mine weren't that different—at least not when it came down to standing firm on our beliefs.

"When you say that in that way, it reminds me of my parents," I admitted. "They're both so into their jobs, they get lost in it and forget about normal life. Seriously. Their anniversary weekend getaway is the only date my parents have each year."

She nodded thoughtfully. "Exactly. My parents live in a cave, surrounding themselves only with people who share the same views. They think they're so great, their cause so righteous, that anyone who disagrees should be banished from Earth." She rolled her eyes. "I'm not kidding. My dad is so one-sided, he would probably tip over if you sneezed on him."

I laughed, thinking about my own sneezing blunder. "I volunteer."

"Be my guest." Lucy smiled, her eyes brimming with shared humor.

Despite my conscience yelling that I was a dumbass for talking to her, that urgent sense of wanting to kiss her returned. *Stop it,* I told myself, cracking my knuckles nervously. "I have to tell you, though, that I'm looking for only one injured bird. The rest are our hunting birds. You sure you still want to come?"

"Yeah, I do. Even though I can never bring your owl back to life, I want to try to help with some of the other things my parents ruined. Okay?" She gazed at me with those sage green eyes with the yellow flecks of sunshine throughout, waiting for my answer.

That was it. Those incredible eyes were my weakness. "All right. Let's hit the road." I took off then, Lucy's arms hugging me tight, finally satisfied she wasn't there to sabotage my efforts. I cruised down the open pasture underneath the high-tension wires, where I'd often seen hawks sitting way up high on the metal scaffolding, scanning the fields for a meal. I asked Lucy to concentrate on the trees to our left, and I'd concentrate on the ones to the right.

For the first time in my life, I felt more like a man than a boy, and it had nothing to do with having a pretty girl plastered to my back. No, this feeling was born out of doing what I wanted to do and what I thought was right. Not backing down, not asking for permission.

It felt good.

We drove along, watching the sky, barely speaking, each of us focused on searching for our birds. I tilted my head toward her so she could hear me over the sound of the engine. "When birds get frightened, they take off and fly until they're out of danger, so they could be anywhere." I turned west on Town Line Road, heading toward the huge deserted field behind the gas station, which was often ripe with quarry. "I guess today will be the big test to see if our hunting birds want to be in the wild or with us."

Lucy started to hit my shoulder repeatedly, pointing. "Wait! Look up on that telephone pole. Is that bird one of yours? It looks pretty big."

My heart skipped a beat. Sure enough, a large bird sat majestically atop the highest crossbeam. "It could be." I stopped and peered through my binoculars. "It's a northern goshawk! It sure looks like my brother's bird." I parked on the grass and hopped off. Lucy followed me as I raced to the back of the ATV to retrieve the equipment I would need from the storage bin. I slid on my leather glove, nabbed a wet hunk of raw meat out of the waist pouch, and stood where I'd be visible to the bird.

While I was holding the bloody flesh in my gloved hand, a few red droplets fell to the ground. "Bella!" I called out. Nothing. The bird flapped once and settled back onto the beam.

What was wrong with me? Had I forgotten everything I knew? I gave one long blast on my whistle, the code to which Lincoln had trained her to respond. I waited only a few seconds before she soared down from the pole, landing on my gloved fist.

"Nice job, Bella!" I gushed, letting her enjoy her reward.

"That's so cool!" Lucy's eyes were as wide as they could go.

"Isn't it?" Grinning with relief, I held on to Bella's jesses so she couldn't take off and walked to the back of the ATV where the carrier had been installed. It made sense that I'd get Bella back. Lincoln had trained her well. A twinge of jealousy rippled through me, a sense of loss over not finding Flip squeezing my heart.

"That was totally amazing!" Lucy said, her voice bright with excitement. "It *chose* to come to you. I can't believe that's how it works!"

I couldn't resist a dig. "There's probably a lot of things animal rights' protesters don't know about falconry. Heck, I've been around it my whole life, and there's still a ton I don't know." I pointed to my backpack jammed next to the bird carrier. "Could you do me a favor and hand me her hood out of there? It's a big brown leather thing with a curlicue on top."

"Sure." Lucy reached into my backpack, holding things up to show me and then putting them back in until she produced the hood I wanted.

"Thanks. Now easy does it, Bella." I reached up and placed the hood on her without a hitch. This bird was a total pro at this falconry stuff. And so was Lincoln, I had to admit. I placed Bella on the perch inside the carrier and hopped back onto the ATV. "Um . . . I need to bring her home now and check on my sister. Do you want to come with me, or do you want to go home?"

Lucy scrunched up her face at me as if I was crazy. "Are you kidding? If I went home now, I think my dad would grab me by the hair and twirl me around the yard. In fact, now that I think of it, you should avoid the main roads. He could be out looking for me."

My stomach dropped. "Do you think he'll go back to my house?"

"Back to the scene of the crime in broad daylight? I don't think so." She brought her hand to her mouth. "Oh my God. Do you think your dad will have them arrested for this?"

I thought he probably would, and secretly I even hoped he would. But I didn't want to tell her that, so I shrugged. "Maybe for vandalism. I don't know."

We were both silent as we got back onto the ATV, each of us probably ruminating about what our parents would do. My thoughts went to Maddie and her little friend Hannah. I tapped my pockets, searching for my cell phone, cursing myself for leaving it at home. Trying to ease both our worries, I announced, "Okay, so one back-roads detour coming up."

Heading toward Benson Woods was our best bet. There probably wouldn't be many people around this early on a Sunday morning, and we'd be able to see her dad's car from far away. Lucy's face pressed up against my neck, sending a romantic shiver ripping through me. "I never saw a hawk close up like that before. Bella sure is beautiful."

I froze, knowing that another cheesy "so are you" moment was available, but definitely not taking it. Not when everything about us as a couple was so completely wrong. I wished someone would tell my body that, because it was reacting to her every touch. "Yeah, they're as beautiful standing still as they are in flight."

As we drove along, Lucy's hands wrapped tightly around my midsection, occasionally shifting positions across my chest. Things continued to stir in places where I knew they shouldn't. How could I even *think* about liking a girl whose family did such horrible things to families like mine? My mind wandered to the Shakespeare piece we had studied in Lit last year: *Romeo and Juliet*.

The story had archaic language that we'd struggled through for weeks, but seeing the movie had brought it all together for me. Even I couldn't deny that the age-old family feud versus stolen romance had me glued. But the ending? Totally sucked. Why didn't Romeo and Juliet just run off together instead of killing themselves? It wasn't as though they lived on an island and couldn't get away from all the haters.

Could Lucy and I be like Romeo and Juliet, but with a different outcome?

I drove down a ravine as we entered the woods, the left side of the ATV higher than the other. Without speaking, we both leaned to the left to prevent tipping. Lucy obviously was telling the truth about growing up with lots of recreational vehicles around. As we got into the clearing, we passed a rustic brown sign with BULLHEAD LAKE TRAIL painted in white letters.

"Want to hear something funny?" Lucy brushed her soft cheek against mine, and I tried to focus only on the road instead of the faint scent of flowers wafting off her hair. "A few years ago my parents ran naked in some race to protest the running of the bulls."

"Did you say 'naked'?" I repeated, positive I'd misheard her over the roar of the motor.

"Yep! Weird, huh?" She giggled, gripping me tightly as we rolled over a bump. "I couldn't believe my mom agreed to do it. When it comes to sports, my mom's a big chicken."

I laughed. "Your mom and I have something in common. When it comes to eating a big chicken, I consider it a sport."

Her voice turned serious. "You do? I thought you gave up meat." She sounded hurt.

I could tell I was opening a wound, but I was done with lying to this girl. Like it or not, I'd tell her what was real about me, and if she didn't like it . . . I sighed, not wanting to worry about that just yet. "Well . . . I did give it up for lunch every day, that part is true. It was really, really hard, but I did it. At home, though, I still ate it."

"Oh." Her hands shifted from my chest to my sides.

I sighed, turning my head toward her. "Sorry I wasn't honest about that, but if you haven't noticed, I can't afford to lose much weight. In the end I decided I needed meat to stay healthy. Kind of like my hawk; no offense."

"Yeah, I understand," she said quietly.

I drove past the lake, still scoping out the fields and trees, praying I'd find Flip there. This place, with its woods and lake and miles of fresh air, reminded me more of Wisconsin than any other place I'd been in Illinois. When Charlie, Reed, and I rode through it, I'd always get a wave of homesickness, but I loved coming here all the same.

We reached the incline that would take us to the highest point, so I revved the engine to get more power. Lucy leaned forward, her hands once again gripping my chest. It was hard to focus on driving and not on the feeling of her chest pressing up against my back or the lilac scent of her hand lotion. When we reached the top of the hill and leveled off, I noticed she hadn't backed away as much as she could have. Her voice wavered as she took in the surroundings. "Wow! It's so pretty up here. This place makes me miss Wisconsin."

Whoosh. As if her heart had pushed through my back and

welded onto mine. Why'd she have to go and say something that was so close to what I was feeling? I hesitated, dying to stop the bike, swap more stories, and kiss those luscious lips of hers, but I didn't. With all of these emotions jumbling inside me, I couldn't sort out what I was feeling. About anything, really. Out tumbled the only words I could manage: "Me too."

"If it wasn't for my parents' big mouths, we'd still be there." Her voice cracked a bit.

The way she said it made it sound accusatory rather than reflective. "Really? Why?"

Wanting to hear her explanation, I slowed the engine a bit, using this opportunity to rub my sweaty palms on my jeans. The intense vibration of the handlebars was relentless.

Lucy sighed, and I could feel her breasts rise and fall against my back. I mentally cautioned myself not to imagine them. "Because they went too far—just like they did last night. It all started when my brother John, who manages Edible Earth Vegan Café out in Fond du Lac, convinced my parents to join HALT. I think they originally did it so they could spend more time with my brother. But then they started getting into it— reading all the literature, going to meetings, attending protests. Before I knew it, they had become like those zombies in the movie, pushing their beliefs on everyone. They got into arguments everywhere they went—at the bowling alley, church socials, even the Piggly Wiggly. I could barely stand to be out in public with them."

I winced, feeling bad for her. My parents might spend too much time working, but they never acted crazy. Not in public, anyway.

"At first, there were a few threatening phone calls, but that didn't faze them. They figured it went with the territory. But then someone set our garage on fire. Almost burned our house down along with it. Freaked my parents out big time. That's why we're here now."

I couldn't believe it. Someone had resorted to arson to get rid of them? Either those criminals were nuts or her parents had really pissed off a lot of people. "Whoa. That must have been scary."

A black bird let out a shriek from high above, interrupting our conversation. "Hold on!" I held up my hand for silence. I stopped the ATV and scoured the skies until I saw what I was looking for. "Yes! There it is!" I pointed, sitting sideways so I could talk to Lucy more easily. "See that bird? I bet you anything it's Troy, my Dad's falcon! Watch what he does next."

Both of us stared in amazement as the peregrine falcon plummeted through the air like a speeding bullet. Seconds later it dive-bombed a low-flying mallard, knocking it to the ground. A familiar scream of triumph erupted from the falcon's mouth, and that's when I knew without a doubt that it was Troy, the little braggart.

"Did you see that?" Lucy asked, her eyes bulging. "That bird attacked that duck!'

"It's called stooping, and it's what peregrines do best. Hang on to me. I'm going to get closer." Sliding back into place, I gunned the engine, speeding toward them. I slid off and grabbed Lucy's hand to help her off the ATV. "Let's go get him!"

Lucy didn't let go of my grip as we raced toward the area I'd last pictured them going down. "It all happened so fast!"

I grinned, squeezing her hand. "Yep, that's falconry for you —the ultimate in fast food."

She slapped my arm. "Not funny, Mercer!"

But I could tell from her smile that she actually did find some humor in my joke. We hurried through the field, still hand in hand, tromping around, searching for Troy. Suddenly there was some rustling in the weeds not ten yards from us.

"There they are." Walking over, I couldn't help smiling when I saw Troy. He had his wings outstretched over the mallard, bobbing up and down in excitement. I could swear there was a look of joy on his face, the same expression a little kid gets when he masters his bike without training wheels for the first time.

Probably how I looked in the movie theater after I'd kissed Lucy.

I let Troy gloat for a few seconds before distracting him with a chunk of meat. The female mallard he'd felled was bleeding from the mouth. Still alive, as evidenced by a few weak wing flaps. Knowing what I had to do next in front of Lucy made me cringe. I froze.

She gasped. "Oh my gosh, Mercer! It's still alive." She clamped a hand over her mouth.

I sighed, shaking my head. "Which means she's still suffering. Sorry, Lucy, but I've got to dispatch it. Look away a second." With Troy still guarding his prey, I reached down, and with one quick twist, broke the mallard's neck, ceasing all of her movement.

"Eeeew!" Lucy grimaced in horror. "That's what you do? Break its neck?"

I spun around, my hand still clutching the mallard's now limp head. "But . . . you . . . I told you to look away!"

"Who looks away when someone says 'look away'?" she said, her eyebrows pinched together, questioning me. "Didn't killing it gross you out?"

I shrugged. "Not really. It's part of being a nature guy, I guess. Besides, Troy would've eaten her alive, which would have been grosser, if you know what I mean."

"Sick!" Lucy made a face as if she was the one who had just eaten a still-living duck.

"It's not sick. It's the food chain." I was tired of being an animal rights guy. "Animals kill each other to eat. That's the circle of life, and personally, I don't think people should mess with it." I was glad when she didn't debate my answer, because right now I needed to get Troy's attention off the mallard before he ripped it to shreds.

I managed to distract Troy and discreetly remove the mallard, but now I was faced with the same dilemma as when Flip had killed the chipmunk. Leave it lay—which in falconer lingo is called wanton waste—or take it and use it? Bothered by either choice, I finally grabbed the mallard by its neck and stuck it in my backpack. Food was food—in season or not.

"Two down, two to go." Holding Troy proudly on my fist, we headed back to the ATV.

"Gosh. He's so darn cute," she cooed. "It looks like he's wearing a little mask."

"He's trying to be incognito," I joked, realizing then we had only one bird carrier on board. Since I couldn't drive with a peregrine falcon parked on my arm, I asked Lucy, "Do you mind driving?"

She grinned. "Mind? Are you kidding? I love anything with an engine."

It took us a few minutes to put Troy's hood on and position ourselves back onto the ATV. With Lucy seated in front of me and Troy on my left fist between us, I needed to squeeze my thighs around Lucy's hips to keep from falling off. I hoped she didn't think I was being a perv. "Hit it, Danica," I joked, referring to a famous female Indy racer, "but not *too* fast. We've got some important passengers on board."

"Cute ones too." Then, looking over her shoulder, she added, "And you're not too bad either, Troy."

I'm pretty sure the adrenaline rush I felt could have fueled our ride home.

She disengaged the parking brake, put the vehicle in drive, and gently pressed the throttle. We drove on, chatting mostly about my role as a falconer: How long did it take to learn? Was it hard? Did I like it? The last question had me nodding emphatically. "Now more than ever. And if Flip is gone for good, it'll suck, but I'm going to try again. If not this season, then next year for sure. I think it's safe to say I'll be doing this for the rest of my life."

We rode along silently then. As we neared my house, she asked, "So . . . what are you going to do with that duck you put in your bag?"

"Donate it to feed the hungry?" I quipped, wondering if she'd fall for it.

Lucy chuckled. "Yeah, right. What are you really going to do with it?"

"You sure you want to know?" When she nodded, I said, "I'll cut it up for my family or our birds to eat."

"*Ew* . . . weird." She shuddered.

"Not as weird as eating crap sprout sandwiches."

"Who you calling weird, Mr. I've Got More Stubble Than a Billy Goat?" She reached back with her hand and patted the side of my face, making me laugh.

"Thaaaat's meeeeean," I said, trotting out my best billy goat impression. I instinctively rubbed my jawline. No wonder she'd called me a goat. Two days without shaving, and I was already in danger of being mistaken for Weasel.

Lucy turned and pulled into my driveway.

That's when I noticed Lincoln's car with the reverse lights on.

My stomach churned like whitewater rapids and my face seared with fear. If Lincoln was as mad as I figured he would be after he'd learned of the break-in, I was as dead as the mallard in my backpack.

TWENTY-SIX ·····➤

LINCOLN WAS BACKING HIS SILVER CADDY DOWN
the driveway with Maddie in the back seat. Thank goodness. The sooner he left, the better. I didn't want to hear him whale on me about what had happened—not now, not in front of Lucy.

My luck ran out the second he spotted me. He threw his car into park and bolted, leaving his driver's door open. He strode toward me at full speed, quickly closing the twenty feet between his vehicle and mine. "Mercer!"

Lucy looked at me, panic in her eyes. "Is that your brother?"

"Yeah," I said with a nod, my voice not recognizable as my own. "Get off and stand back."

Lincoln continued storming toward me. "What the hell happened, Mercer? Did you finally cave and join HALT? Is this some initiation rite?"

"What? No!" I screeched, unable to comprehend how he could even think that.

Lucy leaped off on the side of the ATV away from Lincoln, and I followed, trying to distance myself from him. There was no telling what he might do when he was wild-eyed like this. I'd seen it before—right before he beat some kid up in the school parking lot last year.

"Then what?" he pressed. "How did they know about our birds, huh?"

"Not from me." My mind raced, trying to figure out a way to protect my dignity as well as my face. "At least I got Troy back." As if on command, Troy opened his beak in alarm. "And Bella's in the carrier." I'd hoped that getting this info out into the open might make him chill a little.

"You're lucky!" He stopped on the opposite side of the ATV and glared at me, his hands in fists. He glanced at Lucy, as if seeing her for the first time, and then back at me. "Wait a second. Is *this* the HALT chick you've been drooling over?" Before I could answer, he walked toward her, taking huge strides and pointing his finger at her. "Who did this, huh? Was it you?"

"No!" She backed away, her eyes filled with terror.

"Leave her alone, Lincoln!" I yelled, my anger spiking. I raced toward him as fast as a person could run while balancing a falcon on his arm. I didn't care if he beat the crap out of me, but he needed to stay the hell away from Lucy.

Lincoln grabbed my T-shirt as I neared him, twisting it in his fist. He pulled my face toward his. "How could you screw up this bad? Dad's going to be so pissed!" Though I had him beat in height, he was ten times stronger than me. I held my breath until he let go with a shove. I wished I could sic Troy on Lincoln like in the Alfred Hitchcock movie *The Birds*. I envisioned hundreds of falcons swarming at him, pecking his eyes out as he ran screaming. One look at Lucy's frightened face and I felt like the world's biggest wimp. "You'd better have a good excuse, that's all I have to say."

I couldn't believe my ears. "*I'd* better have a good excuse? What about you? For your information, they broke in sometime last night when you were with Zola. Maybe if you weren't so busy screwing around with her up in your room, you would have heard them break in."

"Liar!" Lincoln's face suddenly turned redder than I'd ever seen on any human before. Troy squawked loudly as I tried desperately to balance him on my fist.

That's when I heard Lauren's voice. "*What* did you say, Mercer?"

I whipped around. Lauren had been in the car? I prayed she hadn't heard exactly what I'd said. If I made something up quickly, maybe I could prevent my brother from strangling me.

Before I could reply, Lincoln called out, "He's rambling, Lauren. Don't listen to him." He walked with his back to Lauren, his teeth clenched as tightly as his fists. "Go put Troy and Bella away and we'll talk about this later, you pansy-ass HALT lover." He spat on the ground as he shot a look of hatred at Lucy.

What a total loser. I hated how my brother treated people, how he thought he was so much better than the rest of us. "Put your own bird away, maggot." I knew that wasn't the best answer to smooth things over, but right then I was done bowing down to the almighty Lincoln. I started walking toward the mews, leaving Bella in the carrier.

"Who the hell is Zola, Lincoln?" Lauren snapped, her heeled boots clacking against the cement as she strode toward him.

Guess she'd heard me after all. Good. Let's see how Lincoln liked people ruining things when a pretty girl was nearby.

He spun around to face her, his arms outstretched. "I have no idea." He shook his head, shrugging. "C'mon, babe. Let's drive Maddie to her party and then we'll go eat lunch. I agreed to work later today, so I still have another thirty minutes for my break."

"Like I'm going anywhere with you?" Lauren's pupils were round and black as buckshot.

"Mercer made that story up because he's mad at me. Go on, Mercer, tell her." Lincoln gave me the look I'd seen a million times — the one that said, *Lie for me or you're dead.*

So Mr. Frisky finally got caught with his pants down, and he wanted me to lie for him? If I remembered correctly, the last time I had covered for Lincoln, I'd ended up with a fat Flip. But this time it would mean a fat lip for me, so I decided to help him out. Again. "I was just kidding, Lauren. There's no one named Zola. I mean, really? Zola is a pirate's name, not a girl's."

She looked at me, unsure if she should believe me or not, when Maddie rolled her window down. "They're both lying, Lauren. Zola is a girl and she was here last night."

"You suck, Lincoln!" Lauren leaned in and snatched her purse from the front seat before storming off down the driveway.

Lincoln whipped open Maddie's door, fury written across his face. "Out!"

"But what about my—"

"Now!" he screamed.

Maddie didn't ask again. She grabbed the birthday gift and almost fell as she scrambled out of the car, running toward me. Lincoln slammed her door and got into the driver's seat. He backed up, wheels squealing, and drove alongside Lauren with his passenger window open, trying to persuade her to get back in while she walked in the street crying.

Lucy went up to Maddie, her voice unsteady. "I was so scared there for a minute. I thought he was going to hit you."

I inhaled deeply, keeping an eye on Lincoln. "Yeah, he's got a wicked temper, all right."

"Like my dad."

That made me think. "Did your dad ever . . ."

"Hit me?" she asked. "No. Not me or my mom. Mostly he yells and stomps around kicking things. And then the next day it's like it never happened."

Maddie's shoulders slumped as she dropped her green-striped gift bag, letting it thunk on the ground. "I hate Lincoln. Now I can't go to my party."

I put my hand on her shoulder. "Yeah, that stinks, Maddie. But I think you did the right thing. Lincoln needs to stick to the truth—like I plan to do from now on." I tossed Lucy a look, not knowing and, really, not even caring all that much if she believed me. I said it more for myself than anyone. Lying about all this stuff made my stomach hurt. I hated covering up who I was and what I stood for just to make someone else happy. Having it all out in the open now took a huge load off my mind. This must be how ex-cons felt once they were released from prison.

Lucy put one foot forward, absent-mindedly making an arc with her toe. "Makes me nervous about what will happen when I get home. I told my parents I hated them before I left."

"Don't worry." I gave her a reassuring smile, dismissing her fears with a wave of my hand. "Lots of kids say that kind of stuff when they're mad."

"Except I followed it with 'And you both deserve to die—just like the owl.'"

I winced. "Ouch. Not good." I continued toward the rehab center. "I've got to put Troy and Bella away and check on the other birds. But then I'm heading back out to look for Bullet and Flip."

Maddie's eyes widened. "Oh my gosh. You don't know?"

"Know what?" A jolt of panic stabbed my heart. I dreaded what other bad news she was going to deliver.

"After Hannah's mom came to pick her up, I found Bullet hopping around behind the rehab center trying to catch a bug. I put on one of those gloves and took him back to his mews."

"You did?" I laughed, giving her a high-five. "Good job, Maddie. I'm proud of you."

She beamed. "Thanks." She picked up the gift bag. "Well, I guess I'll go play with Peanut. She always makes me feel better."

"Good idea," I agreed. Lucy followed me into the rehab

center, which was strewn with overturned tables, broken scales, open bottles of medicine littering the floor, and tons of HALT pamphlets. I watched for her reaction.

"Oh my God! This is so horrible! I can't believe they did this." Lucy held a hand over her mouth as she stepped around Liberty's scale. At least they hadn't broken that. That sucker was expensive.

"Me neither." After putting Troy away, I hurried to check on Liberty. Lucy followed me, peering over my shoulder.

The second I opened the door of Liberty's mews, she kacked loudly at me several times. Noisy birds were ones on the mend. I closed the door behind me with a smile.

"Want to see the rest of our residents?" I asked. When she agreed, I took her on the grand tour. I worried she might side with her parents. Instead, she bubbled over with questions.

"What kind of bird is this?" Lucy peered through Rusty's observation window.

"That's a kestrel, the smallest accipiter there is." As we passed each mews, I told her about all our birds. Lucy said things like "Wow!" and "That's so cool!" making me swell with pride. I purposely skipped Monocle's mews, but Lucy looked inside anyway.

"Oh no! Is that . . . ?" She turned to me, her watery eyes filled with such incredible sadness, it almost made me cry again.

"Yep. That's Monocle. *Was* Monocle," I fought back tears as I moved on toward Flip's mews.

Her voice cracked. "I'm so sorry." Lucy continued to stand at the window and stare, pulling the neckline of her sweatshirt up over her mouth as if to hide somehow.

I couldn't look again, didn't want to talk about Monocle right now. "If you come over here, you can see where my bird, Flip, lives. Or lived. Depending if I find him or not."

"These cages *are* huge," Lucy said, her forehead puckered in surprise. She peeked inside. "And they're not chained up, just like you told Haley."

"Did you think I was lying?" I snapped, but realized I'd done my fair share of that.

"Yeah, actually, I did." Lucy shrugged, not looking away. "So I went on the HALT website yesterday to find out the truth about falconry, and they showed hawks shoved into tiny cages, like the one on the back of your ATV."

"We only use those cages for transport. It's actually safer for the birds; they don't get jostled around," I explained. "I wonder what other false information HALT has on its website."

"I doubt everything's false," Lucy said wistfully. "They do a lot of crazy things, but they do some good things too."

"Perhaps." Now it was my turn to shrug. "Speaking of tiny cages, I need to get Bella. She's been in that carrier for two hours already."

"I'll come with you," Lucy said cheerfully, and followed me.

Seeing how agreeable Lucy was and how objectively she was checking out our birds made me feel more confused than ever about my feelings. Here we'd spent this incredible day together, talking about our views honestly and openly, and yet, because of her family, it was one of the worst days of my life. How was that possible?

When we got to the ATV, I used my English butler voice and bowed slightly at the waist. "Would you like the pleasure of driving the cart to the rear of the facility, madam?"

Lucy dipped her chin daintily and curtsied. "Why, thank you, my dear sir. I shall take you up on your considerate offer. Good thing I wore my royal pajama pants."

She hopped on first and scooched forward so I could sit behind her. Feeling slightly more relaxed, now that more birds were safe, made sitting so close and smelling her hair unbearably attractive. I forced myself to grab the handles on the sides of the seat so I wouldn't wrap my arms around her the way I wanted to. "I'm ready when you are."

Putting the ATV in gear, she cruised smoothly to the back of the house. As she rounded the corner, I couldn't believe my eyes.

Sitting on the very peak of the rehab center like a weathervane come to life was a juvenile red-tailed hawk. "Hey! It's Flip!" I pointed, my voice as happy as when I burst out of school on the last day each year.

"Where?" she asked.

I put my left arm around her shoulder and leaned in close, pointing from her perspective. "Up on the roof. See the bird?"

"Oh my gosh! He came back on his own!" Lucy exclaimed.

When she turned, her lips almost brushed mine by accident, sending another jolt through me. I had to hold myself back from kissing her cheek. "That means Flip's the best bird of all."

"I know. Can you believe it? I'd better call him now before he changes his mind." When I tried to get off the ATV in one swift move, my foot caught on the seat bar and I fell on the ground next to the ATV, bringing up a cloud of dust with me. Real swift.

Lucy gasped, leaning over from behind the driver's seat to see me. "Are you okay?"

I laughed and stood up, brushing off my jeans. "Yeah, except for the fact that I just ruined my tough-guy image."

She giggled. "Sorry, but tough guy doesn't come to mind when I think of you."

"At least you're thinking about me, though," I said with a grin. She smiled but didn't deny it. I threw on a glove and grabbed a rabbit tidbit from my waist pouch as Lucy climbed out to watch. I yelled, "Hup!" once and Flip floated right to my fist, as if he'd been doing it all his life. I snatched up his jesses, mind-blowingly happy that I'd gotten another chance with him. "Yes! Way to go, boy! Flip, meet Lucy. Lucy, meet Flip."

"Pleased to meet you, Flip." Lucy curtsied, bowing her head. She looked at me, her eyes wide and bright. "He's absolutely gorgeous, Mercer."

This time I didn't hold my tongue. "Just like you."

"Aw . . . thanks." She smiled, making her nose crinkle up in a cute way.

Warmth spread across my neck and chest—pride in having the courage to say what was on my mind and also because I was ecstatic to have Flip back. And based on the spark in her eyes, I had a feeling that if I wanted to, I could have Lucy back too. "He's also smart. That's what makes falconry even more interesting—each bird has its own personality, as well as likes and dislikes. It's a puzzle figuring it all out."

Lucy waggled a finger at Flip. "Now don't go eating any chipmunks while I'm here."

When Flip's head turned, his eyes homing in on her finger, I quickly warned, "Careful. He eats fingers as appetizers." Lucy dropped her hand in a flash and I laughed. "Just kidding," I added, but who knew? Flip wasn't much of a rules follower.

As we walked back to the mews, Lucy sucked in her breath suddenly, clapping a hand over her mouth. "Wait a second! I just realized something!"

"What's that?" I somehow hoped she was going to say she knew a passageway into an alternate world, one where we could be together.

"The mouse you got the day I met you, Cinnamon, that really wasn't a pet, was it?" She watched me, waiting for my answer.

I grimaced, feeling awful that I'd been caught in yet another lie. "Sorry. No, it wasn't." Trying to save my reputation, I quickly added, "But none of my birds ate her. I let her go out in the woods. I swear that's true!" I held up two hands in surrender.

"Okay, good!" She held a hand over her heart, as if relieved. "At least she has a chance."

If I had another chance with Lucy, would I take it?

After putting Flip away, I washed up, wishing I had time for a quick shave and a shower so Lucy wouldn't see me like this. I spied a pack of peppermint gum on the ledge next to the sink and nabbed it. Not only was I starving, but I was also an advocate of fresh breath, especially around hot girls. "Would you care for a piece of gum, m'lady?" I offered Lucy a piece and she accepted, folding it into her mouth.

"Mmm . . . heck with manners. This is the best gum ever," she said, chomping noisily.

Patting the top of the worktable twice, I nodded toward the door. "Well, you ready to go?" Not that I wanted Lucy to leave, but Lincoln would be getting back soon, not to mention my parents. Maybe if I could clean up some of the mess before Dad saw it, he wouldn't be quite as mad.

Lucy's shoulders slumped. "Yeah, I guess so. No sense avoiding the inevitable. No matter when I go home, all hell's going to break loose."

I gave her a knowing smile and slid my hand on her back, ushering her toward the door. "Not sure it's any consolation, but I'm in the same boat."

"At least it'll have blue cushions," she joked as we made our way to the ATV.

This time I drove. As we cruised along, I couldn't stop thinking about what I should do and say to her when I dropped her off. But when her fingers suddenly locked across my chest and she pulled me closer, my ability to reason sailed off with the breeze.

I got to the end of her block and parked behind a stand of pines, making sure to keep my ATV out of sight. I put it in park and shut off the engine so we could talk. Lucy placed her hands on my shoulders, slipping out from behind me. She stood next to the ATV, holding on to the handlebar, fiddling with the hand brake. "Thanks for an incredible day, Mercer. It was amazing to watch you work with your birds. Flip is really cool." She looked down the block toward her house, and then back at me. "So what now?" She traced the ridges of my handlebar grip with her fingertip until it reached my hand, and then traced it too. My skin tingled where she touched it, making my heart rate leap, jolting my body into full attention.

Damn. This was going to be harder than I'd thought.

"You mean about us?" I swung my leg over to the other side to face her, resting my elbows on my knees. Because of our height differences, with me still sitting and her standing alongside the ATV, our faces were nearly even. With her this close, I knew I was sunk. No matter what I told myself about how antagonistic our family situations were, I couldn't help being crazy about her.

"Yeah. Do you still want to hang out with me?" She nibbled

on the edge of her fingertip and stared at me. Her expression was one of indecision, as if I were a bottle of poison and she was debating whether to drink me.

I held her hands between mine and paused a moment before allowing myself to glance at her mesmerizing green eyes. "I think you're a really cool girl, awesome, actually, and I wish more than anything that we could hang out, be a couple. But now that you know the real me—the falconer, the meat eater, the nature guy—I know that, as much as I might want to, I can't change that about myself to be with you. With anyone. I'm sorry I lied about those things, but I only did it because I really liked you and wanted you to like me." I swallowed hard and looked down at my hands, dreading saying goodbye.

She moved my hands apart and slipped her waist between them, placing her hands on my shoulders. With her this close, I could barely breathe, and every muscle in my body wanted to pull her close and kiss her. Before I could decide what to do, she said, "I do like you, Mercer. A lot. And after today, I'd never ask you to change." I could sense hesitation in the way she licked her lips, as if she had more to say. "The falconer stuff doesn't bother me at all because it shows you really do love animals." She slid her arms around my neck and looked me in the eye, her face inches from mine.

I knew I should tell her no, deliver the speech that I'd rehearsed in my mind—that we'd have to sneak around all the time and tell lies, and that I just wasn't cut out for that kind of thing. But when she was this close, I couldn't listen to the voice of reason. I pulled her close, wrapping my arms around her waist. The moment I closed my eyes and placed my lips on hers, my heart let loose. Our mouths parted and tongues met gently, teasingly. It felt so good to have her in my arms, to have her responding to my kisses in such a way that I knew she wanted them as much as I did. It was the best feeling I'd ever had in my life.

I don't know how long we were there, but I felt as if I was on a raft with Lucy, floating along on the ocean without a care in the world. My hands skimmed her body and she didn't object. My body roared with anticipation. Finally, when I thought about all the things I'd do if we were in a quiet place, alone, she pulled back, ending our kiss. Her eyes were sleepy and relaxed. "Whoa, that was nice. But I think I'd better go now before we get *too* crazy. Hope everything turns out okay for you at home." She backed up, giving me a wry smile, her hands lingering on my knees.

"You too." I patted her hands gently and sighed. "See you tomorrow in school."

But I knew as sure as anything I'd ever known that everything would not turn out okay. I cranked up the engine and took off toward home, rehearsing what I'd say when I eventually faced my father.

The excitement I'd felt a moment ago was quickly replaced with terror.

TWENTY-SEVEN

AS I REACHED THE WOODEN FENCE AT THE EDGE OF our property line, I could already see Mom's Camaro parked in the driveway alongside Lincoln's car. Part of me wanted to pull a celebrity meltdown—just turn around, drive away, and disappear into the sunset. But since I had no money, no private jet waiting to whisk me away, and the sun was hours away from setting, I was forced to ditch that option. My heart was heavy with shame and apprehension, the way I felt every time I headed into a class for a final that I hadn't prepared for.

Before I had a chance to even think what I was going to say, how to begin the explanation of the course of events, Dad's booming voice came. "Mercer! Get over here *now!*"

Mom, Dad, and Lincoln stood under the open garage door, all of them watching my every step. I gave the ATV some gas, purposely parking it about twenty feet away from them to give me some time to think. As I shut off the engine, Maddie appeared between my parents with her lookalike doll in her arms, her eyes red from crying. Tattleson had probably put on a grand show, crying and exaggerating everything that had happened in retaliation for missing her dumb party.

The second I got off the ATV, Dad barked, "What happened to the rehab center?"

I didn't want to be cocky by saying I was pretty sure he knew already, but I didn't know what he expected me to say. "Um, some people broke in and released the birds."

Wrong answer.

Ballistic Wacko Bird Man appeared, throwing his arms up in the air. He sputtered, "I can see that! What I want to know is why you didn't call me. Criminals break into the rehab center and you don't think that's an emergency? What's wrong with you? With all three of you for that matter? Any one of you could have called us!"

Mom took over from there, crossing her arms. "We were at breakfast this morning and I get a phone call from Hannah's mother, a woman I barely know, saying protesters had come and freed Dad's birds. Imagine our shock!"

"It was all Mercer's fault," Lincoln explained, making a dismissive gesture toward me. "He's been hanging out with that HALT girl behind your backs. I don't even think he cleaned the mews yesterday either."

"Yes, I did, you frickin' liar!" I said indignantly, stunned that I had covered for him twice this past week, and there he was, trying to get me in trouble. Just like Tattleson.

"Watch your language," Mom said. "And I can't believe you were still seeing that HALT girl! She probably used you to get information." She looked at my father. "Do you think they might have done something at my work too?"

"Anything is possible," Dad admitted. "You'd better call."

Mom nodded, pulling out her cell phone from her pocket as she rushed into the house.

"She didn't use me. She's not like that!" I argued, shifting my gaze between Dad and Lincoln. Maddie stood there nibbling on her fingertips. At least she was staying quiet for once.

"Yeah, that's why she was here today. To learn about being a falconer, right?" Lincoln made a face, shaking his head while Dad soaked it all in.

"Screw you, Lincoln." I shot him a dirty look. "Why don't you tell Dad what *you* were doing when he was gone, huh?"

Dad's face reddened. "Don't change the subject, Mercer. You continued a relationship with someone I told you was toxic to my business after you promised not to. Since it appears that you can't distinguish what's more important in your life, I'll distinguish for you. As of this moment, your apprenticeship is done. Go take off all of Flip's jesses so we can release him."

"Wait! I told you I would quit HALT, which I did. I never said I'd stop seeing Lucy," I protested. "That's not fair!"

"Not fair?" Dad bellowed, his thick eyebrows pinched together so tightly, they formed a single row across. "Was it fair to Monocle to lose her life because of you? And to Liberty, who had to suffer a major puncture wound? I'm responsible for their lives, Mercer, and I trusted you to take over that responsibility. You were negligent in your duties, and now you have to suffer the consequences. You know that the DNR is going to be looking into this." He brushed his hair off his forehead and exhaled heavily. "And Maddie, you were told you weren't allowed visitors, so why was Hannah here in the first place?"

Maddie gave Dad her sad look. "Because Mercer said I could."

There goes Tattleson again. Back on the witness stand.

Dad looked confused. "Why'd you ask Mercer when Lincoln was in charge?"

"Because Lincoln was too busy with Zola."

Dad's face ripened to the shade of a cherry bomb. Light the guy up and red smoke would pour out his ears. He faced Lincoln. "You had Zola here? After our conversation?"

"Take it easy, Dad," Lincoln said casually. "I figured the issue was having Zola in the basement with me alone. She stopped over for a little while and ate pizza, that's all. Tell him, Mercer." Lincoln's voice wavered a bit at the end, and I saw how shiny his forehead looked. Poor Lyin' Lincoln was sweating it out now.

I needed a second to think this through. If Lauren hadn't busted out of the car this morning when she did, Lincoln would have thrown a few punches my way. And then a minute ago he'd told Dad that my relationship with Lucy made me solely responsible for the rehab break-in, making Dad take away my apprenticeship. And now he wanted me to cover for him? I might be a wimp, but I'm no doormat.

Dad stared at me, waiting for a response. I shrugged. "Zola and Lincoln were in the kitchen eating pizza—"

"You see, Dad? No biggie." Lincoln smiled at me.

"*After* they were alone up in his room for an hour," I finished. "He even threatened to kill Maddie's hamster if she told." I looked Lincoln in the eye, glad for once I hadn't backed down to him. I wasn't his puny little brother that he could push around. Not anymore.

"Unbelievable!" Dad's face contorted into something resembling a deflated basketball. "This is not a hotel, Lincoln. And since you can't be trusted to follow the rules, you've now lost the privilege of bringing girls here, period."

"Are you serious? Screw this. I'm outta here." Lincoln stormed through the garage and into the house, slamming the door behind him. A can of WD-40 fell off the shelf and rolled across the garage floor. Wow. Lincoln was getting to be as dramatic as Haley.

Dad paced back and forth, smoothing his mustache. "And Maddie? You're grounded for a week for disobeying me."

Maddie nodded, holding her doll tighter. "But don't punish Mercer for letting Hannah stay over. I begged him to say yes and he felt sorry for me."

Maddie was an okay sister after all. I'd thank her later.

"Thanks for telling me," Dad said. "But that's not why he's in the hot seat right now."

Even though Dad was handing out punishments left and right, I felt awful about what had happened and needed to apologize. Whether or not he restored my apprenticeship, there was one thing I needed to clear up. "Dad, I just want to say that I feel as horrible as you do about what happened, but what Lincoln said was a lie. I did everything you asked and walked around before I went to bed to make sure the rehab center was locked up and the night-lights were on. The only reason I didn't call you was because I was more concerned with finding the birds as quickly as possible." I shrugged, mumbling. "In case you don't know, I did get all the birds back. With Maddie's and Hannah's help," I quickly added, hoping Dad might let her off the hook.

He nodded, taking a deep breath. "Lincoln told me you spent the day retrieving them. Thank you for that, but still . . . you should have called. This place is my livelihood. I care about the well-being of those birds almost as much as I care about you kids." Dad looked at me, his face expressionless, as if he was spent. "Does that HALT girl know who did this?"

My insides twisted and compressed like the hood of a car after an accident. I knew I should do the honorable thing and tell Dad that Lucy suspected her parents had broken in and set the birds free. But when I opened my mouth to speak, something came over me and I just couldn't do it. I shook my head. "Her name's Lucy. And no, she said she didn't know."

"Too bad." Dad let out a heavy sigh. "At least you had the sense not to clean up in there, so when the police get here, they can take pictures to use as evidence."

The word "evidence" hit my already crumpled insides like a bowling ball.

Dad looked at his watch. "I want to do another quick check

on the birds. I saw you did a nice job of wrapping Liberty's wound. Excellent falconer instinct on your part to sock her. I think that may have saved her life. Now both of you go inside and get cleaned up, and then, Mercer, I want you to meet me in the rehab center in ten minutes. The police will be here soon."

TWENTY-EIGHT

I TOOK A QUICK, SCALDING-HOT SHOWER TO WIPE OFF the day's grime, debating what to say when the police questioned me about what I knew. I certainly didn't want to get myself in even more trouble by lying to them. This whole thing sucked. All this deception had given me a bad headache to rival the sick feeling in my gut. After wrapping a towel around my waist, I stepped out of the shower stall into the steamy bathroom. I grabbed a few tissues and wiped a circle on the bathroom mirror, hoping to have a nick-free but fast shave.

The bathroom door suddenly creaked open. "Hey, someone's in here!" I called out, glancing over my shoulder.

"I know," Lincoln said, bursting in. Before I knew what was happening, I got a close-up of his fist as it skidded across my right eye, sending me backwards against the sink. Intense pain clouded my vision as I leaned back on the counter, clutching my eye. He punched me two more times, once in my shoulder and the second time, my thigh.

"Stop it, you maggot!" I shouted, sitting on the counter and kicking at him. I know kicking isn't the manliest thing to do, but my legs were a lot longer than my arms. "You told on me first!"

"Payback sucks, doesn't it?" He stormed out of the bathroom with a duffel bag slung over his shoulder.

I ran after him. He was halfway down the stairs when I yelled, "You're right, payback *does* suck. Better hope nothing happens to your tires!" I clutched my throbbing eye, which now made my headache seem like nothing.

He stopped. "If something happens to my tires, you're dead." He pointed at me for a second to let the message sink in before descending the final few stairs.

Lincoln was always getting mad about something, but this was the first time he had ever packed a bag. He'd probably hang out at his buddy Jeff's house and come crawling back tomorrow, expecting everyone to bow down to him. But not me, never again. Not after this. He could rot out there and I wouldn't care.

My eye thudded painfully, so I threw on some jeans, along with a red NEVER TRUST AN ATOM — THEY MAKE UP EVERYTHING T-shirt, and hurried downstairs. I tossed a handful of ice cubes into a Baggie and headed to the rehab center.

When I walked in and saw Dad looking around as if he was lost, my heart dropped. He scratched his head and scanned the room. Without looking up, he said, "Don't touch anything. The police said to leave everything exactly where it was."

"Dad, Lincoln left."

"He'll be back. He just needs time to cool off." He finally

glanced at me, and then did a double take. "What's wrong with your eye?"

"Lincoln's way of saying goodbye." I removed the Baggie so he could see underneath.

"What? He hit you?" Dad's mouth dropped open as he hurried to me, tilting my injured eye toward the light.

"Yeah. So when the police get here, can I report a hit and run?"

Dad must not have caught my joke. "Geez! When's he going to grow up? I'm sick of his tirades, solving all his problems with his fists. Why can't he be more easygoing like you?"

Despite the pain in my eye, I laughed. I couldn't help myself. "You want Lincoln to be more like *me*? Good one, Dad."

He visibly bristled. "Why would you say that?"

"Nothing. Never mind."

"No, tell me. Why did you say that?"

Awkwardness simmered in my throat. "C'mon, Dad. We both know you admire Lincoln. Ever since I was little, you've wanted me to be more like him—confident, cocky, strong as a truck." I tightened my muscles and put my arms in front of me like a bodybuilder.

Dad squinted as though he had no idea what I was talking about. "That's nonsense! I want you to be you."

I gave him a wry smile. "No offense, but you brag about him constantly—what a wonderful apprentice he was, what good techniques he uses in hunting, how great his instinct is. I know that deep down you're even proud about how many girlfriends he's had."

"That's not true!" Dad said indignantly. "Not about the girls, anyway. I'm very disappointed about the choices Lincoln has made, but that's between him and me. But you're not making good choices either, not about what's important in life." Dad picked a glove off the floor and then dropped it back down, realizing his mistake. "Today was a perfect example. You chose to continue to associate with Lucy, and this is the result." He swept his hand across the room, stopping at his smashed laptop on the floor. "I can't believe how cruel some people are."

I swallowed hard, wishing I could have the last forty-eight hours back as a do-over. "I'm sorry—for everything. Lucy didn't do this, Dad. I'm sure of it. But yeah, with all the pamphlets, HALT was obviously behind this." I clenched my fists, pissed that my dad, who had spent so much money to turn this place into a hawk rehabilitation masterpiece, saw it destroyed in one fell swoop.

"The damage they did to the equipment is tremendous, but what has me the most concerned is how the stress of the attack may affect the health of our birds." Dad grimaced as he surveyed the area. It didn't escape my notice that he said "our" birds, giving me a glimmer of hope that there might be a slim chance he could change his mind about my apprenticeship.

He continued, "Not to mention what the DNR will do when I report this incident. They could put major restrictions on my rehabilitation efforts." He shook his head, frowning. "Or, God forbid, blacklist me."

My chest hurt as a huge ball of guilt settled there. "They won't blacklist you, Dad—it wasn't your fault. I'll testify to that too—even if they never let me be a falconer for the rest of my life. You're the best rehabber in the Midwest, maybe even the whole country, and everyone knows it. They'd be stupid to lose you."

He smiled. "Thanks, Mercer. That was nice. But the fault lies with me, no one else. If you kids weren't ready to take on the responsibility of the birds, I shouldn't have left them in your care. If we could figure out who did this and prosecute them, it might make my case stronger."

A shriek, as jarring as Troy's when he was in stoop mode, ripped through my skull. Dad's belief in me made me feel ashamed. Listening to him helped me conclude that my allegiance had to be to my family, not to Lucy, amazing though she was. I couldn't let this incident jeopardize Dad's career, his lifelong dream. His happiness.

"Dad?" I took a deep breath. "What if I told you I'm pretty sure I know who did this?"

His eyes met mine. "Were you involved?"

"Me? No! God, no. Lucy told me a few things, but I was afraid to tell you earlier."

Instead of launching into a tirade about keeping this from him, he simply sighed. "I understand. I was pretty cranky earlier. Can you start at the beginning?"

"Sure."

He pulled up another stool from across the room, and we both sat at the worktable. For the next twenty minutes, I told him the whole story, from what I knew from hanging out at lunch with Lucy and the Veggie Girls to what had happened at the movies, even letting it slip how Reed had gotten mad because he was jealous that I'd kissed Lucy.

Dad smiled a little, nodding, so I went on to tell him how that caused Reed to blab the truth about me being a hunter. He listened the whole time without interrupting. He shook his head when I got to the part about Lucy overhearing her parents talk about his falconry business, and how her dad brought his toolbox into the garage before he and his wife uncharacteristically decided to attend the late show. "Lucy figures that's when they broke in," I added as a final note.

He blew out a heavy sigh. "Whoa. That's quite a story. It appears that I misjudged your friend Lucy. She knew her parents were wrong, yet she showed courage in defying them."

"How about me, Dad?" I asked quietly, concentrating on a small nick on the wooden table. "Can I have the same consideration?"

He looked confused. "About what?"

"Having the courage to defy you when you were wrong." I swallowed hard, waiting for him to erupt in a fit of anger.

"When was I wrong? About what?" He eyed me skeptically, but his voice didn't rise.

"You were wrong when you decided that all HALT people were lunatics," I said. "Some people in that group protest things that are legitimately wrong. And you assumed that there couldn't possibly be any way I would be with a girl with views so different from mine. But if it hadn't been for me and Lucy getting together, you'd never have found out who broke into your place."

He considered this, rubbing his jaw. "On the other hand, they might never have broken in here in the first place if you hadn't started dating her."

"Maybe. Maybe not." I pulled open the drawer next to me and grabbed the awl, using it to clean under my fingernails. "It's not like your falconry business was some big secret. You've practically got a billboard out in front."

He nodded. "Well, you've got a point there."

I knew it was time to go in for the kill, so to speak. "So do you think you can reconsider my apprenticeship? I really want it, Dad. It means a lot to me. More than anything, actually."

He gave me a sideways glance, smoothing his mustache. "You know, I like the way you handled yourself just now. I told you when we started this whole thing that a man is a man when he does what is *right*, not when he does what he wants."

I vaguely remembered making fun of that line. But now I saw it was true.

He took a deep breath, looking me in the eye. "And I think the right thing for me to do in this situation is to continue sponsoring you."

"Yes!" I pounded the tip of the awl into the table with a thud, making it stand on its own.

He quickly added, "But I hope you realize that it's also right to report Lucy's parents."

"Yeah, I know," I agreed, a heaviness settling in my chest. "They broke a lot of expensive equipment that they'll have to reimburse you for."

He tilted his head slightly. "That's true, but that's not the main reason I'm reporting them. If I don't press charges, then HALT members will continue to interfere in people's lives and do destructive things in the name of animal rights without consequences. Everyone has a right to his or her own opinion, but you can't break the law, no matter how noble the cause."

"What about the good things they do?" I asked.

He pulled the awl out of the table and put it back in the drawer. "I do support groups in their fight against cruelty to animals. I've even heard of an organization that raises money to get expensive surgeries for special needs dogs and cats. But destroying personal property in a quest to win an argument? There are better ways of showing you disagree, don't you think?"

I listened, nodding in agreement at the last part. The mostly melted ice in the bag I held swished around noisily with each jerk of my head. I was now as numb on the inside as my eye. It totally sucked that defending our right to be falconers was going to ruin things with the first girl who ever fell for me as much as I did for her.

Maddie ran in, out of breath. "The police are here!"

Standing on the sidelines, I watched five police officers swarm the place. Not much happened in the way of crime in Woodley, so this must have been big news. They gathered evidence for over an hour, taking a ton of pictures and dusting for fingerprints. I overheard one detective tell a policeman that they had enough evidence to bring Lucy's parents in for questioning, along with something about going to a judge to obtain a warrant to search their home.

My chest constricted and my knees felt weak. I leaned against the counter, looking out the window toward the field beyond the mews, picturing Lucy's parents being handcuffed and dragged to the police station. Would Lucy cry and call me names for ratting them out? Would she beg to go to the police station along with them, or be forced to stay home? Picturing that whole scene tore me up inside.

I stumbled up to my bedroom, dizzy and sick. I lay on my bed, staring at the ceiling. As sad as it would be to watch her parents get arrested, remembering that Monocle was now gone made me even sadder. No more herking at me when I went to the mews, no more scratching behind her ears while she closed her eye in pleasure, no more personal time with my favorite bird of all time, period. I pounded my fist on the bed. Screw them. I was glad they were being arrested.

But even if they were wrong and deserved to pay a penalty, how would Lucy react to seeing me at school? And Reed? I was mad at him for opening his big mouth and outing Flip and me, but he had tried to talk Haley out of coming here. And finally, to add more confusion to the bubbling pot of disaster, Lincoln never came home Sunday night. When I finally shut off my lamp around two a.m., I remembered Dad saying I'd done the job of a man.

Sadly, that news didn't make me feel any more ready to face the next day.

TWENTY-NINE ···🦅

WHEN CHARLIE SAW ME IN SCHOOL ON MONDAY, HE whistled, coming up close to examine my bruised eye. "Does this hurt?" he asked as he pressed his finger into the swollen socket, grinning stupidly. I slapped his hand away. "Seriously, Mercer," Charlie said in his rare earnest tone. "What happened? Did Reed sock you one during the movie theater showdown when I wasn't looking?"

"No, worse. You don't know the half of it." As we walked down the hall toward our first class, I filled him in on the horrible and crazy chain of events that had occurred since Friday night —the break-in, Lucy's parents' arrest, Lincoln missing in action.

Charlie's mouth dropped open. "No way! That's crazy. Sorry, man." When the bell rang, he leaned in close to my ear and said, "But guess what? I've got some crazy news of my own." He smiled, elbowing me. "Jeanette and I went bowling yesterday and I didn't strike out, if you get my meaning." He gave me an exaggerated wink and I laughed.

"That's awesome, Charlie. Glad you bowled her over with your charm."

Between classes, I raced through the halls, hoping to avoid almost everyone—even Lucy. I knew that meeting her wouldn't be pretty.

At lunch, I bought a ham sandwich and chips but then stood five feet from the cashier, in a quandary over where to sit. Obviously I wasn't welcome at the Veggie Girls' table, and there was no way I wanted to sit with Reed. When I saw him chowing down at our old table, I walked briskly past him, heading toward the courtyard.

I was nearly at the door when Reed grabbed my arm. "Look, Mercer. I was pissed off at you on Friday and I did some dumb things. But it was only because Lucy is my friend too, and it bothered me that you kept telling her one lie after another — nothing more than that. I'd never go after a girl you liked." He shrugged. "Can't we just forget about it?"

"I don't know. Not right now." I shook off his grip and kept walking. He'd never steal a girl I liked, but spilling beans that weren't ready to be spilled was fine, apparently.

After what he'd done to me, I sensed something had changed between us. Something permanent. Oh, we might ride our ATVs together or hang out at the same party, but our friendship could never go back to the way it was before. It was like trying to glue back the pieces of an expensive vase that had shattered. It might work on the surface, but the vase, like our friendship, would never be as good as the original. You'd always wonder if it was going to leak or somehow fall apart, and because of that, you really couldn't fully trust it anymore.

Using my back to push open the courtyard door, I stepped out to a brisk fifty-two-degree day, opting to sit on the same bench

Lucy and I had shared the week before. This time, however, the experience was completely the opposite. Instead of friendly conversation and excitement over being with Lucy, I was freezing my butt off and feeling sorry for myself. Since I wasn't particularly hungry, I tossed bits of my crusts to a handful of sparrows. I was so lost in thought that I didn't see Lucy until she was right beside me.

"Mercer? Can we talk?" Her voice was soft, sweet, and the fragrance of lilacs wafted in my direction.

"Sure." I breathed in deeply, as if hoping to somehow commit her scent to memory. I quickly wiped a bit of drool from the side of my mouth, realizing I must have been daydreaming.

She perched on the edge of the bench. "What's going on? Are you avoiding me?"

I swallowed hard, allowing myself only a cursory glance in her direction. "Maybe. But only because I figured you didn't want to see me after last night."

Lucy twirled her ring around her finger, as if pausing to collect her thoughts. "It *was* pretty horrible. When the police came, my mom cried hysterically and my dad shouted that he was merely exercising his right to protect wildlife." Her voice cracked a bit, so she looked away a moment before continuing. "Then the police reminded him of his right to remain silent, saying that everything he said could be used in a court of law. He basically stopped talking after that." She let out a sigh.

Picturing the scene, I nodded in sympathy. I would have

loved nothing more than to sit closer and put my arm around her. But the only comfort I could offer was an explanation. "It must have been awful. And I felt really bad ratting out your parents, but I didn't feel I had a choice. At first I told my dad you didn't know anything about it, but when he told me the DNR might be less likely to blacklist him if there was a conviction, I couldn't stay quiet. Just couldn't do it. I'm sorry, Lucy." I reached for her then, placing my hand on the bench as if extending an olive branch.

"I understand, Mercer. You did what you had to. At least my parents are home now." She lifted my hand and scooched closer to me, resting my hand in her lap. She rubbed my thumb with hers, making every nerve in my body wake up. "You want to hear something ironic? Along with vandalism, they charged both my parents with cruelty to animals."

I know that should've pleased me, but somehow their arrest didn't make me feel any better. Monocle was still dead, and the DNR would still be reviewing my dad's case sometime in the future. "That's crazy."

Lucy intertwined our fingers and sighed. Her pink fingernail polish and her Snow White skin looked so perfect against my callused hands and dirt-lined nails. "I've got more bad news. This morning before school, my dad made it more than abundantly clear that I couldn't speak to you or hang out with you ever again." The words left her lips and squeezed my heart, like the bands around our resident raptors' legs. "But you know what?"

She grinned at me and kissed the back of my hand. "What he doesn't know won't hurt him. We can hang out at school, meet at the mall, sneak out to the movies. We just can't be seen together, or my parents will totally flip out."

"They'd 'flip' out? You sure about that?" I smiled at her, despite the fact that every muscle in my body ached with the knowledge of where this conversation was headed. I hated myself for what I was going to say even before I said it.

She laughed, gazing at me with those beautiful green eyes, which made what I had to say all the more difficult. I squeezed her hand, shifting one knee over the opposite side of the bench so I could face her. The way I'd always wanted to do with a girlfriend. I needed her to know that what I was about to say came directly from my heart, even though there wasn't going to be a happy ending.

"Lucy, you know I really, really like you. I think you are the prettiest, coolest, most fun girl I've ever met." She smiled sweetly at me, her eyes sparkling, clearly pleased with my compliment. I continued, "And to be honest, I think my parents could eventually accept that we were going out, especially considering how you told the truth about what happened. Showed them you have values like ours, you know?"

"Uh-huh." She nodded, but her smile started to droop on the edges.

"But the thing is, I did a lot of thinking yesterday. Like hours and hours."

Her grip on my hand lessened, but she didn't let go.

I hesitated for a moment, hating the next part. "And I decided that if I had to sneak around to see you, I didn't want to settle for that." I paused and looked at her. "As much as I like you, it's super stressful to lie all the time about where I'm going and whom I'm seeing. Makes me feel bad inside. Like I'm doing something wrong."

Lucy released my hand and pulled her blond ponytail to one side. "I get it. And I probably even knew it too, but I didn't want to say it." She sighed, nervously stroking her hair. "My dad was so hurt that I told you he . . . he looked like he wanted to cry." She winced, as if reliving the scene. "And after they got home, my mom sobbed all night worrying about the future. It'll be a long time before they get over this, I think."

"The whole situation sucks. I wish things could be different." And it was true. I was giving up the sweetest, prettiest girl around. Part of me wanted to scream, "Kidding!" and kiss her, but the part of me that had spent last night thinking things over knew I was doing what was right for me. For Lucy too, it seemed. My internal organs would thank me as well, because lately all the anxiety over this stuff had made me lose my appetite.

"Me too. And though I understand that what my parents did was wrong, I know that, underneath it all, they're good people. I only wish that our two families weren't such opposites so you and I could . . ." She bit her lip and looked like she was going to cry. A girl crying over me? My heart melted even more.

I touched her shoulder. "How about a hug? No one should have any problem with that, right?" She nodded and we hugged, both of us knowing it was the end of "us."

As we pulled apart, she asked, "So . . . what happened to your eye—a flying squirrel got revenge? Or was Flip hungry for an appetizer?" She grinned, wiping away one solitary tear.

"Nah. It was Lincoln's way of saying thanks for messing things up for him and Lauren."

She winced, peering closer. "No way! Does it hurt?"

"Not as bad as I'm feeling about not being able to see you anymore."

She smiled. "You'll survive. We both will. Starting tomorrow, we need to find a new table to sit at—minus Haley, that is —if you, Charlie, and Reed would like to join us."

Losing Lucy as a girlfriend but keeping her as a friend would be great, at least for the time being. "Of course! But are you saying you're on the outs with Haley?" I quickly added, "Not that I mind or anything."

She laughed. "My parents also made it abundantly clear I can't hang out with her either, per our attorney." She grabbed my hand and pulled me up. "C'mon, the bell's going to ring in a minute."

The weirdest thing was, as Lucy and I walked away, all I felt was relief. All the energy I had spent trying not to talk about the thing I loved most was killing me. I was free to be myself. And just because Lincoln thought lying to girls to get them to hook up with you was perfectly fine, it didn't feel right to me. If that made me a wuss, so be it. So long, Tough Guy.

I decided to put aside the drama for good and start thinking seriously about the big event that I'd been looking forward to my whole life: my first official hunting meet as a falconer. Nothing could lift my spirits more than to show I deserved to win that elusive Best Apprentice pin. Even if I didn't get it, being out in the field with Flip, my mind free to think about nothing but hawking, would be the best healing ointment for my broken heart.

Lincoln finally dragged his sorry butt home Monday night during dinner—probably because he smelled Dad's world-famous beef stroganoff. The sound of the door closing made us all stop and stare as my brother strolled into the kitchen, his eyes darting around from face to face. His clothes were all wrinkly, his face was unshaven, and, even from five feet away, he reeked like the guys' locker room after a round of basketball.

"So you've finally decided to grace us with your presence?" Dad stepped away from the table, his hands on his hips. "I'm so disappointed with you right now that I can't even say I'm glad to see you."

Lincoln leaned against the counter, his face strained with

worry. "Yeah, I don't blame you. I don't even want to see me either. I just want to say that I'm sorry I acted like such a jerk yesterday." He shrugged, shifting his weight from foot to foot.

"Only yesterday?" I shoveled another bite into my mouth. "More like a lifetime. In fact, you should major in Jerk when you go to college — you'd ace it."

"Mercer." Mom placed her fork next to her plate and discreetly shook her head. "Let Dad and me handle this."

"Have you seen my face, Mom?" I pointed to my black eye, but since I also had a huge wad of stroganoff stuffed in my cheek, I probably looked ridiculous, not sympathy worthy. "I believe my injury gives me the right to interrogate the suspect." All this police talk of late had got me going.

"Whoa. I did that?" Lincoln walked up to me to get a closer look, resting his hand on my shoulder as he leaned in.

I instinctively shrugged his hand off. "Exactly where you aimed. Shouldn't be *that* big of a surprise."

He took a deep breath and raked a hand through his hair. "Man, I'm really sorry, Mercer. I'll make it up to you somehow, I swear. Just name it."

At least he seemed way more sincere than Reed had. I rubbed my chin, pretending to consider his offer. "Well . . . I think introducing me to a few of the hundreds of the girls you've rejected over the years might be a start, since I suddenly find myself girl-friend free."

Lincoln scratched his neck and sighed. "You're not the only

one. Turned out Lauren looked up Zola on Facebook to tell her off, but Zola said she didn't know I was two-timing her, either. So now they both hate me. But I'll see what I can do." He winked at me.

A part of me was sad not to have Lauren around anymore, but the other part was glad she'd dumped him. She deserved better than my brother.

"You're going to have to do a lot more than that — both of you." Dad sat down, opening his napkin and placing it on his lap. "Beginning with cleaning up the rehab center. Now that the police are done collecting evidence, you boys need to sweep up, haul out all the trash, and repair any damage."

"You got it," Lincoln said agreeably.

I looked Dad in the eye. "Of course. I can even start tonight." Putting things back in place would make me feel at least a little better about the whole situation.

Dad frowned. "That's not all for you, Lincoln, I'm afraid. In addition to cleaning up the *inside* of the rehab center, I'd like you to give the *outside* of the building a new coat of paint after everything's back in order. Hopefully that will serve as a physical reminder that violence is not an acceptable way to handle problems."

"Yeah, I guess I deserve a little pain in return." Lincoln sighed. "But do you mind if I eat now? I'm starving." He walked toward the dish cabinet when Dad's voice boomed across the room.

"Whoa!" Dad held his hands up. "Go wash up first. You look like you haven't seen a hygiene product for days."

"Guilty as charged." Lincoln smiled, heading toward the sink.

So Lincoln was getting into the whole cop-lingo thing too. After dinner, Dad, Lincoln, and I spent several hours restoring the rehab center close to its original state. Even Maddie and Mom helped out, sweeping and wiping down shelves. Not exactly a family vacation, but it was the first time in a long while that our family felt complete.

That entire week flew by, even faster than I had wanted, since I wasn't entirely sure Flip and I were ready. I worked him tirelessly, but the closer Friday came, the more keyed up I became. I couldn't test Flip by having him go after real quarry because that was illegal until after the official start to the hunting season, but he did keep snagging my lure like a pro.

School wasn't that bad either. It sucked to have lost Lucy as a girlfriend, but we were great at being friends, all of us sitting together. At least Reed knew better than to ask Lucy out, and Charlie kept up with his crazy antics trying to make Jeanette laugh. And without Haley around telling me that I was a horrible person, things were actually pleasant. And I ate meat every day.

On Friday after dinner, Dad and Lincoln had me pack everything. Part of an apprentice's job, they said smugly. After I nearly broke my back lugging all the travel carriers off the storage shelves, they both chipped in, saying they were only kidding about having me do all the work on my own. As we loaded up the truck, we triple-checked the list of things we'd need for the trip. And to end the evening on just the perfect note, Flip even let me stroke his chest feathers a few times without a single repercussion.

At eight thirty, Dad announced that we should hit the sack early. "Two thirty will be here mighty quick."

I got into bed but couldn't sleep—mostly because I never went to bed before eleven, but also because I felt nervous. The gig was up. Time to lay my Flip on the table and show everyone what I had. It felt like I'd slept only ten minutes when Dad switched on the light in my room and told me to get ready. I hopped out of bed even faster than the rabbits that Flip was going to catch later that day.

The hunt was finally here.

THIRTY·····🦅

DRESSING IN LAYERS AS WE ALWAYS DO, I SLIPPED
on my FALCONERS DO IT ON THE FLY T-shirt, followed by
my long-sleeved camouflage shirt, Dad's old vest with my new
whistle and hunting license tucked into the chest pocket, a pair
of old jeans, and Lincoln's army boots. The trick was to wear
clothes that burrs wouldn't cling to because those suckers hurt
when they poked through. I looked out the window and saw Dad
enter the rehab center for our final task: getting our hunting
birds hooded and loaded into the carriers. I dashed downstairs to
help, trying not to wake Mom and Maddie.

I inhaled two doughnuts from the white cardboard box on
the kitchen counter and was reaching for a third when Lincoln
strode in. He snatched a glazed doughnut, ate two bites, and
shoved the rest in his mouth with one push. Charlie would have
been proud.

"What's new, Buddie Boy?" he asked, imitating Dad.

"Not much," I said, realizing right then that Dad hadn't
called me that in a while. "You're still ugly."

Lincoln grabbed my milk and downed the entire glass. He
smiled and let out a huge belch.

"Thanks for finishing that for me." I nodded my approval.

"Mom bought some new cat pee—enriched milk, and I couldn't bring myself to drink it."

"Tasty!" he proclaimed, grinning. Lincoln plucked his lucky red flannel hunting cap off the counter and set it on his head. "Well, off we go. Can't keep those rabbits waiting now, can we?"

"Nope. At least I can't. But you'll be waiting a long time, because Flip's going to catch them all." I wiped my hands on his shirt.

"We'll see about that." Lincoln belched in my face. "Let's go."

We went out to the rehab center, the night air crisp and cool. When dawn came and warmed things up a bit, it would be the perfect temperature for hunting — not too warm, which makes the birds sluggish, and not too cool, which makes the hunters crabby. Dad had already loaded Troy onto his truck and was waiting for me to do the same for Flip. As I carefully secured Flip and his carrier in the truck, I felt like a proud papa preparing his son for his first day of kindergarten.

"That's it. Good job, Mercer," Dad told me, sounding awfully close to a proud papa himself. "Now let's get going. We've got a three-hour drive ahead of us."

Dad got onto I-94 heading north to Wisconsin. Since I was relegated to the back seat, Lincoln poured Dad his coffee, the delectable scent filling the truck. A feeling of exhilaration also permeated the air, and I breathed it in, longing to create a mental picture of this whole weekend to look back on in the future. I felt wide-awake—for about thirty minutes. Then sleep deprivation kicked in, and I dozed the rest of the way. Dad woke me when we reached the edge of Jack Foster's place. Jack had been Dad's sponsor way back in the Triassic period, and his land was prime falconer country.

The sun was beginning to peek above the horizon as we drove down the half-mile entrance onto Jack's four-hundred-acre property. Gorgeous maple trees with leaves in golden, orange, and burgundy hues lined the driveway, reminding me that Wisconsin's change of colors blasted into a sensory explosion about two weeks earlier than in Illinois. I thought about how Lucy would have loved to be there. A twinge of regret coursed through me, but it didn't last long. Trying to outrun all of those lies felt a lot like an executioner was chasing me, the way they always were in *Death Patrol III*.

We parked along the rows of vans and trucks lining the grass in front of the Fosters' enormous log house. My adrenaline kicked in when I stepped out of the truck as a hunter, rather than a helper, for the very first time.

We joined the group of nearly thirty falconers who stood around talking, drinking coffee, and checking out each other's birds. It turned out that all that silly falconer talk was interesting when you knew the lingo. I hung out with Lincoln and some of the other guys we knew, a sense of pride welling up in my chest. Even though I didn't contribute all that much to the conversation, I finally understood all the tips and explanations they spoke about, sucking that information into my brain like a vacuum cleaner.

"Good morning, falconers and friends! Can I get your attention, please?" Jack Foster stood on the second step of his porch, waving his blue plaid hunting cap with the goofy ear flaps above his pure white hair. "I'm thrilled you all could make it to our twenty-fourth annual Midwest Falconers' Club Fall Classic Kickoff. I'd like to welcome all our new members as well as the seasoned ones. It's great seeing so many old faces."

"Yeah, none older than yours," a familiar voice yelled.

"Watch it, Weasel," Jack warned, pointing a gnarled finger, "or I'm gonna sic my bird Esther on you. She likes chewing on smelly, rotten carcasses like yours."

Grinning, I turned and looked at Weasel. He gave me a nod and I gave him one back.

As was customary, Jack had all the sponsors introduce their apprentices. There were three other apprentices on this trip: a fat dude in his mid-twenties, a well-groomed guy in his forties, and a lady hawker around my grandma's age, who sported a well-worn cowboy hat. After she'd been introduced, she tipped her hat. That was cool. Maybe in the future, when Lucy and I were older, she'd want to become a lady hawker too, and we could try again. I'd never admit out loud I had that thought, but somehow the idea that Lucy was a "not now" but a "maybe someday" made me feel better. Dad introduced me then, so I smiled and held my trembling hand in the air, hoping no one would notice how nervous I was.

Jack explained, "We'll see how well you've trained your birds when I award one of you the Best Apprentice pin later on tonight. Now as all of you know, falconry is a rewarding experience that is firmly rooted in camaraderie and teamwork, not competition. We know that none of you would be here today if your sponsor felt you lacked the drive and appreciation for falconry. So as far as that is concerned, we commend all of you for making it this far." He paused for a moment for applause and yelps of support.

"That said, we like to recognize excellence in the field in our first-year apprentices at their very first hunt, which will showcase all that you've learned in the past few months. Your sponsors will complete your score sheets, watching for correct handling techniques, the variety and amount of quarry caught, and the ability to follow directions in the field. Good luck to all of you, and may the best apprentice win!"

Everyone clapped for us, which made me feel both silly and excited. It was only a dumb pin, probably not even worth much, but I knew from experience that the prestige behind the award was the real prize. At every get-together, they talked about the former apprentices, as if winning this pin was the Heisman Trophy of falconry.

It suddenly occurred to me that the other apprentices might

think I was merely a punk teenager riding on his dad's hawk tails, worrying he would exaggerate my score so I would win. Anyone who knew my father, though, would figure out he'd never do that. In fact, my guess was he'd be even harder on me than the other sponsors would be on their apprentices. But after all the progress Flip had made lately, I felt confident that he and I had a decent chance of winning.

When the introductions were over, Jack announced, "All right, people. Meet back at the house at ten thirty if you want to eat the best breakfast in all of Wisconsin. Now it's time to stop the talking and start the hawking!"

"Time to get my ho!" someone yelled, followed by a swell of laughter. Falconers always yelled "Ho! Ho!" when they flushed out some quarry and wanted to alert their bird to chase after it. I didn't know exactly why they used that phrase, but the birds understood it was their cue to shine. Another secret of the four-thousand-year-old culture of falconry.

"With Bella, I'll be ho-ho-ho-ing all day long, but you'll probably need a giant yellow arrow to help Flip find any quarry," Lincoln joked, elbowing me.

I laughed, shoving his arm. "Shut up! Flip's going to kick Bella's butt. Just wait and see."

We were almost at the truck when Weasel patted me on the back. "Good luck, Skinny. Don't come back empty-handed, you hear me?" He winked, his toothpick bobbing up and down in the corner of his mouth.

"If I do, I'll grow a beard like yours," I declared, rubbing my jawline.

He clucked his tongue. "You wouldn't look nearly as good as me, though."

Groups of twos and threes branched off, promising to meet back for breakfast. It had become tradition for Jack's wife and a few other ladies who didn't hunt to cook an enormous meal for us. I couldn't wait until ten thirty, not only because of the amazing food spread they provided. Secretly I was hoping I'd have a cool story to tell everyone about my own first hunt, something I'd been only able to listen to in the past.

We got back into the pickup and drove off to the section of Jack's property Dad called the Hot Spot. It was about fifty acres of hills and fields—perfect for hawking. And with no houses around for miles, tons of critters were waiting to be found, by none other than my very own Flipster. We got our pouches and packs ready before unpacking the birds. When I took Flip out of his carrier and removed his hood, he bobbed his head up and down, searching for prey. He was no dummy—he knew today was different right from the start.

"Hold on, killer," I told him, grinning as if it was picture day. "Another ten minutes and you'll be snatching up juicy mammals by the sackful."

Dad grabbed his and Lincoln's long flushing sticks out of the truck, telling me to find my own. So much for being right up there on the same level with them. Dad said he would hunt with me until he filled out his score sheet and until I felt comfortable before heading back to take Troy out for a few hours.

I wanted to tell him that I'd be fine, that he could leave me to hunt by myself as soon as possible, but deep down, I wanted him there. Although I'd watched him and Lincoln hunt tons of times, somehow doing it by myself for the first time seemed different, harder. I wanted Dad with me so he could steer me in the right direction when I screwed up.

Lincoln buttoned his camouflage coat, picked up his flushing stick, and set Bella on his fist. The way she perched so elegantly —it was almost as if she was posing for a postage stamp. "Good luck winning that Best Apprentice pin, Mercer."

"Hush, Lincoln," Dad said. Then he added, "Don't worry about winning any game pins, Mercer. Concentrate on flushing some decent quarry—that's what's important."

"Whatever you say, Father Nature," Lincoln called out as he walked toward the field of golden grass off to his right. I could see Bella, keenly alert, her eyes darting to the left and right. She looked like a queen, decked out in her adult plumage. "Go for it, Mercer. I still have my Best Apprentice pin, along with all my other game pins, on my dresser. I admire them every day."

I wanted to tell Lincoln where he could cram his game pins, but the truth was, I knew he wasn't trying to brag. I could tell he really wanted me to win, and of course I did too. I was more than ready to kick some butt. Hopefully a few large rabbit butts along with some pheasant butts. Dad and I walked out fifty yards or so, swiping our sticks from side to side as we tromped through the knee-high weeds, not speaking. Dad held his hand up for me to stop when we came across a fallen, half-rotted log—a perfect hiding spot for cottontails.

He nodded at me, and using my foot, I rocked the log back and forth, hoping to send any hiding critters out into the open. Sure enough, a chipmunk bolted out the opposite end and started running like mad.

"Ho! Ho!" I yelled, pointing my stick at the chipmunk. In a flash, Flip was off my fist and after that chipmunk faster than you could say "Alvin, Simon, and Theodore."

Flip flapped his wings hard in pursuit, and not even ten feet later, he swooped down to the ground. I heard the chipmunk's shrill squeak and knew Flip had caught him. Dad shook my shoulder, saying excitedly, "His first kill! Way to go, Mercer!"

I didn't tell him that technically it was his third. What he didn't know wouldn't hurt him. I hurried toward Flip and his catch, happy that Dad was so happy. "Thanks, Dad!"

"We weren't out here even two minutes and you and Flip already caught some quarry. How about that!" Dad whooped with laughter and slapped my back.

Here's the thing: my dad became a different guy when we were out hunting. As though he'd left the serious Joe Falconer at home and brought his fun-loving twin brother instead. "Now, remember, since that prey's so dinky, you probably only have to wait maybe ten seconds before Flip's talons kill it. Otherwise you'll have to step in and dispatch it yourself."

I thought it was a rather large chipmunk myself, a quarter-pounder maybe. But I had all morning ahead of me, so I wasn't worried. Flip would catch something way bigger than this. Dad was right about one thing: I didn't have to put the chipmunk out of its misery, because it was clearly already dead. After distracting Flip, I slid the chipmunk in my pack and continued. We hadn't even walked ten feet when Flip flew off again, chasing something else.

"Holy cow!" Dad roared. "He's really aggressive!"

I ran to Flip and saw him guarding his downed prey. When I bent down to get it away from him, I noticed he had another chipmunk in his grasp. How odd. I'd never heard of any falconers boasting about their birds snagging chipmunks.

I waited until the rodent stopped struggling before distracting Flip again and whisking his bounty into my pouch. Chipmunks were great, but where were all the rabbits? We walked and talked a while longer without success, brushing our sticks from side to side.

"It's a gorgeous day for your first official hunt." Dad's eyes were twinkling with excitement. Or was that pride? A flush of color reddened his cheeks. "Just look at the beauty of this place."

I let go of my anxiety about winning and really scanned the terrain. I took in the splendor of the rolling hills, the sunlight glinting off the pond with thousands of cattails bobbing in the breeze around it, and the trees bursting with intense colors on the back of the property line. "Would it be wimpy to say that I feel like I've already been given a prize just being here?"

Dad laughed. "Not in my book, and I'm the one keeping score. In fact, appreciation of your surroundings is one of the criteria I have to judge you on, so I can safely say you scored the highest level on that category."

"Yes!" I pumped my fist in victory, making Flip adjust his grasp on my wrist. "Sorry, boy." Being here made my decision about breaking up with Lucy even clearer in my mind. Give all this up for a girl? Even a beautiful, amazing, sweet one? No flippin' way. Letting Flip go at the end of hunting season was going to suck, but being here today made me realize that all the crap I had gone through to get here had been worth it. Weasel said there were some things in life that are so central to who you are, you should never give them up — not for anything, or anyone, in the world. I knew that for me, falconry was one of those things.

"It looks like you and Flip have got the hang of it," Dad said, a smile on his face. "And I have enough information to fill out your score sheet. You okay doing this yourself for a bit?"

"Yeah, I'm cool with it."

"Blow three long whistle blasts if you need help, okay? Otherwise, I'll meet you back at the truck at ten fifteen sharp. Good luck." Dad headed toward the truck, stepping carefully so that his footsteps would be soundless. I decided to work on that.

When Dad was way out of my range, I took a deep breath and scanned the field in front of me. Alone at last. To do what I wanted, how I wanted. I set off toward the stream, swiping my stick back and forth, doing my best to keep from stepping on any sticks that might give me away. Flip rode high on my fist like a firefighter in an aerial ladder. We walked and I talked. I told Flip he was a great hunter and mentioned how confident I was that he could handle a big juicy rabbit. "But take my advice and don't go after any rabbits with oddball parents. Trust me. It'll never work out." I chuckled, but Flip didn't laugh with me. Party pooper.

Five minutes later, when yet another chipmunk ran out from under a clump of thick weeds and Flip was on it like a pro wrestler, I had to wonder if this was some secret chipmunk breeding ground. I scooped up the dead 'munk, and Flip and I continued toward the pond. Perhaps some bigger prey would be getting a drink.

There was no way I was blowing that whistle and asking for Dad's advice, but I wanted to know where the honkin' cottontails, the fat, juicy opossums, or even the plump voles were. Anything but stupid chipmunks would be fine. Lincoln probably had ten cottontails by now. Dad and the guys we'd hawked with never had this much bad luck. I can't remember ever coming home empty-handed. Some days were better than others, sure, but out here in the middle of freakin' bunny heaven? Unheard of.

At ten twelve I headed back for the truck, rabbit free and dis-appointed. Dad and Lincoln were already there, waiting for me.

"Hey, hey. There's the Best Apprentice now," Lincoln called out from his lawn chair, Dad's thermos cup in his hand.

"Not quite," I moaned, making my way closer to the truck.

On the ground, lined up side by side along the rear hatch, were three dead cottontails, two pheasants, and four quails. I bet this lot could feed our resident birds for weeks. If we caught a few more pheasants, though, perhaps Dad would make his fa-mous pheasant stew for a football game meal. Another look con-firmed there wasn't a lousy chipmunk in the lot.

"How'd you do?" Dad asked, locking Troy inside his carrier. "Get anything good?"

"I don't see any cottontails hanging from his bag," Lincoln muttered, sipping his coffee.

"It's his first hunt, Lincoln. Cut him some slack."

"He's right, though." I set my pack on the ground by my feet. "No cottontails."

"Show us your quarry, Mercer." Dad ambled toward me smiling, the normally heavy lines on his forehead smooth with contentment. "Did you have a good morning?"

"Disappointing, but not too bad, I guess." I knelt down and unloaded Flip's catch. By the time I got to my fifth chipmunk, Lincoln was howling with laughter.

"What?" I asked, a little irritated. "What's so funny?"

Lincoln raised his eyebrows. "Other than the fact that Flip's got a chipmunk fetish?"

"Guess he's into Chip and Dip, just like you," Dad said.

"With a side of Chips Ahoy!" Lincoln quipped.

When I pulled the ninth and final chipmunk from my bag, Lincoln and Dad were both laughing so hard that Dad had to sit down and hold his chest so he could breathe, and my brother's eyes were watering. "Chippity-do-dah," Lincoln sang, and the laughing fit started all over again.

"I got a good one too." I grumbled to myself. "How about 'shut your chippin' mouths'?"

Dad must have gotten the hint that I was mad because when he saw me, he stopped laughing.

For about two seconds.

After another round of snickers, Dad finally pulled himself together. "I'm so sorry," he said, stifling another chortle. "I haven't laughed this hard in years. It's hard to stop."

"What's the matter, boy?" Lincoln asked Flip, who perched quietly, cleaning himself from atop the T-bar Dad had jury-rigged for the day. "Can't handle anything larger than a pip-squeak?"

"Leave him alone, Lincoln." I yanked Flip's hood out of the supply box, pushing stuff around noisily and trying to send the message that I didn't want to listen to any more crap. I knew I was acting like a big baby, but I couldn't help it. Flip and I had practiced so hard, and now we were the butt of all of the jokes.

"Don't listen to them, Flip," I told him quietly, sliding his hood over his head. "You're a fierce hunter. You happen to know what you like, and that's cool with me." I locked him up in his carrier and headed back to stack all my stupid little chipmunks in the cooler.

As I approached the back of the truck, Dad grabbed my elbow, but I shook his hand off, not in the mood for any more jokes.

He sighed, his eyes lowered, his voice soft. "Look, Mercer. You're right. I'm sorry I laughed. That was not the right move for a sponsor."

I shrugged. "Whatever. It's fine."

"It's not fine. You've got a right to be mad. It's just that I've never heard of such a thing before in my twenty-some years as a falconer. Flip's definitely an excellent hunter, no doubt about it. Four chipmunks would have been impressive, but nine? Completely unfathomable. That's probably some sort of record."

"Really?" I asked, seeing a bit of hope.

"Yep," Lincoln called out. "The Guinness Book of Worst Records."

Dad threw him a look of exasperation, and I went back to shuffling things around in the back of the truck.

"Lighten up, dude." Lincoln said. "No one's going to think you're a bad hunter for bringing in nine chipmunks."

I let out a snort. "Yeah, easy for you to say, Mr. I've Got Three Cottontails, Two Pheasants, and Four Quails to My Name."

"I wish," Lincoln said. "But that quarry was from Troy and Bella combined."

Still. All I felt was embarrassment, but it wasn't as if I could change what had happened. I did my best to shrug it off and act normal, helping load all fifteen tons of quarry into the cooler before heading toward Jack's house for breakfast. On the way there, Dad glanced over his shoulder at me. "Mercer, I know you're upset by your catch today, but it's no reflection on you as a falconer. No one will think badly of you. Trust me."

I didn't trust him, but I wasn't about to tell him that, not when he was trying to be so nice to me. "Thanks, Dad. We'll see." I wondered if he was thinking something else too but couldn't say it aloud.

That he hadn't expected much from me and my bird with the stupid name anyway.

THIRTY-ONE ···🦃

WHEN WE ARRIVED BACK AT JACK'S PLACE, VASES of chrysanthemums sat on picnic tables with checkerboard tablecloths, and half the group was already seated and eating. I got in line and loaded up my plate with freshly scrambled eggs, French toast, hash browns, and pheasant patties until my plate felt as heavy as Flip did. I poured myself a glass of ice-cold milk from the silver pitcher, and then carefully brought my platter of food over to the table. I sat next to Weasel.

"There's my favorite butt-ugly apprentice!" Weasel said, a bit of egg stuck in his beard.

I smiled. "People always say I look like you." A few guys nearby laughed.

Attacking my meal with fervor, I savored every bite. I barely noticed when Lincoln sat down across from us, that is until he proceeded to tell every hunter on Jack Foster's property about Flip's chipmunk feast. Lincoln could really tell a story; I'll give him that. Roars of laughter followed every one of his perfectly timed jabs. I kept my head down, the anger warming my face. My appetite waned with each passing second. I gripped my fork tighter, moving things around on my plate, smiling occasionally but hating every second.

Weasel elbowed me, leaning close to my ear. "Nothing you

can do about piss-poor quarry. It's happened to every one of us. Days like that you just got to laugh it off, Skinny. Come on now, eat your food and join in. You'll feel better if you let it go, Mercer." I looked at him dubiously and he added, "Trust me on this. It's all in good fun. No one means any disrespect."

Somehow, Weasel's declaration made the whole situation seem tolerable. Little by little, I did as he advised—I ate my food and let the worries go. Spurred on by my misfortune, other falconers told some of their own unique hunting experiences.

A military-looking guy named Scott narrated how his hawk had landed a jackrabbit on his first hunt out west, but when he got close enough to grab it, thinking it was nearly dead, the jackrabbit leaped up and kicked his arm so hard that he let go. "And we never did get that sucker back!" Scott laughed. "Boy, was I ever stupid."

"Which goes to show you that some things never change," Dad added. Where had this jokester, formerly known as Dad, come from?

A chubby, white-bearded dude everyone called Santa went next. "Talk about dumb. My sponsor became concerned when I told him my bird freaked a lot after he ate." It turned out that for the first three months of his apprenticeship, Santa mistakenly thought the action of his bird cleaning his beak was called "freaking" instead of "feaking."

"Guess you could say you were a feaking idiot," Weasel teased.

I felt reassured by the fact that most falconers had done ridiculous things as apprentices, but I was even happier that we had finished talking about me. Listening to everyone's stories made me realize that enduring a little ribbing was all part of being a successful falconer.

I had better luck at dusk. Flip caught his first cottontail, along with two dinky voles. Not too shabby. I was more than a little relieved that Flip could catch quarry other than chipmunks.

I wasn't the only one, apparently. When I told Dad, he vigorously rubbed my head, unable to stop grinning. "Way to go, Buddie Boy!"

The excitement of catching a cottontail must have given me temporary insanity, because I started thinking maybe that nickname wasn't so bad after all. Bella landed another cottontail and a grouse. As much as I hated to admit it, Lincoln really was a great falconer, and there was a lot I could learn from him.

We drove to Willie's Lodge and dropped off the birds and the equipment, bringing our suitcases in for the night. Dad and Lincoln went in to take a nap before dinner, but being the lowly apprentice that I was, I had another assignment to complete before I could relax—cutting and bagging the quarry.

I had quartered my third rabbit when Lincoln suddenly appeared, scissors in hand. He said he owed me for my black eye, and, besides, he figured I'd screw things up without him. I rolled my eyes, knowing he was kidding but glad for his help nonetheless.

We sliced and diced while reminiscing about the morning. Lincoln laughed when I imitated the one know-it-all in the group, Ralph Henson, giving me advice about the best way to flush prey. I hunched over, using my old man voice. "'Swipe left, then right, then slap your stick against the ground three times. Works every time.' The guy must think I'm a moron."

Lincoln looked at me thoughtfully. "Uh-huh. And your point is . . . ?" I gave him a dirty look and smeared rabbit blood on his arm, and he flung the intestines on me. Brothers.

As I started preparing one of the pheasants, Lincoln stopped me and showed me a shortcut. He said the best way to remove the legs was to dejoint the hips first by laying the pheasant on its back. When you do it right, he said, it makes a loud popping sound. I tried it the way he showed me, and *pop!* It worked exactly the way he said it would.

I shouted, "Off with his leg, matey!"

When we were finished, we both looked as if we'd been in a slasher movie. We lumbered inside to wash off the grime and blood. I showered, shaved my stubble, and then threw on my DON'T PUT IT OFF — PROCRASTINATE NOW! T-shirt, ready to head out to the award dinner and receive my Best Apprentice pin. Or not. I still wanted it, craved it even, but somehow, somewhere, its significance had changed for me during the hunt. I realized that instead of wanting to prove I was the best, I had wanted to prove I knew what I was doing and could handle the job. Not only to Dad and Lincoln, but also to myself.

I figured I'd already accomplished that goal.

Dad drove us to our falconer club's regular hangout, a great restaurant called Adam's Ribs. It was your typical Wisconsin eatery: lots of knotty pine, Packers memorabilia, and locals milling around on the barstools. They drank beers, ate pickled eggs from the large glass jar, and watched college football. The noise usually got so loud that by the end of the night my ears hurt. But I wouldn't have wanted to be anywhere else in the world, busted eardrums and all.

Because there were so many of us, the bar owners always gave us our own private room in the back. I sat at the end of a long table with Dad next to me, Lincoln and Weasel across from us. It took a while for the waitress to take all our orders and even longer to serve them, so by the time she brought me my dinner, I was starving. I scarfed down an entire slab of barbecue ribs; a baked potato swimming in butter, sour cream, and chives; and two servings of baked beans. The pitchers of beer and soda flowed freely, and so did the stories.

After the plates were cleared, Jack Foster announced that it was time to hand out the awards. He walked to the front table, where the pewter game pins and shiny ribbons had been laid out for everyone to ogle. There were six categories of game pins: cottontails, squirrels, ducks, pheasants, quails, grouse, and miscellaneous. They were given for success in catching a certain type of quarry, not for the largest head count in that division. I admired all the bling, at last spying what I was looking for in the far right corner of the display: a large pin of a hawk with a ribbon in its mouth with BEST APPRENTICE inscribed on it — exactly like the one I'd gazed at many a time atop Lincoln's dresser.

Now as I leaned back on the heels of my chair, I was full of food but, as lame as it sounded, also with the knowledge that these hunters accepted me as one of their own. As was the customary practice, Jack asked the general falconers to come up to the table and grab their game pins, which had been doled out based on the quarry sheets they'd turned in to the weathering yard warden. Dad reminded me to stay at the table because next they'd be calling first-time apprentices to the front for prizes.

When Dad, Lincoln, and Weasel came back to the table with their game pins in hand, I gave them a round of fist bumps, happy for their success.

Then it was our turn. Jack called us up to the stage one by one to receive our game pins. Proudly I accepted one for Flip's cottontail and one for miscellaneous, relieved when Jack didn't specify what my odd capture was. After all the ribbing this morning, I'd expected the guys to tease me even more, but from what I could tell, everyone just looked pleased. Flip's nine chipmunks might have been a bit freaky, but I had decided that, being a bit odd myself, we were perfect partners.

Jack cleared his throat. "And now, for the final award of the evening, we would like to hand out the Best Apprentice pin." He put on his glasses, rifling through a few sheets of paper. "The score sheets have all been tallied and discussed among the board.

We have some fabulous sponsors who did a great job of teaching these apprentices, and it shows. Let's give a hand to the four sponsors out there: Scott, Santa, Rick, and Jeff." I clapped heartily, knowing how hard it was for Dad to be patient with me. I gave him a pat on the back. "Thanks for everything, Dad. I mean that."

Dad smiled at me and took a sip of his beer. He looked a little—I don't know—sentimental, which kind of shocked me. I hadn't thought he really cared all that much about how I felt about him. Guess I was wrong. I turned my attention back to Jack as he continued, "Today was truly a banner day. The weather was perfect, the quarry plentiful—"

"And so was the beer!" someone yelled out.

"I'll take one if you're buying, Mitch." Jack paused a second, pretending to hold his hand over the microphone. "Methinks Mitch may have had one too many already." Everyone laughed and Jack continued, "As I was saying, we had some good times out there today. But nothing quite matches the thrill of your very first hunt as a falconer, as I'm sure you can all attest to."

I squirmed in my chair, trying not to care about who won but desperately wanting this particular recognition anyway. Dad elbowed me, but I didn't want to look away and miss anything.

"This final award is the one all our first-years look forward to: the Best Apprentice pin. It was a very close call this year, but we do have a clear winner. This apprentice worked hard, listened to his sponsor, and caught a nice amount of quarry to boot."

That could have been me. He didn't say what type of quarry, just that there was quite a bit. I squeezed the sides of my chair.

"And so, without further ado, the Best Apprentice award for this year's Fall Classic Kickoff goes to"—I held my breath— "Sam Hawkins and his red-tailed hawk, Chico, who snagged two rabbits and a quail this morning."

I smiled, trying not to let my disappointment show as Sam Hawkins strode up to receive his pin. "I bet his last name influenced the judges," I joked to Dad, winking.

Dad gently tapped my back. "Don't worry, Mercer. You're still the best apprentice in my book."

Weasel stroked his beard, nodding slowly. "You done good, boy."

"Yeah, dude." Lincoln leaned forward from across the table, looking thoughtful. "You got totally chipped off, I mean ripped off." He snickered as he took a sip of his Coke.

I dunked my fingertips into my water and flicked it in his face.

"I'll let you all in on a secret." Dad waved the three of us closer to him. "I happen to know that Mercer's scores were higher than what Lincoln's were the year he won."

"What?" Lincoln slammed down his glass in mock anger. "You told me I was the best apprentice who ever lived! No way little bro-mite over here beat me."

My mouth dropped open, a grin on my face. Talk about

ironic. The three people I'd wanted to impress by winning the award were the three guys who basically said I already had.

Jack tapped on the microphone. "Excuse me, folks. I made a mistake. We do have one final award for tonight. Will Mercer Buddie please come up here?"

What was this about? I strode to the front table, curious about what I'd won.

"Mercer, in addition to your two game pins today, the Midwest Falconers' Club is awarding you a trophy."

Did he say a trophy? Lincoln had never won a trophy. Everyone cheered, making me feel pretty darn smug. That is until I saw what Jack held in his hands—a cardboard trophy cut into the shape of a chipmunk stuck in a wad of clay. Scrawled in black marker across the chipmunk's belly were the words "Chipmunk Off the Old Block."

When I glanced at Dad, there was a weird look on his face. I prayed it was all the cigar smoke in the room that was making his eyes watery, not this dumb-joke trophy. I accepted my chipmunk award and held it up over my head, the way a boxer does after he wins the championship belt, making the heckling begin all over again. When everyone quieted down, I said, "I accept this trophy in my hawk's honor and just realized that Flip gave me something to give to all of you guys too."

I reached into my pocket, grunting and struggling a bit, as if trying to pull something that was wedged in there. "Oh, here it is," I said, dramatically sliding my hand out my pocket and flipping them all the bird. The place was rocking after that.

When I got back to my seat, Weasel was in it, so I sat in Weasel's empty chair, next to Lincoln.

"That was hilarious, Mercer." Lincoln smiled, his teeth glinting yellow and green from the neon Packers light behind me. For the next hour, we talked about all kinds of things, but mostly girls. Lincoln even told me a story about the time he got a D in Spanish, and Evelyn Hamilton made out with him at McDonald's because she felt sorry for him.

"Man, I hope I get a D in French next quarter," I joked. I swirled my ice around in my glass, suddenly uncomfortable. "Speaking of girls, I never said I was sorry about messing things up between you and Lauren." I tipped my glass back and tossed a few ice chips into my mouth. Ha, ice chips. Even the ice was poking fun at me today.

Lincoln sighed. "Nah, it was my own fault for trying to fool her. But I couldn't pass up the opportunity with Zola. She practically begged me to go out with her."

I shook my head, laughing. "You are one lucky jerk; you know that?"

"Not lucky, smooth," he corrected.

"You got a handbook on smooth? 'Cause I don't think I'll ever have chicks fighting over me like they do over you."

"You're so dumb, Mercer."

347

"Thanks," I said, hurt that he was ruining our great time by insulting me.

"Don't you get it? You don't need smooth, Mercer. You got something else all the girls want." He took a sip of drink and watched as a cute waitress walked by.

I swallowed hard. Did he think I knew what he was talking about? "Wait. What do I have that all the girls want? A hole in my back pocket so my money falls out? What?"

The sound of Dad and Weasel whooping it up made me turn my head. Seeing Dad laugh so much led me to think that he needed to get out more often — as in *way* more often.

Lincoln smacked me on the back of my head. "Hey, pay attention when I'm telling you my secrets of snagging women. People pay for this information, you know."

I raised and lowered my hands and head in unison, as if bowing to him. "Oh, Smooth Man, please tell ole Chipmunk Boy the answer to the question I seek."

He grinned. "Better. The secret is that every person has his own secret. And yours is that you're funny. Nice too. You always make people laugh. There are a lot of girls who dig nice guys who are funny, so stop trying to change."

I scrunched up my face as if he'd just insulted me. "That's it? You think being funny is gonna get me anywhere? Girls want strong guys with big guns, jocks who win a lot of ball games, or good-looking guys with tons of money."

Lincoln put his hand on his chest and smirked. "Fortunately, I've got the whole package." He shrugged and I rolled my eyes. "Come on, Mercer. Seriously. As hard as it may seem, some girls would rather go out with a guy like you than a guy like me."

The cute waitress came by. "Are you done with these drinks, guys?"

"We sure are." Lincoln handed her our empty glasses. "So how's business tonight?"

She smiled. "Pretty crazy, but I think it's finally slowing down." She vigorously wiped the table with a moist bar cloth. "Luckily, my break is in five minutes." She hurried off toward the bar with her tray of empty glasses.

Lincoln cocked a thumb in her direction. "*Some* girls like nice guys, but not this chick. 'My break is in five minutes' is code for 'I want you, Lincoln.'" He stood up and stretched. "Off I go to work my magic on that poor, exhausted waitress. Later, dude." He walked off, leaving me shaking my head and smiling at his self-confidence.

I thought that for a conceited jerk, he had given me some good advice. I had somehow managed to attract the hottest freshman at Woodley High by being a funny, nice guy, so potentially there would be others. I only needed to find one who didn't have such bizarre parents.

One thing was certain. I'd never lie about who I was to impress a girl again. There were worse things in life than being a nice guy who was funny. Maybe I could even forget about those twenty-pound weights altogether and find a girl who chose humor over muscles.

I got up to play arcade games, reaching for the mound of coins nestled in my pocket. I crossed the bar to the far corner, past the electronic darts and pool table, and stopped in front of *Extreme Wildlife Hunting*. I slid a quarter into the slot, lifted one of the plastic orange rifles into position, and lined my eye with the front sight.

The graphics started up, and I found myself in a thick forest, facing wildlife of various sizes and speeds — lumbering grizzlies, rambling badgers, and sprinting deer — all the while avoiding clueless hunters wandering among the trees. I was nailing critters left and right and was well on my way to earning a high score when someone bumped my arm, making me miss my shot wide right. The grizzly rushed forward and attacked my video double, ending my turn.

"Hey!" I spun around to give the jerk a dirty look but saw a pretty redhead of about my age standing there. I quickly softened my approach. "You made me miss my shot and the bear ate me. Now I'm dead and it's all your fault." I clutched my heart in mock dismay.

"My fault?" The redhead raised her eyebrows. "Sorry, but if you missed the bear, you suck. The grizzlies are the biggest, slowest targets in the whole game."

I dropped my jaw, pretending to be insulted. "Excuse me,

but you're speaking to the greatest hunter who ever lived. Wild animals run for cover when I show up."

"Run away laughing, maybe." A cute giggle escaped her lips. Mr. Nice Guy didn't need to join a club to figure out that this girl was flirting with me.

"Laughing at me, eh?" I asked, smirking. "Sounds like a challenge." I picked up one rifle and held the other out toward her. "You game?"

"Always." She grabbed the rifle out of my hand. "Prepare to lose, pal."

I slid a couple of quarters into the slot and smiled at her. "We'll see about that, won't we?" As I lifted the rifle to my shoulder, she smiled back.

Maybe I had learned a thing or two about girls after all.

ACKNOWLEDGMENTS

So you've come to the end of the book, and I've come to the end of writing it, which is an amazing, yet bittersweet place to be. Sweet — because I'm sending this book out into the world with the hope that others will connect with it as much as I did, and bitter — because I have to release *Flip* out into the world to be free, pushing my fledgling book out of the nest to greet life on its own.

Flip the Bird has lived in my heart (and on my computer) for many years. Like parents assessing their love for their children, authors are not supposed to have a favorite. But the more deeply I delved into the fascinating sport of falconry and spent time with characters I grew to love, the more this book resonated in my heart like no other. (Please keep this between us. I'd feel very guilty if my other books found out.)

Accolades to my wonderful agent, Eric Myers, for his continual diligence and guidance, and especially to my editor, Julie Tibbott, whose love of falconry, along with a passion for children's literature, made her the perfect champion for this novel. I'm in awe of her brilliant guidance that made this novel so much better than when it began. Additional kudos to the many others at Houghton Mifflin Harcourt Books for Young Readers who had a hand in making *Flip the Bird* soar. This talented team's attention to detail blew me away.

I have so many people to thank—people who helped with the research for this novel—that it's difficult to know where to begin. I'll start with George and Bernadette Richter, licensed master falconers and rehabilitators, who run an amazing place called SOAR-Illinois (Save Our American Raptors), the raptor sanctuary that I modeled the Buddie Bird Rehab Center after. The love the Richters have for the multitude of raptors in their care was evident in the hours upon hours of falconry apprentice lessons I took under their tutelage. This book would not have been nearly as richly detailed without their help, and I'm so thankful to have met and worked with them. Bernadette was also my "go-to" falconer during final revisions, and I am eternally grateful for her wisdom and patience during this process.

Through George and Bernadette, I met a falconer who lived in my area, Troy Moritz. He let me hang out with him and his goshawk, Helena. I asked him a billion questions while observing his mews and the proper care of his bird. He was even a beta reader for my book long ago, guiding me about specifics when I went off track about falconry practices. (Yep! The peregrine falcon in my story is named after this kind man.) Later on, I was lucky enough to be invited to be a bush beater during a hunt with a group of falconers in central Illinois, which allowed me to experience firsthand the magic and respect falconers have for the most beautiful and majestic birds on earth.

Excellent books on falconry by authors Emma Ford, Frank Beebe, Phillip Glasier, and Bill Oakes also contributed to my understanding of this sport, as well as advice by Joe Nelson from Florida Falconers and the kind souls on the forum of the North American Falconers Association. Thank you for your guidance.

Any mistakes about the proper methods of falconry in this novel are mine alone, however. If, after reading *Flip the Bird*, any readers want to become falconers, you'll need to take apprentice lessons and find a sponsor in your area. As I'm sure you have gathered, falconry is a very specialized passion that demands the supervision of professionals, along with an extreme commitment to the proper care of your birds.

I'd also like to give a giant hug to Jeanette Ruby,

my brilliant friend and biologist, who enlightened me about the necessity and procedural practices of animal experimentation as determined by the FDA for drug approval. I'm forever indebted to friend and freelance editor Maria Mooshil, who combed through the novel before submission and got all the tangles out. Thanks also to Sergeant Rick Kappelman of the Arlington Heights Police Department, who instructed me about the rights of protesters to assemble peaceably and what charges might be filed when activists go too far.

Without supportive friends and family, my life would be a sad and lonely place. Thanks especially to my closest author buddies and confidantes, Cherie Colyer, Katie Sparks, and Veronica Rundell for their intuitiveness, enthusiasm, and guidance. Showers of appreciation go out to the rest of my Wednesday night SCBWI writing pals as well.

On the home front, I need to give a friendly pat to my two lapdogs, Sophie and Kahlua, as well as an enthusiastic shout-out to my loving parents, Rita and OB, my two older brothers, Keith and Kevin (who were my inspiration for the sibling bond in this novel), my three gorgeous daughters, Kaitlin, Emily, and Karly, and to my hunky giant of a husband, John. My life is infinitely better whenever any of you are around. Thanks for cheering me on every step of the way. My love for all of you is never-ending.

And last, and most important, eternal gratitude to our heavenly Father, who continues to bless me beyond what I deserve and whose faithful guidance I couldn't live without.